TRUE ROMANCE

TRUE ROMANCE

A Noir Anthology

Edited by

TROY LAMBERT & VINCENT ZANDRI

True Romance: A Noir Anthology

Edited by Troy Lambert and Vincent Zandri

Copyright © 2026 Alibi Syndicate Press

Stories Copyright © 2026 by:

Reed Farrel Coleman	Danica Favorite
Rebelry Stone	J.E. Fishman
Charles Salzberg	Lawrence Kelter
Samantha Ripley	Paul D. Brazill
Troy Lambert	Scott Kikkawa
Vincent Zandri	Frank Zafiro

Library of Congress Control Number: 2026905761

paperback: 978-1-971773-09-4

ePub: 978-1-971773-10-0

Published by:

Alibi Syndicate Press – Nampa, ID USA

https://alibisyndicatepress.com

CONTENTS

ABOUT THE AUTHORS

FOREWORD

Last year, Vincent Zandri and I looked at each other through a video screen and made a decision. After two publishers offered to help us with an anthology, one that turned out not to be viable, the other, which seemed unsure they could help us the way we needed them to (and later went out of business, more on that in a moment), we decided to create it on our own.

That became our first successful Kickstarter, *True Pulp*. Our idea was that this would become a series of "True Kickstarters" with varying genres and a variety of authors. Just under a year later, a lot has happened.

As mentioned, a major noir publisher went out of business. So my business partner, Stacey Smekofske, got together with Vincent as our "managing editor" and founded Alibi Syndicate Press. This is a neo noir press publishing noir and pulp, mystery and thriller, and horror. We're what we would call a boutique, micro publisher, and plan to put out 20-30 titles a year, at least for now.

And this is our first Kickstarter as a publisher. The second successful "True Kickstarter." We're excited to have a fully funded project, and that encourages us to keep creating great anthologies like this one.

Vincent and I contacted authors we know and love, collected stories from them, and pulled them together. From Reed Ferrell Coleman, a giant in the genre, to Danica Favorite, a well-known romance author who is switching genre gears in her career, and newbies like Samantha Ripley, there are a variety of voices alongside regular favorites like myself, Vincent, Charles, Frank,

Larry, Scott, and the rest of the crew. You'll meet them in the following pages.

You'll also meet deep characters in dark places and maybe learn that love isn't always all it's cracked up to be. Or maybe it is (see "Knives and Velvet", by Rebelry Stone). These types of stories are what we're all about at Alibi. We hope you enjoy reading them as much as we did.

We also hope you find love, the love of the stories inside these pages, and your own version of love outside of them. After all, love is what makes life worth living. Or is it?

Troy Lambert
Co-Owner and Managing Editor, Alibi Syndicate Press

Stacey Smekofske
Co-Owner and Manager, Alibi Syndicate Press

AN EVEN THREE

REED FARREL COLEMAN

SUSAN KINER GAZED out her classroom window in Striker Hall at the cloyingly scenic setting of Halleyton College and groused to herself about how far she had failed to come.

"Nice place to be buried," she'd said to Henry Corbin during her interview. Corbin was her former student and current Dean of Humanities at Halleyton.

She kept a pleasant expression as she watched Henry laugh off the remark. Susan was sure that like everyone else, he was chalking it up to her famously prickly personality and sarcastic sense humor. "She makes Dorothy Parker seem like Mother Teresa. Susan's a handful," she had once overheard her a Vice Provost at Arizona State say to a donor. She knew Henry still bore some scars her biting remarks had left when she was his thesis advisor and lover at UW, Madison. But Susan had been perfectly serious, because buried is what she was. This small liberal arts college surrounded by the endless evergreens and grass carpeted mountains of northern New England was her last stop, the pine scented sarcophagus in which her career in academia would be put to rest.

Her late husband, the Nobel Prize-winning economist Max Schlegel, used to joke during Passover Seders that the holiday should serve both as a celebration of the Jews' emancipation from slavery in Egypt and as a testament to how many times his wife had failed to get tenure.

"Dear, Jesus, Susan, talk about being passed over. First Wisconsin, then ASU, and NYU. You've missed the cut more times than a shaky handed surgeon." And that was before it happened again at Princeton. Comments like that helped account for Max no longer being part of her life.

Now as she waited for her Ethics 1 class to show, the flavor of her own bile soured the last pleasant grace notes of her morning latte. *Bitter.* She had much to be bitter about. Sure, at the beginning of her career, when she was just learning how to navigate the maze of departmental politics, she bought into the bullshit that women did not get tenure, especially in philosophy departments. But the bitterness was less about her own complicity and more about the way she had degraded herself in order to move her career along. It killed her to think about the men she had forced herself to sleep with in order to get their votes for tenure, the men who always had excuses when the votes in her favor fell short. Their bad teeth and body odor, dandruff and ineptitude. *God, their ineptitude!*

She saw her reflection in the pane of glass. *I'm still pretty sexy for an old bird,* she thought without joy. And for a woman in her late fifties, Susan Kiner certainly was still awfully attractive, in the vein of the mature Lauren Bacall. Unfortunately, pretty continued to be a curse for smart women. The * * *metoo movement hadn't changed that. Her male classmates and colleagues thought she hadn't seen the bathroom graffiti or heard their whispered locker room witticisms. Of course she had, from her first day in graduate school until her last days at Princeton. *The woman who put the pussy in Ph.D. The girl who put the cunt in Kant.* Where had her looks gotten her? Where had the politicking and bad sex gotten her? Where had the scholarship and publications gotten her? Halleyton fucking College, that's where!

The creaking of the huge oak classroom door broke her bile-infused trance. She turned away from her fir tree framed reflection to see a procession of sleepy-faced eighteen and nineteen year-olds zombie walk to their seats. There were twelve of them, seven girls and five boys. Eco-friendly coffee cups in one hand, unfortunately ironic cell phones in the other. Susan had to confess she liked the small class size. You could do some actual teaching in a small class, really get to know your students this way. She dispensed with introductions and got right to it. This had always been her style. *Attack!*

"The Trolley Dilemma, have any of you heard of it?"

A girl in the front row raised her hand and spoke without waiting to be acknowledged, "Is that anything like a subway dilemma? Because in New York, we face that all the time."

A few of them laughed. Some rolled their eyes. Some were still panicked at the thought of being away from their helicopter and bulldozer parents for the first time.

"Nice," Susan said, "but no. So, on to the Trolley—"

"Aren't we going to introduce ourselves to each other?" It was a slender boy in the second row, handsome. His demeanor was that odd late teenage combination of shy and cocky. "It's rude, isn't it, to just start this way?"

Susan could feel her gut burning. She had no respect for modern students, students who grew up in a participation-trophy world. Students who couldn't sit on the toilet without wearing a safety belt or a motorcycle helmet. Spoiled, coddled, risk aversive little twats whose feelings got bruised more easily than the orange flesh of an overripe mango. The burn in her belly and her expression of it is what had been the final nail of her coffin at Princeton. *Don't react! Don't react!* It had become her mantra a little too late to save her job there.

When he was interviewing her, Henry Corbin recalled several stories that were part of the lore of Susan Kiner. She smirked when, with a nervous cough, Henry broached the subject. *He would never have had the balls to bring this stuff up when he was my student,* she thought, *or when he was in my bed. But now that he's got me pinned and wriggling ...*

"Susan, did you actually throw a student out of your classroom for arguing with you about causality?"

She laughed, remembering the incident as clearly as if it'd happened ten minutes earlier. "I was using the example of a shooter, a gun, a bullet, and the victim's resulting death. This kid interrupts me to say, 'The victim didn't die from the bullet wound. He died because he believed the bullet would kill him.' She laughed again. "I told him to get the fuck out of my classroom and that if he ever said anything so unreasoned and stupid in my class again, I'd fail his ass. Kid got an A and the rest of the class got the message. Philosophy class isn't a place for bullshit. It's exactly the opposite."

Susan could see that Corbin was genuinely horrified at the obvious glee she took in relating the story. She enjoyed his discomfort.

"And the Valencia Captree Award, did you really—"

"Ah, yes, Valencia Captree." Susan's face fairly glowed at the mention. "When I was an undergrad at Columbia, there was a question on my metaphysics midterm asking us to define a believer. Our prof, Mitch Schare—you remember Mitch. Anyway, he read the answers aloud before returning our booklets. Valencia Captree defined a believer as 'One who doubted the existence of God.' To this day, I have never heard a stupider answer to any question, and that's saying something. So for years, I'd give out the Valencia Captree Award to the student who gave the dumbest test answer of the term. It was all in good fun."

Her pleasure was short-lived. Corbin's expression turned icy. "Not here, Susan. No Valencia Captree Awards. No kicking kids out of class. No cursing. You use the pronouns students ask you to use when addressing them. You warn them if the subjects you are going discuss involve race, religion, sex, and/or violence. We believe in safe spaces and microaggressions at Halleyton."

"You're kidding me, right?"

But one glance across the desk and she knew Corbin wasn't kidding. "I owe you a lot for helping me get my degree and for introducing me to the joys of earthly delights, but I don't owe you my career. You're brilliant, Susan, but you're a pain in the ass. This is your last roundup. I think we both understand that."

That was months back and though she didn't much like the

rules, she accepted that they were going to be strictly enforced and she had better toe the line.

"There are five people tied to the tracks of a trolley line," she said to the class, the stern warnings during the interview with Corbin now only a vague memory.

A boy in the back seemed perplexed. "Trolley. What's a trolley?"

"Like in San Francisco, man," a girl in the class answered. "Like the light rail system between here and town."

"There are five people tied to the tracks of a trolley line," Susan began again. "If nothing is done to divert the trolley, the five people tied to the track will surely die beneath the wheels of the trolley car." She was careful not to point at any of the students. "*You* are alone, standing by the track switch, but notice that there is a single person tied to the track onto which you would divert the trolley. Your choice is clear. If you don't act to divert the trolley, five people will die. If you do divert the trolley, one person will die. What decision do you make and why do you make it?"

These kids are bright, she thought. They asked the right questions. *Can we know anything about the people tied to the tracks? What if the five people tied to the main track are all violent felons and the one tied to the side track is a cancer researcher?* She actually enjoyed the discussion in spite of the fact that she had taught this class and used this example for over thirty years. She stopped the discussion when there was a natural lull, taking that as a cue to do the perfunctory introductions, explain about tests and papers, and to give the reading list. She ended by saying, "We will return to the Trolley Dilemma throughout the term to see if your attitudes are changed by your reading and research on the subject."

When she headed to her office, Susan Kiner was optimistic that this green and pleasant land wouldn't be the soul crushing purgatory she feared it might be. Her optimism lasted until about four that afternoon when there was a knock on her office door. It was a contrite, embarrassed-looking Henry Corbin. Contrite and embarrassed, but displeased. She gestured for him to sit, but he declined. The air went right out of her.

"Okay, what is it, Henry? I thought my two classes went very well."

"I had a visit from one of your Ethics students."

"Which one?"

He shook his head. "Who is irrelevant. It's what that matters."

"In English, please, Henry. Or does the code of conduct not permit you discuss things I am not allowed to discuss? Am I supposed to intuit the substance of the complaint through your body language?"

He laughed despite himself. "Frankly, I find the complaint ridiculous, but ..."

"But the parents of these students pay a fortune, education and the rules of normal human behavior be damned."

"Something like that, yes. The Trolley Dilemma, you should have warned the students that there was potential violence involved in the discussion."

"You're putting me on, right?" She got up from her desk and looked behind the door, checked her bookcases. "This is like *Punked* or *Candid Camera*, right? You're recording this, hoping you'll get a rise out of me to show at some faculty dinner."

"I wish it was a joke and I hate even having to bring it up, Susan, but I'm serious. There are six potential deaths involved in the Trolley Dilemma, violent deaths. Keep that in mind in the future. Fortunately, I've convinced the student not to make the complaint a formal one."

She was tempted to demand to know the complaining student's identity and at other points in her career she might have been willing to go to any length to force it out of him. *What do you think the president of the college and the executive board would think of their Dean of Humanities if I told them you enjoyed choking me when we fucked? Or that you used to beg me to let you watch another man fuck me while you masturbated.* But she didn't go there except in her head. She was grateful to Henry and she already thought she knew who the student in question was. Drew Bishop was the handsome boy from the Ethics class, the one with the shy/cocky affect and the one who was disappointed at her rudeness.

"Thank you, Henry, it won't happy again. I'm sure you understand I'm a little new to this level of oversight. Forgive me."

He seemed heartened by her response. "No need for that, Susan. You know how much I admire you. Why don't you come for dinner tonight? Peg would love to see you."

"Thanks for the invite, but I have to say no. Another night, okay? I've got plans."

She hadn't had plans until Henry Corbin walked into her office. She had them now because, finally, she had had enough. She had taken all the crap she was going to take and the time had come to give it back.

Men liked to think themselves enigmatic creatures, mistaking their own emotional confusion for complexity. Susan Kiner had a very different view of the male of the species. Women were complex. Men were simple and the younger they were, the more they believed themselves complicated masters of the universe. That made them easy targets. She had only a solitary target in mind. Step one was to find out if he was straight. Given how Drew returned the admiring glances of the girls in class, Susan was confident he was. If he was gay, that would make things more difficult. Not impossible, but it would mean getting at least one more person involved. She had no desire to do that nor would she let herself be pushed.

She would take her time. It was her experience that hurrying things along led to mistakes and a quick victory was also an unsatisfying one. No, she would not be rushed. She would no longer suppress nor swallow, accommodate nor accept the indignities, the hurts, the lies, the false promises, the rejections, the faithlessness and disloyalty visited upon her. She would let the burn in her belly smolder, let it rage until it would nearly consume her. Then, and only then, would she take her revenge. As her late husband had found, there would be nothing micro about her aggression.

Absurdly, wonderfully, Halleyton made itself complicit in her plan. Due to the small size of the student body and the school's philosophy, the kids were compelled to visit with their individual professors in the professors' offices for a half hour every two weeks. Susan had made sure to schedule Drew early in week two, but at the end of the day so no appointments would follow.

"Hello, Drew, please have a seat," Susan said, without looking up from her desk.

She listened, making sure to let him sit in silence for a bit. Silence, she had found over the course of her career, was very telling. Some silences were loud and expressive. Some still and uncomfortable. Most people, Millennials in particular, were ill at ease with it. She wondered how long it would be before he pulled out his pacifier cell phone to occupy himself. One thing she noticed immediately was the overwhelming blast of Drew's grassy cologne. *Teenage boys and cologne! It took them until their mid-twenties to understand that a little bit went a long way.* But she was encouraged. *He wants to impress me, to be attractive to me. Boys and older women.* She had always thought Freud a bit of a pompous clown, but she had to confess that maybe he had something right about men and their mothers.

Susan and Max hadn't had children, one decision they got right. They both understood there would never be enough oxygen in the room for a child of their making. There was barely enough breathable air when they were in a room together. Funny that she should think about Max—a man with a Nobel Prize and a Nobel Prize worthy cock—with this boy sitting across from her. But then again, no. The bedroom was really the only honest place in a house. The one place where all the artifice, awards, and degrees became moot. The place in the house that gave completely different meanings to supply and demand and to the categorical imperative.

She looked up. "Hello, Drew."

He tried not to smile, failed miserably. He was already hooked, but she was going to slow walk it. They made some small talk, then moved on to the readings she had assigned and to a discussion of how to approach his first paper. Before he left, she made a point of apologizing for failing to do proper introductions during their first class and for not warning the students about the violent nature of the Trolley Dilemma.

"Oh, that's okay, Professor Kiner."

He was hooked, alright.

After their second class, she had "accidently" let her hand brush against his as she passed him in the hallway. After the third class meeting of Ethics 1, she dropped some papers on the floor as he was leaving. Dutifully as a dog, he stopped, turned, and helped her gather them. When she thanked him, she made certain there was more in her voice than simple appreciation. She let her stare linger. But it wasn't until their third office visit that she moved beyond the occasional longing look and flirty comments.

"Drew, I know this can get me fired, but …" She was properly hesitant. "Would you like to have dinner with me tonight? Oh, God …" She acted embarrassed, her face blushing red. "Please, I'm sorry if—"

"I'd love that," he said. The hero saving the damsel from distress.

Dinner went uneaten that evening. Susan even enjoyed herself some. She had forgotten about the staying power and endurance of young men. He was unskilled but enthusiastic and not utterly inept. Mostly he was smitten and that was the point.

"Please, Drew, you can't tell anyone about us. I mean it," she whispered, licking his ear, playfully biting it. "We'll both be kicked out of here and I can't—"

He squeezed her tight, stroking her hair. "Never."

On his fourth office visit, she locked the door behind Drew and cleaned off her desktop. Drew didn't need to be told what to do. In bed the next night, she asked him a favor.

"I need some help with a paper I'm working on."

She had him interested. "A paper?"

"I still do get published, you know."

He looked a little panicked and was quick to apologize. "Sorry. What's it about?"

"The Ethical Dilemma of Suicide."

His eyes got big. "What is it you need me to do?"

She swung her legs off the bed, but slyly stopped herself, leaned back and kissed him hard on the mouth. Only fifteen minutes later did she finally climb out of bed.

She brought back a list of publications. "I'm so busy, I can't do all the research I need to do. If you help me, I'll name you as one of my co-authors and you'll have your first publication credit."

His eyes got big with excitement. "Really? You'd do that?"

"For you, lover, anything. Oh, and one last thing." She handed him a second piece of paper. "This is a suicide note written by a student at MIT and it presents the dilemma perfectly. You'll see. Do me a favor, make a file of it on your computer. My office printer isn't working and this is the only copy I have."

He put the research list and the copy of the handwritten letter on the nightstand before pulling Susan back into bed.

It was the day after the Ethics 1 final exam when she put the terminal steps into play. The timing was perfect as there was a snowstorm predicted for the morning. The snow would help obscure any potential mistakes or evidence left behind. For two weeks now, they had been meeting for nighttime walks in different wooded areas off campus. He was initially hesitant, but Susan knew how to deal with that.

"But, Sooz, aren't you afraid we'll get caught?" he asked, looking over his shoulder during the first of their little hikes.

"I'm a little ashamed, Drew, but I've got an intense fantasy about having you out in the open air." And before he could say another word in objection, she dropped to her knees.

He never again asked about getting caught.

That last night, they met at a rocky spot called Blind Bend. She got there ahead of him and when Drew arrived, Susan handed him a glass of champagne.

"To us, lover."

"To us."

They clinked glasses and drank. She poured him another glass.

"What are we celebrating?"

"Our paper on the Ethical Dilemma of Suicide … it was accepted for publication." She hugged him tightly, kissed him.

"That's fucking great, Sooz. Wow!"

"I'll tell you what's great, the way your mouth tastes of champagne. One more glass and I'm going to make you feel like you've never felt before."

He drank that glass in a single gulp. She saw the recognition in his eyes that something wasn't right. She saw it and felt a cold burn inside, a jolt more electric than handing out a thousand Valencia Captree Awards. Drew became unsteady, his eyes rolled up into his head. It appeared to her that his wobbly legs were losing their will to hold him upright.

"My head is all cottony, Sooz," he said. "Your face is … droopy. I don't feel good."

She was laughing now, enjoying the fruits of her labor.

"Why … why are … you laughing?"

That halting question was to be his epitaph. His eyes closed. Gravity grabbed him by the hair and yanked him toward the center of the earth.

Susan unfolded the tarp she had hidden behind a big glacial boulder, rolled Drew and the champagne bottle onto it, and carefully pulled them down the hill to the light rail tracks. This is why she had chosen Blind Bend. When the train came around the curve, it would be for impossible for the engineer to see the body on the tracks and stop. Susan had timed it and tested it with a road kill raccoon. She checked her watch. *Ten minutes.* She removed Drew's gloves and formed his right hand around the neck of the bottle. Pressed his lips to the bottle top, poured some more of the drugged liquid into his mouth and onto his coat. She dropped the bottle far enough away from the tracks to make certain it would be found intact, then folded up the tarp and made her way back up the hill to watch.

At her perch, she collected the plastic glass from which Drew had been drinking and checked for any other objects that might give her away. When the light rail train blew its horn, Susan smiled and said. "Hello, Trolley. Goodbye, lover." Susan found the little split of untampered champagne she had poured her drinks from and made a silent toast to the sacrificial lamb who had died in lieu of all the assholes who had conspired to steal her career and dignity from her. The horn blew again. Breaks screeched and ... Snow was already falling as she made her way back to campus.

Because Drew had died so near the end of term, the memorial service was held the first week of the Spring semester. Susan sat to Henry Corbin's right on the other side of the aisle from the kid's family.

"Did you know he was so depressed?" Corbin asked in a whisper.

She shook her head. "I had no clue."

"He was apparently obsessed with suicide. The police found all sorts of research on the subject on his computer and a file with a suicide note."

"That's terrible."

"He mixed himself up quite a cocktail in that champagne bottle and just laid down across the tracks. Made sure he did it where the train couldn't help but kill him."

"So sad."

There was a loud sob from behind them and they both turned to see Ella Farnboro nearly fainting with grief. Ella had been in Susan's Ethics 1 class with Drew.

"That bitch!" Corbin's whisper had grown fangs.

Even Susan was taken aback. "Bitch?"

"She's the one who complained about you and the violence of the Trolley Dilemma. She's complained about every one of her professors for either being racist, sexist, ageist … There seems to be no end to what that girl finds offensive."

"Why put up with her?"

"Her father's an important alum and a huge contributor to our endowment. Three and a half more years of that girl and I think I'll do what Drew did."

Susan said nothing. She felt no guilt. Whether Drew had been the real offending party or not was beside the point. She did, however, enjoy the notion of ridding the world of Ella Farnboro. Ella would make it an even three. There was a certain symmetry in groups of three that appealed to the human aesthetic. It certainly appealed to hers.

She stifled a laugh, thinking about how cleanly she had managed victims one and two. At least there had been some perks and challenges in murdering Drew. Max … Max had been almost too easy. Twenty-five years Susan's senior, he had been suffering the onset of dementia. That, along with a chronic heart condition—"He didn't have one, a heart," Susan was wont to say—made it all rather simple. No one raised any questions when it was determined Max's death was due to his overmedicating himself.

She looked back once more at Ella the Grieving and smiled on the inside. Susan Kiner had returned to Halleyton unhappy at the prospect of a second term of teaching the brats, a term without intrigue or plans. Ella had rescued her from her fate and for that much she was grateful to the girl. Halleyton was, as Susan anticipated, a burial ground. Only it would not be hers.

A CONVENIENT MURDER

DANICA FAVORITE

CHAPTER ONE

THE MERCEDES' brakes screeched, matching Serena Barrett's rage as she spotted the convoy of black SUVs choking her driveway like a funeral procession. Julian's funeral procession, if her wish came true. She'd fantasized about it enough times: the somber faces, the crocodile tears, the blessed silence where his voice used to be. But instead, here was Toby Sinclair's vulgar display of excess, the parasitic lawyer from L.A. who'd slithered back into town like he always did when there was blood money to be made. The merger. Thousands of jobs sacrificed so Julian and his pet shark could add another zero to their offshore accounts. Her husband had the audacity to ask her—no, to *tell* her—to leave the Mercedes at the pool house for Toby's convenience, as if she were the goddamn valet. As if she were just another piece of property he owned.

Well, there was nowhere to park now anyway. Fine. She'd leave the car on the street like some common visitor to her own home and walk around the long way. Her kickboxing class was cancelled, and God knows she needed to hit something. Since Julian's face wasn't available, the pavement would have to do.

The air had a sharp bite with a twinge of manure that meant snow wasn't far off, always the best way to tell the weather in the Front Range. All of Denver could smell Greeley. Clouds hung low and heavy, the kind that swallowed the sun and muted the world.

She pulled her coat tighter and told herself she was imagining the tension in the air, but something about the silence felt off.

She steeled herself for whatever fresh hell awaited her in the main house. With the housekeeper off for the day to take care of a sick relative, and the retinue in front of the pool house, no doubt Julian would be in a mood.

Cutting through the side gate and into the garden, Serena took a moment to do a quick meditation, her own version of the Serenity Prayer.

Whatever higher power is out there, please give me the grace to endure whatever nonsense this man comes up with tonight, the wisdom to keep my mouth shut at his ridiculousness, and if I'm given a weapon, the restraint to not kill him.

Serena took a deep breath and let out a long sigh. She'd made a deal with the devil when she married Julian, and the only reason she didn't leave were the three faces smiling at her from the screensaver on her phone. Alistair and Kate away at college, and sweet Sophie studying at the boarding school she'd tried talking Julian out of. But God forbid a Barrett raise their own children. Which left her here, sitting in a hidden corner of the garden, not ready to paste on a smile and act like the perfect wife.

Technically, she wasn't due home for another hour or so, since Julian thought she was at class. But it was getting too cold, with the storm brewing, and at least the chill in her home didn't come with precipitation.

If only she'd been able to take out her frustrations on an inanimate object as she'd planned.

She paused at the side door, noticing her old BMW parked in the driveway. Odd. It was supposed to be at the garage for service, which was why she'd been asked to leave the Mercedes for Toby.

Oh well. Not her circus, not her monkeys. As long as she didn't have to listen to Julian grouse about it. Tonight was already looking like a Valium night, two if she was going to have to have Toby at the house for dinner.

Once inside, she found it eerily quiet. She should be used to the silence by now, since the kids had gone away at the end of last month, but today felt different.

Noises from Julian's office made her pause. She heard a woman's voice, to be precise. Julian didn't usually bring his dalliances home, but he wasn't expecting Serena to be here, either. Lord only knew what he did when she was gone. One more indiscretion to pretend wasn't happening. The woman's voice grew louder, but Serena couldn't make out the words. The breakup, then.

Idly, she wondered how much this one would cost, and which guilt gift she'd receive. Not that she needed more jewelry, but it was always interesting to see what price Julian put on her silence.

She entered the bedroom, pausing at the closet to decide which outfit best suited the role of a wife pretending she didn't notice that her husband had yet again broken the rule not to bring home his mistresses. She sighed. What was that about not killing him again? Right. Orange wasn't her color.

A gunshot rang out, and she froze.

Gunshot?

In her home?

Julian had done a lot of idiotic things in their marriage, but this… this was too far.

She flung open the bedroom door and started for his office, just in time to see a blonde woman slip out the back.

Well, at least one of the women Julian screwed over finally found the backbone Serena could never muster.

When she entered his office, Julian was sprawled on the floor, a gunshot wound to his head, clearly dead.

So much for not killing him.

Someone else had gotten to him first.

CHAPTER TWO

Part of Serena said to call 911. But the part that was married to Julian reminded her he was already dead, and whatever this was, it was going to get messier than the blood on her Turkish carpet before it was over. As much as she detested Toby, she should talk to him first.

Leaving Julian in his pool of blood, she noticed how little she felt at seeing her husband dead. Was this what shock felt like? Or maybe it was freedom? Weird that she didn't feel the slightest bit guilty, and even felt glad.

She left the house the way she'd come in, through the side door, and it occurred to her it was probably a good thing, because when the police came, they could get the killer's fingerprints off the back door. Yes, she'd watched enough police procedurals to know that was going to happen. Already, she was piecing together where to tell the police to look for evidence of the identity of the mystery woman. It wouldn't be hard, since Julian had never been discreet in his affairs.

As she reached the side of the pool house, Serena heard voices.

"It's done," a woman with a Russian accent said. "Just make sure the housekeeper gets back here to see me getting into the BMW holding the gun."

Serena stilled. Toby was in on it?

She crept closer to the open window and spotted Polina Sorokin lounging in a chair, a blonde wig framing her face as she spoke to Toby. "The back cameras are off, so they'll only get footage from the front ones, which will show me looking like her leaving, right?"

"Yes. Her class finishes in about an hour, so we have time to set the scene. The mechanic will call and ask her to pick up the car, which you will drop off there when you leave. By the time she arrives at home to find Julian's body, the police will be there and have eyewitnesses who say they saw her leaving earlier with the gun."

For a moment, Serena couldn't breathe. Their words blurred together, impossible to make sense of. Then her body caught up— her pulse slammed in her throat, knees weakening as if someone had kicked them from behind.

They were talking about her. Her car. Her house. Her husband's body.

And worse, if Polina had killed Julian, that meant only one thing: somehow, Julian had crossed his friends in the Russian mob.

Her stomach churned as Toby laughed. "Good. That little bitch deserves it for telling Julian she didn't think the merger was a good idea. He was going to vote against it, which would have cost me millions."

"I don't care about the fucking merger." Viktor Varlamov said, stepping into view. Of course Viktor was involved. Polina was his favorite mistress, and also his favorite assassin. "This is about my Evochka."

Evochka? His daughter, Eva? Who had grown up with Kate and spent summers with them at the lake house?

No. Julian couldn't. Wouldn't.

Serena closed her eyes.

Of course he would. Boundaries meant nothing to him, and the bigger the challenge, the more he relished in the victory. His mobster business partner's off-limits daughter was the kind of thing he lived for.

Toby practically bowed to him and said, "I know, sir. The estate is going to be tied up for a while... with his death. But don't worry. Once the kid's born, the child will get a share, and that will provide compensation for what's been done."

A baby?

Serena pressed her fist to her mouth to keep herself from crying out. If Julian had gotten Eva pregnant, this was bad, very bad. Julian had gotten others pregnant, and they'd all been given compensation, along with an escort to the nearest abortion clinic. Viktor was notoriously anti-abortion, so this was not a problem

Julian could make go away. Especially when it came to a mobster's nineteen-year-old daughter.

"Compensation?" Viktor shouted. "My Evochka is supposed to marry Sergei Orlov, and he's expecting a virgin. This will create a war between our families, and you think money will solve it?"

"It's all right," Polina said, standing and placing her hand on Viktor's chest. "Back when I was running my girls, we had a surgeon who could make it seem like they were still virgins. I sold the same girls over and over, and no one ever knew. We send Eva away, she has the baby, it gets adopted, Eva gets the surgery, and Sergei will be none the wiser."

Viktor brushed her hand away. "And what do I tell Lena? She's already not going to like the arranged marriage, but she won't be able to handle knowing our Evochka is pregnant, nor will she allow me to take away the baby."

Lena. At least she wasn't involved. Viktor's wife had become a friend of sorts to Serena, and they'd bonded over their unhappy marriages.

"I could take care of her," Polina said suggestively.

"Idiot." Viktor made a noise. "Do you think if that were an option, I wouldn't have done it already? That woman is a pain in my ass. But I need her, and she knows it. Still, your idea of sending Evochka away, then giving her surgery has merit."

"Everything is set," A man said, entering the room.

Serena glanced at the new arrival. Sheriff Jack Evans, as in the actual Sheriff. Not a lackey, the man the good mayor of Denver appointed, whose campaign had benefitted from a great deal of Barrett money. Apparently, his appointee was not averse to taking money from the Russian mob as well.

"Good," Polina said. "It's about time I make my appearance carrying the gun to the car and leaving. You can meet me around the block to pick it up, so you have it for evidence. You'll make sure her fingerprints get on it?"

Sheriff Evans laughed. "I know you Rooskies don't have rodeos in the good old homeland, but I can assure you, this isn't my first one. My men will have enough evidence to put Serena Barrett away for a long time."

For a moment, Serena squeezed her eyes shut. Then they snapped open with perfect clarity.

All this time, she'd been the one with restraint. She'd imagined it a thousand times: her hands around Julian's throat, a pillow over his face, poison in his scotch, but she'd never done it. Someone else had stolen that satisfaction from her, and now she'd pay the price anyway.

Not a chance in hell.

She'd spent years playing the dutiful wife, swallowing her rage, making herself small. That woman would have waited here in the shadows, paralyzed, until they dragged her away in handcuffs. But that woman had died the moment she'd seen Julian's body sprawled across the floor, denying her the revenge she'd longed for all these years.

Serena pressed her palm against the wall and rose to her feet, her legs steady beneath her. She had maybe an hour before they "discovered" the body and people started looking for her. Just enough time to temporarily disappear until she could find a way out of this mess.

She wasn't going down for Julian's murder, and she'd be damned if these snakes got to reap the rewards while she rotted in prison.

CHAPTER THREE

Two weeks later, Serena Barrett paused at the alley door, glancing at the piece of paper in her hand. Surely this couldn't be right? But this is where GPS had led her. She glanced around to make sure, once again, it was safe.

People like her didn't come to places like this, the forgotten parts of Denver, where even the police feared going. A gust of wind blew another stream of snow across Serena's face, as she contemplated the door. She pulled her coat tighter against her, cursing Chase for having chosen the worst neighborhood in the metro area to lick his wounds over a drug bust gone wrong.

She tentatively knocked on the door, then chided herself for being so timid. No one inside would hear her.

Maybe this was a sign the plan was a complete waste of her time.

But what other choice did she have?

Before she could raise her fist to knock again or decide to run away, the door opened a crack.

"What are you doing here?"

"I didn't know where else to go," she confessed. "The police are—"

"Yeah, I know," he said, making a noise in the back of his throat. "And you thought coming to see a police officer in the dead of night was the right answer?"

"We were friends once." Serena shifted her weight at the edge of the building, the chill seeping through her coat as she waited for him to unlatch the door. But instead, his voice came muffled through the crack.

"Friends." The word snapped out of him, sharp as ice, followed by one of those low, sardonic noises she remembered far too well—half laugh, half snort. The sound hit her right in the sternum. "I suppose if you mean doing the horizontal mambo multiple times, the first time being prom night, I guess that means we used to be friends."

She flinched, though she couldn't tell if it was the crude phrasing or the casual venom that caused it. Through the small gap, she saw the shadow of his profile, jaw tight, shoulders angled as if he was holding the door closed with his whole body.

"Funny how you pretended not to know me once you got your billionaire boyfriend," he went on, his tone flattening into something that wasn't quite angry, just tired. "But I guess you did okay for yourself. He married you. Then you killed him."

The bitter chuckle that followed stabbed the air between them. It sounded older than she remembered. Worn down.

Her throat tightened. She wanted to say *Chase, please,* but the words froze in her throat.

Then he leaned just close enough to the door that his next words slid through like a knife.

"So why'd you do it?"

The silence after was deafening, heavier than her own guilt. But she didn't have any other options.

"I didn't," Serena said, tears rolling down her cheeks. The snow masked most of them anyway, streaking her face and stinging her lips with salt. "And I need you to help me prove it."

"Why would I do that?"

He cracked open the door a bit more, standing half in the doorway, half out, the interior light catching the hard edges of his face. He'd aged since she'd last seen him in the news, face filled with harsher lines, eyes that didn't seem to rest anywhere for long.

"I know you got suspended for shooting an undercover cop while trying to take down the Russian mafia," she said, desperate. "You'd do anything to get back in the department's good graces."

"Which is why I should turn you in." His jaw flexed. "Look, I broke a lot of rules. I know that. I'm not proud of what happened. But I also didn't kill Manny. As soon as the investigation is complete, I'll be exonerated."

She stepped closer, shivering. The wind had picked up, plastering her hair against her skin. "So you know what it's like to be wrongfully accused of murder. I didn't kill Julian." Her voice cracked, raw and pleading. "You know me. You know I wouldn't ever kill anyone."

He snorted, the sound bitter enough to make her stomach twist. "Yeah, I knew you. I also thought you were loving, faithful, and kind. That went right out the window when you met that billionaire. How much do you get now that he's dead?"

"Not enough, and nothing if I'm convicted," she cried. The words burst out like something broken loose inside her. "Not enough for it to have been worth everything I went through. What they're doing now…"

He looked her over then, long enough that the weight of his silence felt heavier than his words.

"And you're still crazy enough to think I'd help you."

The snow came down harder, pelting the roof in uneven sheets.

"Please," she whispered. "Can I come in?"

He exhaled through his nose, a weary sound she remembered from nights long gone. Then he opened the door another few inches.

"You have five minutes before I call you in."

The inside of his apartment was dark, dingy, but as her eyes adjusted, Serena realized it wasn't dirty. Everything was arranged with precision, deliberate and spare. The couch had a military hospital-cornered blanket folded on it, and the counters empty except for a drip coffee maker and a single mug. It looked less like a home and more like a bunker someone refused to abandon.

"This is where you live?" she asked softly.

He shrugged, stepping past her to flip on a lamp. The light didn't do much to chase away the shadows.

"I gave up everything to go undercover. This is one of the safe houses I had that wasn't compromised. It's not just the police I made an enemy of. The Russian cartel has a price on my head. Things are better and safer this way for me. At least until I'm cleared."

His tone was matter of fact, but she heard the weariness underneath.

"I could help with that," she said. "I've got money. Even without having to wait for things to clear probate with Julian's estate."

He snorted. "Yeah, you don't think the Russians told me that when they asked me to join them? And also? Bribing a police officer? That's another charge to add to your rap sheet. What else you got?"

"No, I mean it," she said quickly. "Yes, I am relying on your fond memories of our friendship to at least hear me out. But when this is over, I will pay you. I will help you with that new life. I will help you with whatever you want. I don't have anywhere else to go."

He leaned against the wall, watching her too carefully. "The news says you're holed up in some private island retreat. You can stay there, no extradition, or spend that money on one of your fancy lawyers. One of them will arrange for you to be handed over peacefully, without fanfare. That you've been on the run for so long adds more difficulty to things. But with your connections and your money, I'm sure they can get it down to house arrest."

Serena shook her head, water from the snow still dripping from her hair onto the carpet. "You don't get it. His lawyer? He's in on it. So's the sheriff."

He straightened slightly. She could see him slip from jaded ex-cop to investigator again, his eyes sharpening.

He scratched his chin, the faintest ghost of interest breaking through the cynicism. "Now this, this could be interesting," he said. "What makes you believe that?"

Her breath caught. This was the hardest part. The thing she hadn't told anyone. And why she'd been on the run.

"That day I got home and I found his body," she said slowly, "it didn't happen the way the news outlets say."

He waited. Silent, still, but she could feel the question coiling between them.

"When I got to the house…" She swallowed, her pulse hammering against her throat. "Julian was still alive."

"I arrived home early," she continued. Her voice trembled, but her eyes stayed fixed on the floor between them. "And I saw a woman dressed like me... shoot him."

Chase blinked, disbelief flickering across his face. "You saw a woman dressed like you?"

"Yes."

"Why didn't you call the police?"

Serena drew in a shaky breath. "Well, that's just it. Julian is working on contracts for the company, some new business venture he's getting into. Toby Sinclair, his lawyer, was staying in the guest house. Flew in from L.A. the day before."

She hesitated then, twisting the damp cuff of her sleeve. "I got to the guest house—"

He stopped her, staring hard. "So, you see a woman shoot your husband, and your first instinct is not to call 911? Not to go to the police? But to go to the lawyer?"

A small, bitter laugh escaped her. "He was already dead. What would calling 911 have accomplished? I needed to talk to our attorney to see what to do. I thought I was protecting our assets, our interests. Julian's company was in the middle of a big merger, and I was thinking we needed to get ahead of the situation before it hit the news."

"Your husband's dead, and you're more concerned about the price of a merger?"

"Look, there were a lot of people not in favor of this merger, and Julian wasn't exactly the most popular man. I thought I was doing the right thing. As it turns out, it was."

He rubbed a hand over his jaw. "Alright, fine," he said finally. "You go to talk to the lawyer. Then what?"

"When I got to the pool house, there was a woman in a wig—a blonde wig to look like me. Polina Sorokin. Do you know who she is?"

Chase's head snapped up, everything in his body on alert. "Viktor Varlamov's mistress?"

"Bingo. And guess who else was there? Viktor himself."

The name seemed to hit him like a gut punch. His jaw flexed, the muscle there twitched once before he spoke.

"Hold up. They're involved?"

"Yes."

He exhaled through his nose, a tight, controlled sound—anger under pressure. "Could you have led with that? We're talking about the man whose criminal activities almost got me killed, cost the life of my partner. And I still might lose my badge over it."

"That's why you should help me."

"Again, lead with that. God, could you be any more dense?"

"Are you done insulting me, or do you want to hear the rest? Because this is exactly what you need to know." Then her voice softened. "I just thought it would be helpful if you knew I was actually innocent."

He shrugged. "Not particularly. I'll admit, I had a sick thrill at the thought of you in prison."

His words hit like a slap. For a second, Serena's breath caught and heat flashed up her neck. She steadied herself, forcing her voice to stay even.

"I guess I thought you'd have fonder memories of me."

"Yeah, well. It takes a special kind of masochist to have fondness for what you did."

The words sliced deeper than she expected. Beneath the hard edges of his voice, she finally heard what he'd been trying to tell her all along. He hadn't forgotten the pain she'd caused him, and just as she'd been selfish back then, she was doing it again and asking him to put himself at risk to save her.

Her chest tightened. The anger she'd been clinging to drained away, replaced by something heavier.

"I'm sorry," she said quietly. "I should have realized how much I hurt you. Can you forgive me?"

When he finally spoke, his voice came out low and rough.

"Don't do that. Don't bring us into this. Whatever happened back then, it's dead and buried. I'm not interested in ancient history. I just want to know what you know about Viktor."

But even as he said it, his tone betrayed him. Chase would not let go of his grudge easily, and the only reason he'd help her was the fact that his grudge against Viktor was stronger.

Serena told him what she'd seen, as well as the conversation she'd overheard. Even as she spoke, it felt almost unreal.

Chase leaned back, absorbing the words. "Okay, okay," he nodded slowly. "So you're telling me your husband was having an affair with Viktor's daughter... and she got pregnant? So Viktor ordered a hit?"

Serena shrugged, exhaustion pulling at her shoulders. "Sounds like it."

"Did you know he was having an affair?"

"Of course." She hated the weariness in her voice, the way it came out flat and defeated. But how did she explain to this man—this man who had once loved her—what her choices had cost her?

"Of course?"

The disbelief in his tone made heat climb into her face. Ashamed of the incredulous look he gave her, Serena scrambled for words, her mouth suddenly dry. "Look. He got bored easily. There were always women. Some fancy jewelry, a couple hundred thousand and an NDA, and he could have whoever he wanted."

"But not the only daughter of the world's biggest drug lord," he challenged. "Do you know how protective he is of her?"

Serena's stomach twisted. She met his stare but couldn't hold it for long. "Everyone knew. I just didn't know it would get my husband killed," she said with a bitter exhale. The words tasted like metal.

"Men weren't even allowed to look at her, let alone touch her. So for your husband to have had access—let alone get her pregnant?"

She folded her arms, more out of self-defense than confidence. "My husband and Viktor may have done business together."

"What do you mean 'may have'?"

"We went out to the island a few times. Family things."

"You've been to Viktor's island?"

"Yeah. I've gone shopping with his wife, Lena. Had spa days."

"You had spa days with the wife of one of the most feared drug lords in the world?"

"I learned not to ask questions early in our marriage. Besides, Lena's actually a pretty nice woman. I liked her. Still do."

Serena exhaled tightly, rubbing her palms together to ground herself. The motion did little to ease the tremor winding through her chest. Her mouth felt dry. Her ribs ached from the effort of holding everything in. "Yes, Julian comes from old money, but he's always had other business interests. Obsidian Construction Group? It's a front. There are other dealings and other businesses —I wasn't supposed to know."

He didn't interrupt, but his silence pressed at her, thick and heavy. She could feel his skepticism sitting in the room with them, a weight she couldn't shake. And once she started talking, her words simply spilled out.

"Listen. Julian and I had an agreement. He did his events, I went as his wife, smiled for the cameras, and we kept up appearances." Her voice caught, but she forced it steady. "Married to Julian, I was the perfect showpiece and mother to his children. He had... other hobbies. And I turned a blind eye."

The quiet that followed wasn't kind. It scraped at her skin, made her wish she'd saved some part of herself instead of laying it all bare. Chase's expression didn't change, but she could almost feel him dissecting every word like he would a suspect's statement.

When she finally spoke again, her voice had lost all its armor. "But I didn't kill him."

"How do you think I can help you with this?" Chase asked. "I've been working on the Varlamov case for the better part of a decade, and when I finally get a shot at breaking it wide open, my partner ends up dead and I'm on suspension because Varlamov made it look like I did it."

He blew out a long breath, jaw tightening. "I was so busy

tending my partner that the one shot I got off at Viktor only wounded him. I couldn't even kill the bastard."

"Too bad you didn't. I wouldn't be in this mess if you had."

Chase glared at her. "Really? You want to put that on me too?"

The heat in his words stung. Serena swallowed hard, realizing she'd gone too far. "Sorry," she said softly. "I was trying to make a joke to ease the tension, but I clearly messed up. I apologize."

He didn't answer right away, the silence pressing in so thick she could hear the hum of the refrigerator across the room.

Straightening, Serena said, "The fact that you were able to get so close to him makes me think you know enough to get close again. Because of the nature of Viktor's work, Lena's phone number is constantly changing. I don't have a way to reach her, but I think if I could just talk to her, she would help. She'd be furious if she knew about Viktor's plans for Eva."

Serena exhaled, the weight of desperation sitting heavy in her chest. "I've exhausted every possible resource. You're my last hope. Lena's in town this week for a charity fundraiser. I need you to help me get some time alone with her, which means circumventing her security detail."

Chase barked out a dry laugh. "I'm sorry, did you just ask me to participate in a murder-suicide? Because that's what you're asking. Getting to Lena would be suicide. The fact that you're asking me to do it is setting me up to be killed."

Serena held his gaze. "Maybe. But you've gone up against worse for less."

For a moment neither spoke. Outside, the wind rattled against the window, the temperature dropping another few degrees—a reminder that the storm wasn't far off.

CHAPTER FOUR

They huddled behind boxes in the empty storeroom, waiting for their opportunity to talk to Lena.

"You're sure Lena is going to help you," Chase whispered, scanning the shadows. "She's not going to be mad about your husband was screwing her baby girl?"

Serena exhaled slowly. "Oh, she'll be mad," she said. "But Lena? She's the kind of mad that plots revenge. She'd have wanted to cut Julian's balls off herself."

Chase raised a brow, but she kept going.

"She'll help because Viktor broke his word. Eva was supposed to be off-limits. The one kid who'd get out. Her own life. Her choice of husband. But when Lena learns what Viktor has planned for her, she'll be furious with him. I wouldn't be surprised if Lena cuts off Viktor's balls for this."

Chase gave a dry grunt. "I'd settle for putting him behind bars."

Serena glanced at him. "I'd settle for watching him burn."

"And you're sure Lena will be here today?" Chase asked, glancing toward the door as footsteps echoed faintly beyond it. "I didn't see her name on the client list."

He held up a printed appointment schedule they'd snagged from an adjacent treatment room.

Serena sighed. "She'll be here. She always comes after a charity event. Trust me."

"There's that T word again," he muttered. "I don't think you understand what that word means, because you keep using it in wildly inappropriate ways."

Serena shot him a look. "Last night Lena attended a charity fundraiser. Every time they're in town for it, the next day she comes here alone without her driver and guards. She says she needs to unwind. She says it's to wash off the stench of her husband. And honestly? After what Viktor's done this time... she might need bleach."

A name on the appointment schedule jumped out at her. "Zarya Bloom. That's her. Lena wanted to start a cosmetics company, and that's what she was going to name it—until Viktor said no."

"Sounds like a real peach," Chase said. "You've got to wonder why anyone would stay married to a man like that."

Serena glared at him. "Are you talking about her or me?" she asked coldly. "Because in either case, you're just as naïve as you keep accusing me of being if you think we had a choice."

The flicker in his expression told her the shot had landed exactly where she meant it to. Good. Let him sit with it for once. She wasn't the monster Chase believed her to be.

"Just a few more minutes, so we should get ready," she said, grabbing the wig they'd bought to make her harder to recognize.

"Look at you—a brunette," Chase muttered as he helped her settle the fake hair on her head. He didn't press the conversation. For once, he seemed to understand this wasn't the time to poke old wounds.

"Not bad." He gave a low whistle, just enough mischief in it to ease the tension.

Serena shook her head slowly. "Stop."

Once he made sure the hallway was clear, Chase opened the door, and Serena slipped out, leading him across the corridor to Lena's treatment room.

"I told you people not to bother me. I'm fine," Lena said, clearly irritated. She was wrapped in seaweed, eyes covered with a thick green face mask.

"Lena, it's me. Serena."

"What the—?" Lena struggled against the wrap for a beat, then stilled. "What are you doing here?"

"I need your help."

"Help? Me? How?" Lena's voice sharpened with annoyance. "The police are looking for you. Though I'm not sure I'll turn you in. You killed your husband. Good for you! Finally, a woman in this godforsaken place accomplished something."

She snorted. "At least one of us is rid of our miserable husband. Viktor tried to feel me up last night. Can you believe it? The man's drowning in mistresses but still thinks he's gonna get milk from this cow? I don't think so."

Chase chuckled under his breath. Lena turned her head toward the sound.

"Who is that?"

"He's a friend who's helping me. I didn't kill Julian."

Lena muttered a curse in Russian. "So what do you want from me?"

"Viktor ordered the hit."

Her head tipped slightly. "You are screwed," she said bluntly, then paused. "Wait. Why would Viktor order the hit? He had no reason to kill Julian. They were about to make a ton of money together. Good deals don't get people dead—bad blood does. Viktor was pissed when the deal fell through."

"It was an act," Serena said. "When you hear what I have to tell you, it'll make sense."

Lena let out a breath, her tone laced with exasperation. "Good God. What has that man done this time? What did your asshole do to my asshole to make him want to kill him?"

"Julian was sleeping with Eva."

There was a beat of silence. Then Lena froze, lips parting beneath the face mask. "Wait—my *Evochka*?" her voice cracked upward, laced with disbelief. "That bastard. I'll rip his balls off myself. Let's dig up his grave."

Serena didn't flinch. "Well, it gets worse."

"What do you mean worse?"

"He got Eva pregnant."

Lena jerked forward instinctively, her seaweed wrap peeling and pulling in damp strands. She clawed at her body. "Ugh, get me out of this thing. I need to think."

Serena rushed to her side and peeled off the eye mask. Lena sat back, breathing hard, green goop smeared across her temples like war paint.

Once she could see, Lena focused on the man standing behind Serena.

"So *you're* the one helping her," she said, fixing Chase with a disdainful once-over. "Useless man. My husband was handed to you on a silver platter, and you couldn't even kill him. What good are men anyway?"

Chase opened his mouth, then seemed to think better of it and stepped back.

Lena pivoted her attention back to Serena, eyes fiery with rage. "You say *Polina* killed Julian? So it even took a woman to kill your stupid husband. Now, help me finish getting out of this."

Serena motioned for Chase to move to the other side. He hesitated, then knelt and began tugging loose the damp layers of seaweed wrap, mimicking the technique Serena remembered from her own treatments. Lena grunted and wriggled, clearly impatient to be free.

As they reached the last layer, Chase froze. "Uh... are you wearing anything underneath this?"

"What?" Lena snapped, lifting her head slightly. "So you're a prude *and* a lousy shot? God, it's like you've never seen a naked woman before. There's a robe over there."

He turned, grabbed the robe, and avoided making eye contact as they helped her into it. Once Lena was settled and sitting upright, green residue still streaked across her hairline, Serena told her what they'd uncovered.

By the time she finished, Lena sat stone still.

"I'm going to kill him myself," she muttered. But then her face crumpled slightly. "Are you sure this is true? Our children grew up together. My sweet girl would never..."

Serena looked away, shame radiating off her like heat. "Eva did spend a lot of time at our cottage over the summer. I didn't think much of it. Our daughters had always been so close. I never imagined..." She trailed off, voice cracking. "I thought he was finally showing interest in the kids and their friends. I didn't see it. I should have."

Lena let out a sharp, bitter snort. "None of us would have. Disgusting old man with his saggy balls." There was venom in her voice, but then, a chuckle. "Did you know the last time Julian came to the house, he and Viktor were discussing plastic surgery… for their balls? Like, *lifts*."

She shook her head in disbelief. "How could my daughter fall for someone like that?" Her disgust cracked into something softer, a half-sob. "My baby. Having a baby. She's just a baby herself. Only twenty years old." Her mouth twisted. "I'm glad Viktor killed him."

Then, suddenly, confusion returned to her expression. She turned to Serena. "But why frame you? It's not your fault your husband was a pig."

Serena shrugged, jaw tight. "I wasn't happy with the merger. Julian considered backing out, and Toby was pissed."

Lena nodded thoughtfully. "Viktor would've lost money too. That company's one of his few businesses that actually runs clean. Good for the laundry." A pause. "Who runs his companies now?"

"It's supposed to be me," Serena said. "But with the whole murder accusation… Toby was next in line. He'll run it least until the kids are older. That's how we structured the trust."

Lena sighed, dragging a hand through her damp hair. "And now that he's doing Viktor's bidding…" She made a noise of disgust. "Ugh. Men are so useless and predictable. We should chop off all their balls."

She turned to Chase, eyes narrowing with mock consideration. "Not you. You won't miss next time you get a shot at my husband, correct?"

Chase shifted where he stood, discomfort flickering across his face. "I'm still technically a police officer," he said carefully. "I can't kill him in cold blood."

"And what good has *that* done you, huh?" Lena muttered. She rolled her eyes, waving him off with a flick of her hand. "Useless men."

She turned back to Serena, the sharpness in her expression softening—just barely.

"It's always up to the women," she said. "Viktor took the one last sacred thing from me." Her voice dropped. "He's broken every promise he's ever made. To make up for it, he's going to turn that little slut—and the evidence she killed Julian—over to the authorities."

She paused, her gaze drifting back to Chase, this time with calculation in her eyes. Watching Lena was like seeing the version of herself Serena had never dared to be—until now. Serena might not want to chop off all men's balls, after all, they could be of *some* use, but seeing the conviction in Lena strengthened her own resolve.

"You might have some use after all," Lena said. "Now I just have to figure out how I'm going to make Viktor pay for what he did."

Looking pleased with herself, Lena primped in the mirror, adjusting the robe like armor.

"The attendants will be back soon," she said, lips curling. "I'll help you."

"Thank you, Lena. I appreciate your help."

"Please," she scoffed, eyes glinting. "It'll be a pleasure to ruin Viktor's plans. And now I can keep my daughter—and my grandchild—safe."

At the door, Serena hesitated. "I'm truly sorry for what Julian did to your daughter."

"It's not your fault," Lena said, her tone softening. "You could no more control your husband than I can control mine."

A familiar sadness passed over her face like a shadow, the kind Serena recognized too well. The kind that came with being married to powerful, dangerous men. Men the world feared, envied, but never truly understood. Especially not men like Chase, who saw their world in black and white.

Lena gave a little wave, as if brushing away all of it—all the mistakes, all the bitterness. "You remember that little park we used to take the kids to when they were young?"

"Of course," Serena said.

"Meet me there tonight. Midnight. No, let's say 11:30. God, I'm too old for this bullshit anymore. Viktor and the boys have their night at the club. He's still sulking because I turned him down last night. And apparently... they've got some pretty new dancer he's going to 'check out.'"

She muttered under her breath as she turned back to the mirror. "Good for him. Good for him. And good for me too. Maybe he'll leave me alone for a while. If I let him live."

Once more, Serena was struck with sympathy and a bitter sense of kinship. They existed in different prisons, but with the same bars. She glanced at Chase. The look in his eyes was softer now, more complicated. Less judgmental.

"Thanks, Lena. I really appreciate it." Even though they had no idea what the final solution would be, Serena couldn't help thinking her nightmare might finally be nearing its end.

"How do we know this isn't an ambush?" Chase asked.

Lena laughed. "You don't. You might die tonight. You might live. It'll be fun to find out."

Her smile turned feral. "But I promise you this. If Viktor thinks he's walking away from this mess with his balls intact, he's dumber than I thought."

She waved them toward the door, already dismissing them. "Now get out before the attendants see you. I need to look my best to destroy my husband's life."

CHAPTER FIVE

Serena and Chase sat huddled on the bench against the cold. The park was mostly dark, the distant glare from the streetlights barely touching the edges of the gravel path.

Chase glanced sideways at her. "This feels like it could be a trap."

Serena shrugged. "Could be. But it's not like we had better options." She paused. "Besides, I'd like to think our friendship meant something to Lena. And we have a common enemy."

"You were hoping she'd want to murder her husband, weren't you?"

"At the very least, she'll chop off his balls and the poor bastard will kill himself." Serena's smile was cold. "Men only seem capable of thinking with their lower brain most times."

"You're aware you're talking to a man?"

The laugh that escaped was more bitter than she expected. "Says the man whose first concern about helping me was the offense I gave to his nether regions." She shook her head. "Look, let's not pretend tonight ends with a peaceful resolution."

Chase dropped his gaze.

She turned to face him fully. "If what's about to go down offends your black and white sensibilities, leave now. You helped me contact Lena. I got what I needed. But if you want to be part of whatever justice gets meted out to Viktor, come with me. I can assure you he'll never see the inside of a jail cell."

Chase didn't answer. Instead, he gestured toward a line of SUVs headed their way.

"They didn't spare any money on armor now, did they?" Chase muttered, eyeing the glossy black vehicles.

The door to the first in line swung open. A large man in a tailored coat stepped out, silent and unreadable, then motioned for them to be frisked.

Chase raised his arms without protest, as if he'd known this was coming.

The guard reached under his coat and quickly located the gun.

"See?" Serena said under her breath. "I told you not to bring that."

"I always have my gun," Chase replied evenly.

Once disarmed, they were motioned into the back of the SUV.

"So good to see you," Lena greeted them as they climbed in. She was already lounging inside, radiant in a fur-lined coat, a glass of something clear and cold in one manicured hand. "Tonight is going to be so much fun. Have you been to the club?"

She laughed, the sound sharp and bright.

"Of course you have, Chase. Yes, that's where you shot my husband and your friend died, isn't it?" Her voice was a silk-wrapped weapon. "Next time you try to kill Viktor, don't miss."

The quick draw of breath from the cop seated nearby made Serena stifle a laugh, until the mirth in Lena's eyes made it hard to resist joining in.

"Your guy took my gun," Chase said, gesturing at the hulking man seated beside Lena.

"You won't need it for a while," Lena replied, smiling sweetly. "We'll have a nice chat. Drink some vodka. Check out Viktor's latest—"

She paused, a smile teasing the edge of her lips.

"—plaything. Mistress. Companion. Whatever term the young girls prefer these days. Then maybe help you arrest the whore he uses to do his dirty work. Easy peasy."

She held out her hand to the security guard without looking at him. Wordlessly, he placed Chase's gun in her palm.

"Thank you," Lena said, slipping it into her designer handbag like it was a compact mirror.

"Please be careful with that," Chase said, watching her with a mix of irritation and disbelief.

"Oh, is it special to you?" Lena asked, raising a brow. "That's so cute, the way you men love your guns."

"It's loaded," Chase said evenly.

Lena laughed, unbothered. "It's fine. Don't you worry. You

think it's the only gun I've had in my handbag? I feel like Prada was made for this. Not enough women take advantage of that."

She gave Serena a wink, then settled back into her seat, deadly calm and freshly amused. Her expression shifted. "I've spoken to Evochka," she said quietly. "It took some doing, but I know where she is now. She's safe."

Serena's breath caught.

"She confirmed everything you told me—the affair, the pregnancy." Lena's lip curled slightly. "The little idiot even admitted she thought Julian would leave you and marry her. She went to Viktor, thinking *he'd* talk Julian into it. Can you imagine?"

Her tone twisted, caught between disbelief and fury.

Unfortunately, Serena could imagine. Eva wasn't the first who'd thought Julian would marry them. She'd witnessed enough emotional scenes and received the obligatory apology diamonds to know it was just another one of her late husband's lies. But that didn't help the angry woman sitting with her, so Serena gave a sympathetic murmur as Lena continued.

"She's devastated now. Upset that her father would order a hit on the father of her child." Lena shook her head as if trying to dispel the absurdity of it all.

Slowly, Lena straightened her spine, regaining every inch of her imperious posture. Then she held her hand out to Serena.

"You will not go down for your husband's murder."

Lena's hand dropped back into her lap, the warmth in her voice cooling just slightly as her thoughts shifted gears.

A beat of silence passed. Then, her tone sharpened, laced with practicality.

"I'm assuming the child... some portion of Julian's estate will given them upon the conclusion of the legal proceedings? You are the executor, correct?"

Serena nodded. "It's not the baby's fault Julian was such a scumbag. Julian had more money than any sane person had a right to, and I've always wanted to give more to charity. It will be my pleasure to make sure Eva and the baby have everything they need."

Was it weird that she was talking so easily about giving her late husband's money to his illegitimate child? Probably no more so than being framed for his murder.

"Very good," Lena said. "So that is settled. My daughter and her little baby will be fine."

Lena's turned to Chase then.

"I will get you your arrests. But we do this on my terms."

Chase met her gaze with hard skepticism. "I don't negotiate with drug lords."

Lena's smile was sharp and humorless. "I'm not a drug lord. I'm *just the wife*. But I can give you enough evidence to destroy him and half a dozen of his associates. But in exchange, you will protect the rest of my family."

They arrived at Viktor's club as the city's neon pulse reflected off the tinted SUV windows. As the vehicle rolled to a stop, Lena turned to them.

"I'll do all the talking. Just follow my lead."

They entered through the VIP entrance—Lena leading with Chase, and Serena in tow, surrounded by her security detail. The guards at the door straightened when they saw her, clearly surprised, but said nothing.

Lena offered them a cool smile. "They're with me," she said simply.

No one argued.

The group was escorted down a narrow hallway into the back rooms. Serena had never been this far inside. She'd always been told the club "wasn't for refined ladies like her."

Now she could see why.

Everything was dripping in gaudy imitation luxury: crushed velvet, mirrored walls, and just enough gold trim to make her teeth hurt. Lena had once affectionately called the aesthetic *Tacky Russian Chic,* and it lived up—or down—to the name.

They stopped at a heavy door. As it opened, Viktor looked up, seated in a leather armchair surrounded by his usual entourage.

He didn't appear surprised to see them.

Serena could sense Chase's tension simmering under his skin. He was watching for exits, calculating angles, still half-convinced this would all go sideways. But at this point, she figured, if it was a trap, it was one they'd already chosen to walk into.

Let him stew. They wanted the same thing: justice.

Viktor lounged with a glass in hand, flanked by two men. He didn't rise.

"What are you doing here, Lena?" he asked, voice casual but laced with tension. "The boys said you were on your way, but I didn't believe it. And who's this with you?"

As he raised his glass, the man beside him leaned in and whispered something in his ear.

Viktor's smile didn't move, but his eyes darkened, just slightly.

"Serena," he said, voice lazy with mock amusement, "I hear the police are looking for you."

She stared at him and said nothing.

He laughed, turning to Chase with a glint in his eye. "Aren't you going to arrest her? Maybe they'll let you back on the force. You know, issuing parking tickets or something."

Next to her, Chase tensed, jaw clenched.

Serena nudged him—just a small, deliberate pressure against his arm. *Don't take the bait.*

Lena let out a sharp noise in the back of her throat. "God. Stop acting like such a child." She rolled her eyes at Viktor. "You're lucky the stupid man missed. I hope next time his aim is better ."

Then, as if suddenly remembering, she looked around the room. Her voice sharpened. "Where's that bitch, Polina?"

The woman in question emerged from behind a velvet-draped table, moving with calculated grace. She draped herself against Viktor's arm, smiling like she owned the room.

"Do not address me unless it's with respect," she said stiffly. "Did you want something?"

"I do," Lena said, lifting her hand to the overhead light, her oversized wedding ring catching gold and diamond fire. Her eyes flicked from Viktor to Polina.

"Would you be so kind as to tell us all," Lena continued, her tone casual, "why you disguised yourself as my dear friend Serena and killed her husband, Julian, effectively framing someone who's always been so good to our family for murder?"

The air in the room shifted.

Polina's smile faltered. Her eyes widened. "How do you know this?"

"I saw it," Serena said, voice dark and steady. "I saw you."

Her words hung in the air, heavier than she expected. She'd held them in for so long, afraid they would sound like grief or rage or madness. But now, in this room, surrounded by those who had tried to bury her, she felt strong in the truth.

"I saw you," she said again, meeting Polina's gaze. "I saw you."

Polina's expression twisted. "Prove it," she hissed.

"She won't need to," Lena said, her smile razor-sharp. "Because you're going to confess."

Viktor laughed. "Why would she do that? You're crazy, Lena. Go back to your spa. Clearly, today's session did nothing to improve your mood."

"I don't think so." Lena's gaze shifted to one of the men near Viktor—older, heavyset, his shirt open nearly to his belly and straining at the fabric, revealing a thick patch of graying chest hair tangled with several oversized gold chains. He looked exactly like the type of man this club was built for.

"You know," Lena said, syrup-sweet, "I had an interesting chat with Evochka today. Would you two like me to fill you in on the details? Particularly you, Sergei, as she is, I understand, your bride-to-be."

Viktor stood abruptly. "Lena, please. Our family matters should be discussed in private."

Serena caught the flicker of tension across Chase's face. She kept her posture controlled, but her hands curled slightly at her sides.

Lena gave a dry laugh. "Private? Like all the things you've been keeping from me?"

She turned toward Sergei. Her voice was calm, but Serena felt the silence in the room tighten.

"My daughter won't be marrying you. She's pregnant with another man's baby."

Sergei needed only a few seconds to process the words. His face turned a violent shade of red.

"You bastard," he shouted at Viktor. "You bring shame to my family. We're leaving," he barked at his men. "Come on."

They stormed out, the threat hovering thick in the air.

Viktor's focus returned to Lena. "You may have just started a war with a family I've spent years trying to win over. You will pay for that."

"Oh no, I won't. You will," Lena said calmly, putting her hands in her coat pockets as though she was getting ready to take a casual stroll.

Serena had known this woman for years, but she had never seen her this still. Everything about Lena in that moment radiated control.

Viktor narrowed his eyes. "What's that supposed to mean?"

"You have broken every promise you've ever made to me. And then, you framed a dear friend of mine for murder."

"Lena, please. You don't understand," Viktor said, changing his tone.

"Oh, I understand. What I understand is that you have betrayed a dear family friend, and you have betrayed me. Therefore, you will get Polina to confess. You will give me the evidence I need to prove it, because I know you have stashed it in case you need to ensure her compliance. The police will have an airtight case."

Polina's voice trembled. "Lena, please."

"No, Polina. Please don't. Did you or did you not kill Julian?"

"I... I did," Polina said. Her voice cracked. "But you have to understand. I did it because he asked me to."

"Enough," Viktor said sharply. "Polina, you've said too much."

Lena didn't flinch.

"That's right. She's supposed to confess, but not say you put her up to it. Isn't that right, darling?"

Serena felt the weight of it all settle in. Days of shame, isolation, running, and second-guessing, now ended with a single confession.

"What were you thinking?" Lena demanded.

"What I was thinking is our daughter's innocence was stolen by a pig who would never appreciate her. I wanted him dead."

"So you had Polina kill him? I could appreciate that," Lena replied, her voice edged with ice. "Only you had to frame one of the few friends I have in this world."

She glanced at Serena then, and for a moment, every shard of fear Serena had felt in coming here dissolved. Lena's rage ran deeper than just a daughter who'd been wronged. And despite everything, Serena knew she'd made the right choice.

"Friends," Viktor said, snorting. "Friends don't impregnate your daughter."

A bitter laugh escaped Lena. "But you have no problem marrying her off to some lecherous old goat. You broke the one promise you kept all these years. You will ensure Polina is punished for murdering Julian. And Serena goes free."

"Fine." Viktor sighed deeply. "I'll give you the evidence to prove Polina did it."

"No!" Polina screamed, her voice cracking. "Viktor, after everything I've done for you—everything we've shared. The others I've killed for you..."

Her tears streamed down her face. For a brief moment, Serena actually felt sorry for her.

Beside her, Chase remained still, focused. She knew what this meant for him. This would be the arrest that would bring him back, and restore his reputation.

Until Viktor opened his mouth.

"Shut it, bitch." He pulled out a gun and fired.

Polina collapsed onto the velvet table, blood pooling around her.

Viktor looked at Chase, almost apologetically. "I can't risk her talking, you know. But I'll turn over enough evidence to prove she did it. Acting on her own, of course. Jealousy. Rage. Classic story. Julian wouldn't leave Serena for her. By the time I'm done, it will appear to be a suicide. I've done it before."

Serena's stomach turned.

She glanced at Lena, who stood eerily still.

"You murder so casually," Lena said softly. "Even though I know she was one of your favorite mistresses."

Viktor's expression twisted. "Woman, I grow weary of you. Cease talking before I shut you up permanently as well."

"You wouldn't dare," Lena said.

"Oh, wouldn't I?"

He stared at the gun in his hands and grinned.

There was a tense moment. And then, Lena's voice changed. "Put your gun away. Don't shoot. Please don't kill me, Viktor."

She fumbled in her purse as if panicked. But Serena knew better. She remembered the moment Lena had slipped Chase's gun into her bag like it was nothing.

And before anyone could stop her, Lena leveled the barrel at her husband and fired.

The shot echoed through the room.

Viktor dropped where he stood, a clean bullet straight through his forehead.

"And that is why you don't rely on a stupid man to do a woman's work." Lena wiped the gun clean of prints, then handed it to Chase.

"Now, shoot a hole in the wall so there's gunshot residue on your hands. When the police come, we'll tell them you shot him to stop him from killing me, after you witnessed him shoot Polina."

She pulled her phone from her pocket and held it up. "I recorded the whole thing on my voice recorder app."

Then she turned to the bodyguard who'd been in the room the entire time. "You will tell the others to stand down. The police will be called."

She nodded toward Chase. "You may call that in. Congratulations. I believe your prior mistake in failing to kill my husband has now been rectified."

Then she turned back to the bodyguard. "Very soon, this place will be crawling with police. I suggest they find nothing of interest. They are to assume this was a domestic dispute. That's all. I don't want any reason for them to look further. Am I clear?"

"Yes, Madam," he said. He was already dialing.

He stepped away, speaking briskly into his phone, leaving the rest of them in silence, staring down at Viktor's body.

Lena let out a long sigh. "I really wanted to shoot him in the balls, but I couldn't risk him shooting one of us first. Do you think it'll look bad if I do it now?"

Chase gave a dry laugh. "We're already tampering with evidence. Let's not add a mysterious gunshot wound to the groin to the report."

"What about kicking him in the balls?" Lena asked. "Will that show up on an autopsy? Serena and I both deserve a turn."

Chase sighed. "Please do not kick the victim in the balls. I'm still not entirely sure how to explain what just happened."

"You'll say exactly what I told you to," Lena replied with a shrug. "You saved my life, officer. I'll be forever grateful."

She repeated the line slowly, deliberately.

"You saved my life."

She looked over at Serena and smiled. "Between the recording and all of us giving the same statement, it'll be an open and shut case. Serena gets her freedom, you get your badge back, and I'm rid of my husband."

Her smile widened. "We both are."

Serena allowed herself to smile.

Lena exhaled, deeper now, her posture softening just a little. "But honestly, this husband-killing business is exhausting. It's way past my bedtime."

"Mine, too," Serena said.

"Tomorrow, we go for a spa day. We'll need a good scrubbing to wash the stench of these idiot men off our skin."

Then she touched Serena's hair. "That, and your roots need a touchup. God, the trials we endure. After tomorrow"—her smile sharpened—"we take over their poorly run business empires. Finally, we'll get something useful done around here."

Serena smiled, feeling lighter than she had in years. "I think I'm going to enjoy being a widow."

The End

KNIVES AND VELVET

REBELRY STONE

LOU

THE CITY WAS HOLDING its breath when I parked two blocks shy of the card house.

Not the polite kind of breath—this one tasted like copper and old prayers, the way a church smells after the candles drown themselves.

I watched the street the way I watch men who think they're invisible. One black sedan that should've been on the west corner wasn't. A white van with no logo had circled twice, then vanished like a magic trick performed with a body. The doorman's posture had changed by an inch… A tell so small you needed to have survived a dozen ambushes to read it. His right foot faced the alley, not the street. Exit ready. Run poised.

Something had shifted under the Salvator floorboards.

I texted the ghost channel—three dots, two slashes—then shut my phone off and slid the spare blade into my boot. I could feel the night inside my ribs, pacing. Domenico, the Don, ruled this city like a hymn written in cut glass. Matteo, his brother, enforced it like the steady beat beneath the music that keeps the dancers from falling. Two versions of control. Two kinds of danger. I knew which one I preferred to touch.

Somewhere out there, Valentina's name had started moving like rumor-smoke again. The kind men pretend not to believe until they're standing in the ash of their own certainty.

I tasted for lies, found too many, and smiled anyway. If the house was a trap, better I spring it than the boys. Better I bleed than the woman who taught me how to wear a crown without showing the blade hidden in the velvet.

I stepped into the alley and let the dark shut behind me like a mouth.

I was almost to the servant's door when the first shot sounded —muffled, mean. It punched the night in the teeth. A second shot answered. Then silence. Pain flared along my ribs, but it looked like a graze. I'd deal with it later.

Nothing is more dangerous than a room that pretends to be quiet after it's done screaming.

I palmed the latch, counted to seven in Italian, and flowed through.

The smoke met me first. Then the dead. And then him.

Matteo.

The night made a new shape around my name.

I tasted blood in the air before I saw him clearly.

Gun smoke licked the dark like a tongue, teasing the wreckage of the poker room. Men I'd trained bled into the Persian rug. A chandelier swung on one chain, throwing knives of light across overturned chairs. The house had been quiet when I slipped in through the servant's corridor. But quiet never survives a Salvator.

"Drop the blade, songbird."

His voice came from the blind corner... low, amused, entirely in control. It slid under my skin like a blade in a silk sheath. I smelled him: gun oil, expensive soap, a hint of cigar he didn't smoke but everyone offered him anyway. Matteo Salvator had a reputation for switching from charm to brutality faster than a heartbeat, faster than the way my pulse went traitor at the sound of him.

"You're making a mess," I said, and stepped into the light.

He leaned against an overturned billiards table, shirt sleeves shoved to his elbows, tattoos stark on his forearms, black hair mussed. His gun hung loose in his hand, muzzle down. A smear of someone else's blood stained the edge of his jaw. He wore it like a badge.

"And you're late." His eyes dropped to the knife at my thigh. "You promised me the head of the man who sold us out."

"I promised you his silence." I arched a brow. "Heads don't stay quiet. Tongues do—if cut correctly."

He grinned, wolfish. "I always forget you're nastier than me."

"That's why I'm the insurance policy," I said. "And you're the accident I love to watch."

A body groaned near the bar. Matteo flicked his gun and ended the sound without looking. Clean. Efficient. Ruthless.

I should've hated him.

He strode toward me, loose and lethal. Outside, sirens curled up the night and rolled away—ours, not theirs. I watched him the way you watch an ocean in a storm: calculating the pull, respecting the undertow, already building the desire to drown.

"Lou." He stopped close enough for heat to cross the inch between us. "You're bleeding."

I glanced down. A line of red laced my ribcage where a bullet had kissed me. "Barely. He nicked me because you took too long."

"I was disposing of liabilities." Matteo tucked two fingers under the hem of my top. His skin brushed mine. I hissed on reflex, not from pain. He went still, reading me, that dangerous focus pinning me to the moment. His fingers were rough from triggers and rope. I'd felt both.

"Look at me." His voice went softer, a paradox in a throat that had just ordered death. "Tell me if you're dizzy."

"I'm fine."

"Tell me because I asked, not because you're stubborn."

My mouth tilted. "You don't get to own all my obedience, Matteo."

"I don't want all of it," he said, and it was a lie, but a pretty one. "I only want what you crave to give."

His thumb traced the edge of the cut, slow as a promise. Heat slid through me. Danger hummed in the room like electricity caught under glass.

I met his eyes. "Then ask better."

His mouth quirked. "Would you let me take care of you, songbird?"

The nickname hit low. Too tender for a man like him to use out loud. Too accurate—if I were a song, I'd be the kind that lured sailors to their deaths then kissed the salt from their lips as they sank.

"Yes," I said. "On a condition."

His brows lifted. "Name it."

"I want him." I nodded to the back room, where the traitor was hog-tied with a nice double-column knot I'd taught the boys for fun and contingencies. Blood dripped off his fingers, painting the floor in patience. "He's mine."

Matteo's expression didn't change. But something sharp flickered through his gaze... approval, hunger, possession. "We'll do it together."

I smiled. My knife smiled with me.

We ended the traitor quick. You can be cruel without being sloppy; you can be merciful without being soft. When it was done, Matteo signed the room back to our men and pulled me into the hallway like I was the only thing he needed to carry out of that house.

"Med bay," he said into his comm. "Keep it hot."

"Always is when you're in it," I murmured.

He shot me a look that dragged my pulse to my throat. "Careful."

"Of you?" I licked a drop of blood from my thumb. "Never."

Of how much I wanted to belong to him? Constantly.

Outside, the night clenched its jaw and swallowed us.

***

The safehouse sat in the bones of a church that had burned down and rebuilt itself in steel and secrecy. Stained glass had been replaced with blacked-out panes. The altar was a stainless-steel island with medical-grade drawers. Sanctity had traded with sin, and both of them knew they'd gotten the better end.

Matteo led me to the edge of the steel like he was taking me to communion. The lights hummed awake, bright enough to turn the room into a confession booth where every lie would glare.

"Shirt," he said.

"Bossy," I grumbled, but my hands were already on the hem. The steel island kissed the backs of my thighs, cold and unyielding, and for a heartbeat I wanted to be either. I peeled the fabric up and off, slow enough to make him impatient.

"Sit," he ordered.

I didn't. "You don't give me orders."

His gaze didn't move. "I do when you're leaving red on the floor."

"The floor deserves it."

"The floor didn't save your life."

"I did that."

"I know." He softened the words without losing the edge. "Sit, Lou."

I stayed standing because I needed to feel the tremor in my legs, needed to choose it. He read the stubborn in my spine and adjusted like a man who'd built a cathedral out of other people's resistance. Matteo set the kit down, unclipped my braid with one hand, and dragged the other over the steel to show me its sterilized shine.

Still not going to sit. Time passed until he gave in.

"Then lean," he said. "On me."

A little surge of triumph flared low in my body. I exhaled. Leaned.

The antiseptic sting bit. I hissed. His body went taut, and for a second I wanted to say the word just to hear him stop the world for me—Winter—but I didn't. He breathed, slow and deliberate, until my pulse obediently matched his.

"You're shaking," he murmured.

"I'm furious," I said.

"Same thing in our family."

I laughed once, ugly and honest. "You were late."

His jaw ticked. "Someone moved a piece off my board. Someone I trusted to stay where I left them." He pressed gauze to the cut. "You like me when I'm late?"

"I like you when you admit you're human."

"Dangerous rumor." He checked the gauze, hands heartbreakingly careful. "Turn."

I turned. His palm landed high on my spine, warm and steady. The weight said stay better than any rope. He held my eyes over my shoulder, and the room quieted the way a church does when a sinner finally sits down.

"Color?" he asked.

"Green," I said, and tasted the heat that came with it.

He reached to the tray and lifted the leather cuffs like a priest raising a chalice. My pulse shivered. He hesitated… Just a breath, just long enough to say *your call* without words.

"Ask me," I said.

His mouth twitched. "Lou. May I restrain you so I can stop the bleeding and keep you here with me a little longer?"

My laugh broke on a sound no one else gets to hear. "Yes, Matteo."

"Safeword?"

"Winter."

"Show me."

"Winter," I whispered, a blade in velvet.

He buckled the leather, snug but not cruel, the chain short enough that I couldn't use my hands to run. The restraint didn't make me smaller. It made me precise.

He kissed my shoulder, just once. It burned like absolution. "Good girl."

The praise cracked something under my ribs, a frozen river finding a way to flow. I wanted to sink to my knees and I wanted to put my knife to his throat and tell him not to call me that unless he meant to keep me, both, both, always both. He felt the riot like men feel weather before it hits.

"Breathe with me," he said.

I did.

When he was finished stitching me, he unhooked the chain but left the cuffs on, thumbs smoothing the skin they'd circled. "I'll take them off if you want."

"I don't," I said. "Not yet." We always played this game. Both wanting more, but knowing it would never work.

The grin he tried to smother rewired me. "Then I'll hold you with something that can hold you back."

His words promised something deeper. My gaze flitted away, landing on the stitches.

The smear of blood on my skin looked obscene and pretty against the black lace of my bra. Matteo's hands bracketed my hips, warm and heavy, anchoring me.

"You like me here," I said, and tossed my head to get hair out of my face.

"You like that I like you here," he countered. "You like that the world goes quiet when I tell you to be still."

"Arrogant."

"Accurate." He cleaned around the new angry stitches with steady precision. The sting made my breath hitch; the way his thumb stroked my side made my bones go molten. When he dressed the wound, his mouth brushed my shoulder, a kiss or a check for fever. His breath turned my skin to a prayer.

"You bleed pretty," he murmured.

"I don't bleed for you."

His gaze snapped to mine. That hunger again. The one that said he would eat the world if it tried to put space between us.

"Not yet," he said.

That's the problem with men like Matteo. They build a need

inside you and then they worship it until you confuse their hands for your own hunger.

His gaze roamed over me, then he nodded, satisfied. His hand slid into my hair, and his mouth took mine.

Heat shuddered through me. The kiss went pornographic fast, messy and hungry and not a bit polite. He tasted like metal and power and a sin I'd begged to repeat too many times. I moaned into him. His fingers tightened at the nape of my neck. The chain clinked between my wrists like an exhale.

"On your knees," he said against my mouth. "Show me your devotion."

My knees hit the steel, cold and beautiful. I sank for him not because he told me, but because surrender felt like lighting a match inside an ocean. Controlled fire. Voluntary drown.

I didn't worship Matteo with prayers. I used my teeth and tongue, my gaze locked to his, my wrists bound in trust in front of me as leverage. He came apart like he rarely let himself, a velvet violence in the clutch of his hands on my skull, an oath broken and remade on my tongue. When he was done, he pulled me up and kissed me like he was taking back everything he'd given and then deciding to give it again, anyway. He unbuckled the leather and massaged my wrists, careful and reverent.

"You're a problem," he said, breathing roughly.

"I'm your solution," I said, breath ragged.

I expected him to laugh, but he didn't. He framed my face like a man memorizing the map to his own survival. "Stay with me tonight."

The word slotted into the crack in my chest where a home should've been, and I pretended I didn't feel it fit.

"Not tonight," I said.

His smile was small and savage. "I knew you'd say that. That's why I'm asking, not ordering."

"I thought you liked ordering."

"I like you choosing to obey more." His thumb traced my mouth, smearing the taste of him across my lower lip. "Water," he said, already reaching. He crouched to my level, offered the bottle like it was expensive and sacred.

I drank. He watched my throat work like a man starving at a feast.

"Again," he said, and when I grinned around the rim, he flushed, then laughed—quick, rare, young. It undid me faster than his mouth ever could. He caught my face between his hands, foreheads pressed.

"Tell me something true," he said.

"I don't like sleeping in the dark," I answered, surprised by my own admission. "So, I keep the bathroom light on." I paused. "The fan too. It lies to me about being alone."

He kissed my cheek like he was closing a wound. "I keep a radio playing in the kitchen, even when I'm not home." He swallowed. "It lies to me about being wanted."

I slid my fingers under his collar and felt his pulse say everything his voice wouldn't. "You are wanted." And yet neither of us could commit outside of these adrenaline trysts we always seemed to find ourselves in.

"Say it again when the sun's up," he said. "Say it when I look like my brother and not like myself."

"You never look like Domenico," I said. "You look like the man who tells a room to calm down and it listens. Even me."

He smiled against my mouth. "Especially you."

We breathed together until my muscles stopped shouting. When he moved to clean the steel, I caught his hand.

"Leave it," I said. "Let the ghosts have proof."

He stilled. "You want proof?"

"I want the night to know we survived it."

His phone buzzed against the tray, a rude little vibration that turned the room thin. He didn't look at it. Not yet. He brushed hair from my face and tucked his need somewhere I could find again later.

"Ready?" he asked.

"For you? Always," I said, and meant it.

He checked the screen.

The light in his eyes changed temperature.

———

"Domenico?" I asked, already knowing from the bits of the conversation.

He nodded once as he ended the call. "Valentina."

Her name pushed splinters under my nails. Not because I feared her. Because I loved what she'd become... a flame with a spine, a woman who learned to use the silk noose as a sash. I saw her in my head, sitting posture-perfect in a room built to break her, and deciding the room would have to try harder.

"What does he want?" My voice went flat as a blade.

"For her to be found without starting a war," Matteo said. "He knows that's impossible."

"Then he's calling you to do what he won't. Again."

Matteo's jaw flexed. "He's calling me to keep the family from eating itself."

"And if the family is already chewing?" I stood. The world tilted, then obeyed. "I'm going."

"You're not." The command came easy. Habit. Fear wearing authority like armor.

My smile had more teeth than mercy. "Try to stop me."

He stepped in. So did I. We met at the fault line.

"You'll die for her," he said.

"You'll die trying to keep me safe," I said.

The truth landed between us, hot and bright. His hands hovered an inch from my hips, like a man who knows touching the stove will burn and touches it anyway.

"I don't want you to run toward a bullet meant for the Salvators," he said.

"I don't run," I said. "I hunt. And if they're aiming at Valentina, they're aiming at the wrong queen."

Something like reverence crossed his face. "You think she's a queen."

"I know she is," I said. "And I don't let anyone dethrone the women I've sworn to."

He closed his eyes like a prayer he'd never learned was finally echoing back. When he opened them, the enforcer looked out, but softer around the edges, as if my fingerprints had smudged his outline.

"Then we go together," he said. "But you listen when I say move, and you say Winter before your hands shake."

"My hands don't shake."

"They did when I kissed you," he said, wicked and tender. "And it made me feel like a god."

"That's because you're arrogant," I said.

"That's because you're divine," he countered.

I would've kissed him again, but the room already had too much ego in it.

He pulled a clean shirt from a shoulder bag and helped me into it like the kind of man who puts armor on his saint before he sends her back into hell.

"Lou." He waited until I met his eyes. "If it comes to choosing between you and the family—"

"You'll choose me," I said.

"And then deal with the fire after," he finished, a vow, a threat, a map.

And that was what I was worried about. I could never make him choose. One day, I'd have to make the choice for both of us.

MATTEO

The night bled danger as Lou and I stalked the alley behind the east docks, following the last thread of a rumor so thin most men wouldn't have bothered. But Valentina wasn't most people. She was my brother's wife. And Lou wasn't someone I let walk blind into a trap.

A door slammed up ahead. Heavy footsteps.

"Corner rat," Lou murmured beside me.

"That's our messenger," I said.

"Doesn't look smart enough to spell messenger."

"He doesn't need to spell it." I stepped in front of her. "He needs to scream it."

We caught him before he reached the chain-link fence. Lou struck first—blade to his thigh, clean enough to avoid the artery, cruel enough to get his attention. He collapsed with a wet sound, palms slapping pavement.

I crouched with a cruel smile.

"Evening," I said, voice low enough to make him understand I wasn't here for theatrics. "You've been whispering about a woman. Valentina. My family's business."

His panic steamed the air. "I—I didn't know she was yours—"

"She's not mine." I smiled because it scared him more. "But she belongs to someone who is. So if she's hurt, I'll make sure your soul doesn't recognize the body it left behind."

Lou leaned against the wall, wiping her blade on her thigh. "Ask him the easy way first. You know how I get when it gets boring."

One punch, carefully aimed, then I grabbed the man by the collar and slammed him against the dumpster. "Talk."

He spat bloody spit down his chin. "They—they moved her. I only heard… I swear I only heard—"

I hit him once. Sternum crack. Enough to knock the breath out, not enough to silence him.

"Say the name," I growled.

"Alonzo Sacco!" he shrieked. "He took her—he wants leverage —he said you Salvators were getting soft, that he'd carve power out of your bones—"

Lou's eyes glittered. "He's going to regret using the word soft."

"Where?" I asked.

The man's breath rattled like loose bolts. "Warehouse… six…

under the trestle bridge. The old cannery. They've got her locked in the freezer room—cold… said cold keeps her quiet—"

My blood turned molten.

Someone had put their hands on Valentina.

Someone had locked her in a freezer like she was inventory.

I stood. Dialed Domenico.

He picked up on the first ring. "Report."

"Alonzo Sacco has her," I said. "Old cannery. Back freezer. He thinks he can freeze a Salvator asset into obedience."

Silence. Then my brother's voice, razor-thin. "Do what needs doing, Matteo. Bring her home."

"Gladly."

I hung up and crouched again. The man was shaking so hard his teeth chattered.

"Please," he whispered. "I told you everything. Please—don't—"

Lou clicked her tongue. "Tell him the rule."

I cupped his jaw, forcing him to meet my eyes. "You don't get to breathe after betraying my family. You only get to choose how fast you stop."

He sobbed. "I'm begging you—"

"I know," I said.

And I killed him quickly, because Lou likes precision and because there's no honor in letting a coward die slow. Besides, there wasn't anyone to leave a warning for.

When his body slid to the ground, Lou stepped beside me, shoulder brushing mine. "Freezer room?"

"Freezer room," I echoed.

She smiled like a knife warming under a flame. "Good. I'm burning up."

I grabbed her hand. She let me. Maybe she was ready to let me in.

"We move now," I said.

"Lead," she murmured. "I'll paint the floor."

We left the alley without looking back—two monsters walking

toward the fire we intended to start, and the man who thought stealing Valentina wouldn't cost him his empire.

The stench of ammonia and rot curled through the hallways. Ice machines hummed somewhere deep inside—steady, cold, and cruel. My hands itched. Men who locked women in freezers didn't deserve mercy; they deserved to be peeled open like fruit.

Lou tapped my shoulder once: movement.

Two guards leaned against a pallet of crates, arguing about something stupid. I stepped into their peripheral like a shadow with a vendetta.

One opened his mouth.

He didn't finish the breath.

I snapped his neck with one hand and shoved his collapsing body into the other guard, who barely had time to register panic before Lou slit his throat clean enough to keep the blood from spraying the crates.

Teamwork.

We pushed deeper. A cluster of refrigerators buzzed like a hive of metal bees. Frost crawled up the walls, thicker with every step. Lou shivered but didn't comment.

I did. "Cold?"

"Only for them," she said.

The last guard near the freezer door raised his gun. Lou was already airborne.

Her boot struck his wrist. The shot went wide. I caught his face, drove him into the floor, and crushed his windpipe.

He twitched once, twice, then stilled.

Lou wiped her blade on his shirt. "Your turn."

I keyed in the override code with numb fingers. My breath fogged. Rage churned under my ribs like a broken engine.

If Valentina was dead, war wouldn't be a big enough word for what I'd unleash.

The lock clicked.

The freezer door swung open with a groan.

And there she was.

Valentina sat on a metal stool, hands bound behind her, jacket missing, skin pale with cold but spine straight as a royal decree. Her breath curled in the icy air. Her eyes—glacier-sharp—snapped to mine.

"Matteo," she said. "You're late."

Lou exhaled a sound that was half laugh, half prayer.

I pushed inside, ripped the rope off Valentina's wrists, and shrugged my coat around her shoulders. Relief nearly knocked me to my knees.

"Are you hurt?" I asked.

Her smile cut like a blade. "Only my patience."

Lou stepped forward. "Queen."

Valentina's gaze softened around the edges when it landed on her. "Lou."

I touched Valentina's jaw, turning her face toward the light. No bruises. No split lip. No swelling at the throat. They'd chilled her. But they hadn't dared touch her.

Smart.

Or cowardly.

Both die the same.

"Can you walk?" I asked.

"I can run," she said.

Lou snorted. "Show-out."

Valentina's lips twitched. "Thank you for coming."

"You're family," I said.

"Family is often the problem," she murmured. "But I'm glad you're mine."

I ignored the way the words settled under my ribs like a vow I wasn't ready to examine.

Lou touched Valentina's shoulder. "We need to move. Sacco's men will notice their friends went quiet."

"I'll notify Domenico," I said.

I dialed before my brain finished the thought. My brother answered with a tension stripped down to bare wire.

"Well?" he asked.

"She's alive," I said. "Cold, pissed, and ready to make someone regret breathing."

Valentina's eyes glittered wickedly.

Domenico exhaled. For a man who didn't believe in God, it sounded like a prayer. "Bring her home."

"On our way."

I hung up.

Lou already had the route mapped in her head. "North stairs. Fire escape. Rooftop exit. Cleaner than retracing."

"Agreed," I said.

But before we moved, I turned back toward the freezer.

A man huddled in the corner, hands zip-tied, teeth chattering from cold and fear. He was the guard who'd been assigned to "watch inventory." He'd stayed silent, hoping we wouldn't notice him.

Bad plan.

I dragged him out by the collar. He squealed. Valentina arched a brow.

"Matteo," she said. "I'm fine."

"I know," I replied. "He still dies."

The man sobbed. Lou leaned beside me with a savage little smile. "Ask him why they kept her in the cold."

I did.

He babbled nothing but excuses—orders from above, whispers of psychological leverage, claims he'd tried to keep her warm with a blanket.

Valentina snorted. "He tossed it in after threatening to wrap it around my throat."

That was enough.

"Matteo—" Valentina started.

"This isn't about you," I said quietly. "This is about reminding the world who we are."

The man begged until he couldn't anymore.

When the body hit the floor, Lou stepped closer, brushing her fingers against my hand. Not a mercy—just acknowledgment.

Valentina nodded once, regal even in a borrowed coat. "You two are terrifying."

"Thank you," Lou said, proud.

"Not a compliment," Valentina murmured.

But she smiled.

Dominico breathed murder and revenge, but also relief when we brought Valentina home.

Not wanting to intrude on their reunion, I whisked Lou off. It wasn't the Salvator penthouse. Home is where I can defend the walls and predict the angles, and a favorite safehouse of mine gave me both. I should've sent Lou to sleep. I should've put her under three locks and one of my quietest killers. I did none of it.

Instead, I poured us whiskey in tumblers that cost more than a small car and watched her walk barefoot across the polished concrete floors, shirt hanging open where she didn't care to button it, wound neatly dressed, mouth swollen from my selfishness.

"You're staring," she said, amused.

"I'm plotting," I said.

"At my death or at my surrender?"

"Yes."

She snorted, pretty and lethal. "You Salvators. Everything's a chessboard until it's a bed."

"Sometimes it's both."

Her gaze darkened. "That's why I haven't tried to kill you in your sleep."

"You'd miss," I teased.

She gave me that look that wired me straight into the wall socket. "I don't miss."

I believed her. I also believed she'd never take the shot. Not at me. Not after the way I made her come undone by my mouth. When violence writes itself into the script of your nerves, tenderness becomes the plot twist you can't predict and don't want to stop.

Lou came close. The whiskey on her breath warmed the cold place under my ribs where loyalty and loneliness sit back-to-back. "What do you need, Matteo?"

No one asked me that. People need me. People obey me. People fear me. She offered me everything I pretend I don't want.

"I need you to stop sleeping with a knife under your pillow," I said.

Her smile was all teeth. "No."

"I need you to stop offering yourself up like a saint for our sins."

"Also no."

"I need you to wear my ring sometimes. Or all the time."

Silence bloomed. Her mouth parted. Something soft and terrified moved under her eyes, a fox looking across a field and seeing the trap.

"A ring?" she asked. "Is that what this is?"

"This is me trying to make the monster inside me behave." My voice came out rougher than I intended. "This is me wanting everyone to know I'll unmake their bloodlines if they touch you."

Her laugh cracked. "Touch-her-and-die energy. Very on brand."

"Say yes," I said. It came out huskier than I cared to admit. "Say you'll let me drag you toward something that looks like a future."

"We don't get futures," she said quietly. "We get nights like this and mornings if we're lucky."

"Then be mine for the nights and the mornings," I said. "Be mine when it's ugly. Be mine when it's exquisite. Be mine when we don't deserve it and when we do."

She looked down at the leather on the table—the cuffs I'd set out, the chain coiled like a promise. Her throat moved. "What does this look like, Matteo?"

"It looks like a contract we don't put on paper," I said. "It looks like protocols. It looks like you eating at least one real meal a day. It looks like you using our word before the first tear. It looks like me meeting you at the door when the night spits you back and washing the blood from your hands."

Her breath seized. My hands shook.

"It looks like rope sometimes," I added softly. "And knives. And my hand around your throat to remind you where you are when the past drags you somewhere you don't want to go."

"Show me," she whispered. "Show me what belonging costs."

I moved slow because you should always go slow when the thing you want most is tilting toward you. I took the cuffs and set them aside, because tonight we needed a different weight. I pulled open the drawer and took out a length of midnight rope, soft as sin; she watched my hands and the hunger in her gaze grew.

"Color?" I asked.

Her smile was the kind of feral that gets worshiped in old stories. "Green."

I wrapped her wrists behind her back, neat and symmetrical, each knot a sentence in the language we'd invented together. The rope slid over her skin and her shoulders softened. I circled her chest, pinned the end with a bite of pressure that made her eyes flutter closed.

"Okay?" I checked.

"Perfect."

I palmed the knife she loved, flipped it, offered the hilt. "Yours."

She took it. I took her throat, fingers firm on the side where the nerve whispers to the brain… This is yours, you are safe, you can drop the armor. Her pulse tripped against my fingertips. I pressed my mouth to her ear.

"You belong to me," I murmured. "By your choice, not my claim."

"Yes, Matteo," she breathed, surrender and sin twined.

I kissed her with the rope under my fingers and the knife in her hand, with the world burning.

We tore into each other like two creatures who'd spent their whole lives pretending they weren't starving. The rope bit into her skin, her breath hitched with every drag of my hands, and the world narrowed to the sound she made when I pushed her past the last piece of control she tried to keep.

When her body seized around my name, I followed her into the dark—hard, fast, with a reverence that felt like sin dressed as devotion.

After, she collapsed onto her side, the rope still warm on her skin, her pulse shivering under my fingertips. Her hair spilled across the mattress like a shadow trying to hold its shape. She was flushed, trembling slightly, her breath drifting out in uneven exorcisms.

I exhaled like I'd been drowning and didn't know it until the air clawed back into my lungs.

Slowly—careful in a way I'm not with anyone else—I eased her against my chest. Her body fit there like she'd been carved from my missing ribs. She let me pull her closer, let me wrap an arm over her waist, let me tuck her knees toward mine so I could bracket her completely.

I held her tighter.

Not possessive.

Not violent.

Not even dominant.

Just… held her.

Like if I loosened my grip, the night would steal her the way it tries to steal everything good I've ever touched.

"Stay," I said into her hair.

"Tomorrow night," she teased, voice hoarse.

"Tonight," I said, a man reduced to a puddle by the woman he loved. "Please."

Silence, then: "Okay."

I didn't sleep. I watched her breathe, my rope marks fading

from her skin. When the sky showed its first bruise of morning, Lou rolled into me and spoke into my chest. "If I say yes to a ring, it doesn't make me yours."

"I know," I said.

"It makes you mine."

I smiled, teeth against her hair. "I plan on that."

"Good." She pressed a kiss over my heartbeat. "Because right after we put a ring on anything, I want Alonzo Sacco's mouth sewn shut with your family crest."

"You always know the precise want of my heart."

"I know the shape of your rage," she said. "And I love you for it."

The word landed and detonated, throwing light through all the dark places inside me. The ceiling didn't crack. The city didn't go quiet. But my pulse said kneel and I almost did.

"Say it again," I said.

"No," she said, wicked. "But I'll show you."

She did.

When I finally left the bed to take the call from Domenico— another emergency, of course; there's always another—I looked back at her with possession in her gaze, her knife on the nightstand, and my heartbeat inside her mouth.

Home, I thought, and knew I'd be killing for that word for the rest of my life.

THE END

CHILI GIRL

BY J.E. FISHMAN

"WHY DO you want to find her so bad?"

The whore rolled over onto her back, exposing her breasts. Nothing I hadn't seen before, the last time three minutes ago.

"I told you. I'm on a job."

"Who has a job like that?"

I considered. "Guys like me, I guess. Reckless guys."

We were speaking Spanish. I won't bore you with that and I don't do accents. I'm an Italian "who don't speak Italian," and I speak Spanish with a thick New York attitude. The word "reckless" was a deep reach. *Temerario.* I'm not sure I got the emphasis on the right syllable, to tell you the truth, but the whore didn't question.

Her name was Lucía. Pretty Mexican girl. "Woman," I should say, well past the age of consent, although figuring the maturity of prostitutes was not among my specialties. People with hard lives can age fast. I was looking for information, but she insisted on charging, so I figured I may as well get my money's worth. Lucía had lips like a bass. Gobble-you-up lips. She knew how to use them, too. But now we were done with her business and onto mine.

Aldo's my name. Aldo Macchiarulo. Macchiarulo means "stained." *Stained.* Ironic because the name came from the old country but I'm the one with a port-wine birthmark covering a third of my face. Nobody I know has one, but perhaps it runs in the family all the way back to Calabria.

Anyway, that's all the Italian I know, if you don't count the foods and the curse words. The Spanish I picked up from high school and college, where I was a good student at a crummy school. Major in criminal justice, minor in Spanish. I thought they would both come in handy in the line of work I aspired to. Also, the chair of the Languages department had a way about her.

Lucía learned what little of this I communicated in the course of the night. On the other side of the equation, I thought she might know a thing or two about matters of interest to me. Specifically, the whereabouts of a young woman who fled the altar on a wealthy client of mine. I am not using the word "altar" metaphorically here. She literally bolted in a wedding dress from St. Patrick's Cathedral. She was a small-time actress, I was told, but apparently with an eye for Oscar-level drama. You can look her up in the IMDB if you want: Mara Baye. That's a stage name. Her real name was Shaina Weinstein.

Mara's father was a mid-level executive at a fragrance firm. Her mother ostensibly worked as an editor at a small press but saw her real job as stage mother and chief matchmaker. She must have been good at it—or Mara was good at living up to it—because the jilted groom was none other than Sean Russo, whose father was the two hundredth richest person in the world with a real estate fortune based on storage units. I guess no one ever went broke overestimating the amount of crap Americans accumulate in a lifetime, and some made bank.

It was the father who'd approached me to "go see about the girl." He asked about my methods, and I told him I don't kill people. Also I'm not a spy.

He looked at the distinguishing mark on my face and replied, "That figures. I just want to give my son the chance to talk to her, maybe come to understand…"

I was sure I could locate her. The aborted wedding had only failed to go off the day before. The cake hadn't even turned stale yet. And I don't work slow. Some detectives use subterfuge, but that can take forever. I just come on like a freight train.

It took me all of twelve hours to trace Mara to Cabo San Lucas, where she'd briefly checked into the highest of high-end resorts for a little pampering. Before that, she'd ditched the wedding dress in her apartment, packed a bag small enough to carry on the plane, slept overnight in the first-class lounge at JFK, and boarded the next flight west with a one-way ticket. I caught a Boeing in the same direction just fourteen hours behind her.

People are generally pretty bad at running and hiding. They have to eat, and their weary bodies require a place to rest. These days, they can't make much headway without cell phones and credit cards, both of which can be used to closely track their movements. And a woman trying to hide her appearance on short notice has few options, with no chance at introducing facial hair like guys can. It's basically down to a dye job, sunglasses, and a big hat, unless she decides to go full burka. I didn't see Mara taking it that far, not on the Baja Peninsula. For one thing, she would have died of heat stroke. It was mid-June and ninety in the shade.

The hotel manager wouldn't give me the time of day. A few pesos in the palm of a busboy revealed that Mara had checked out that morning. That was all I got. The livelihoods of people who work in the tourist trade rely on discretion. I wouldn't waste more time with them. I had to go low, so I went to the easiest door a stranger could open and asked the kid for the nearest brothel. That's how I ended up in Lucía's bed. The whores in town know everything that happens in the street, and the street feels every disturbance in the matrix. Some single woman checks into a two-grand-a-night hotel alone and checks out the next morning, that stands out. A gringo with a port-wine stain on his face starts asking questions immediately afterwards? The underground's tremors turn into an earthquake. Fine. Let it get back to Mara that someone was on her trail. That kind of buzz makes amateurs panic and do stupid things.

"How am I supposed to know what happened to some random chica?" the whore asked, rolling onto her side.

"I don't expect you to know," I said. I rose from bed naked, fished five hundred American dollars out of my jeans, and laid it neatly on her exposed hip. "I think you can find out. Time is of the essence. Go now."

With those instructions still on my lips, I headed for the ratty shower. Just to be safe, I took my clothes and my sling bag into the bathroom.

Ten minutes later I emerged fully dressed and freshly shaved. Feeling a little anxious, I stood in my Mexican cowboy boots looking through the greasy window onto a Cabo side street. This was not one of those streets most tourists see. The pungent smell of roasting peppers wafted in. A couple of abuelas leaned on the sills of open windows, eyeing the whole block. Down on the sidewalk, a few men stood apart from one another, smoking cigarettes unhurriedly. They all appeared to be watching for trouble or opportunity, two things that often come in similar packages.

I heard the door open and turned slowly to see Lucía entering the room. Those sensuous lips widened into a broad smile. My God. I could stare at those lips forever, watch them frown and smirk and pout and pucker. I could lose myself in them until the tides overtook Baja California. But that part of our transaction had concluded. The job I came for beckoned.

"There's a man named Javier here in the barrio who specializes in changing identities," she explained.

"Oh? And she came to him?"

"No. But he has people up and down the peninsula who scout for him. They tell him when people arrive who have the vibe like they're meaning to disappear. Let me see the picture again."

There were two pictures, actually. The first was Mara's headshot from a second-rate modeling agency. The other was a candid of her talking at a cocktail party, waist up, revealing a lithe figure. In both she had shoulder-length hair the color of polished mahogany, large cerulean eyes, and plump but not fat cheeks. I'd spent several hours absorbing the photos on the plane ride out. There was nothing exotic in them, but I'd passed so much time staring into those eyes I nearly cast a spell over myself. Now I slipped the photos from my wallet and handed them to Lucía.

She looked only briefly and nodded her head. "The girl is in San Cristóbal."

"San Cristóbal," I repeated to help me remember.

"Someone saw her in the camel place."

"You're putting me on. Camels in Mexico?"

"It's a resort on the west coast, half an hour from here."

I thanked her and picked up my sling bag, but she closed in on me, rubbing her chest against my ribs and coquettishly looking up past my chin.

"I think I'm good at this, *Temerario*. Maybe I could help more."

This offer stirred a feeling in my gut that I chose not to indulge. "I have no budget for an assistant," I quickly replied. And when she looked genuinely disappointed, I added, "You're good at the job you already have, and it's steadier work."

She recovered herself quickly and began to unbutton my shirt, but I saw it for what it meant to her: opportunity, not affection. I stopped her hand and slipped another hundred bucks into her palm, squeezing her fingers closed around the bill.

Then I opened the door and stepped out into the hallway. When I turned to close it, Lucía was occupied remaking the bed. My gaze must have lingered a moment too long, or maybe she'd cultivated that sense many women have of knowing when a man is staring.

"Take care of yourself, *Temerario*," she said with a flash of her glistening brown eyes. "The girl could be armed and dangerous."

I smiled at the tease as I pulled the door closed behind me.

After renting a car and working my way out of town, I found myself parked near the beach in sleepy San Cristóbal, where I watched with astonishment as a line of mounted camels worked their way in my direction. When they grew closer, I walked through the sand to intercept them, slipped a few bucks into the palm of the guide without a word, and passed the pictures around to the elevated tourists, none of whom looked especially comfortable so far off the ground. Some had seen Mara eating breakfast in the restaurant a couple hours earlier. They said she seemed well put together and not in any kind of distress. After breakfast, she climbed into a taxi with her Gucci carry-on and her Birkin handbag. Those were the things that really caught the tourists' eyes, these tourists being a group of commissioned fashion reps from L.A., off on a sales junket.

"Every American in Cabo," Lucía had said between romps, "makes themselves look richer than they are." Perhaps Mara was the exception, perhaps not.

She might be returning to Cabo, but my gut told me she would be heading up the coast, bouncing among fishing villages. She had stopped for sustenance, not to ride camels.

It only took me five more hours to find her—five hours of spreading baksheesh around one sleepy town after another to no effect until I stopped for a late lunch at a sit-down taqueria in the small village of Puerto Chale. She was munching on corn chips too daintily for a local, grasping them between two fingers and biting into them with her incisors as if to avoid messing up her nail polish and her lipstick, although she wore neither. The soft linen dress she sported, however, looked straight out of an East Hamptons boutique, betraying her standing in society to anyone who knew about such things.

She saw me come in and get seated by the host, a short, thick, square man who looked one hundred percent Mayan. Our eyes met, followed by the slightest nod of the head, merely an acknowledgment that we were the only two gringos in the place. But I had to work to pry my gaze from her.

I found her to be much more beautiful than her pictures, so stunning in fact that a lump formed in my throat, and I could understand immediately why the son of a billionaire would want to possess her.

The tacos were quite good, but the hot sauce was liquid fire, made apparent by a quick wave each of us made for the next *cerveza* as soon as we ran dry. It required several paper napkins to dab the sweat off my forehead, a gesture I tried to hide from Mara in a way that made me feel like a teenaged boy struggling desperately not to make a bad first impression in the lunchroom.

Once the third beer appeared to have loosened her up, I sauntered over to her table and laid a hand on the back of the chair across from her.

"May I?"

She gave the most subtle shrug I ever saw in my life, which I decided to take as absolute permission.

The petite waitress came over, no more than a teenager. She wore an Evinrude Outboard Motors t-shirt three sizes too large that came down to the edges of her cutoff jean shorts. I asked for another round and ordered two more tacos—one for me and one for the lady.

"You'll want to try the *lengua*," I told Mara. "It doesn't get more authentic than that."

"Ah," she said, "authenticity. Is that your jam?"

The tacos with their pink content landed before I could protest. She took one look, and both corners of her mouth rose, her smile telling me she wouldn't be that easily grossed out.

"I'm from New York," she said, chewing. "I grew up eating *lengua* in Jewish delis. We just called it tongue. See the tastebuds there?" She pointed.

I had no follow-up. "Bravo," I said. "Pass the hot sauce."

She slid the sticky squeeze bottle across the table. Instead of letting go, she tipped it over and spurted out a generous helping. This is the kind of woman, I thought, who leaves a man at the altar. Although my tongue felt permanently damaged, I refused to touch my beer until she took her own swig. She smiled at me, making fun, totally onto my nagging insecurity. If I didn't shake off my schoolboy crush, Mara would get the better of me before sundown, and how would I explain that to the billionaire?

"What brings you here?" I asked.

"I came for the tongue," she replied without hesitation. "You?"

There was no point in not fessing up. "The Russo family sent me." I watched her blue eyes closely and they betrayed nothing. At this point, she had a number of options, but they all boiled down to some version of cooperating or trying to lose me. But why bother with the latter? It wasn't like she was under arrest.

"Lunch is on you," Mara said.

"Fair enough. It's a big per diem and tacos are cheap."

She stood abruptly, which made me flinch. Then she shuffle-marched across the restaurant in her black leather mules on her way to the ladies' room, leaving her large handbag behind. The Birkin—most expensive handbag on the planet, so far as I knew. I wondered whether she hoped to catch me rifling through it, but I had only needed to find her, and I'd accomplished that already.

As she bunched up her dress to escape the table, I noticed she had scars on her knees, the kind one gets from an active childhood, the kind I presume fashion photographers touch up, doing their bit for the perfection machine that conspires to create icons where once we had women. I thought for a moment of Lucía's lips and wondered how they'd play in magazine ads. Quite well, I decided, no touchup required.

Mara returned and sat down again, pushing the plate with her half-eaten tacos aside. She looked at her bag and briefly back at me, then smirked. But I had her this time—from the grin I returned she knew in a moment that I hadn't rummaged the purse. All of this in an instant. She opened it and took out a compact, checking her teeth and fluffing her hair. An old habit, I thought. You could easily imagine her doing this at lunch on Park Avenue.

"A woman who is beautiful inside doesn't have to look at herself in the mirror," Lucía had said as she dressed.

As she returned the compact to her bag and zipped it closed, Mara said, "You wouldn't find my phone in there, or anywhere.

One day a thousand years from now some plumber's going to find it back at the hotel in the toilet tank of Room 245 and wonder whether a drug deal went down or some shit."

"What would I do with your phone? I have my own."

"Information is power." She paused and we sat in silence for a minute. "Did you see those signs on the way in? For the whale watching?"

"Of course," I lied.

"Let's see if we can catch a boat."

She didn't wait for me. I threw a couple of American twenties down on the table and hustled after her as the Mayan host laughed.

"I'm not your puppy," I said, climbing into the broiling-hot passenger seat of her rented Ford.

"Oh, no? Well, I'm not the one who's following *you*."

She started the car and headed for the ocean, which was only a mile away, not enough time to cool down the interior.

Fifteen minutes later, she had negotiated for a private tour in a Boston whaler with a canopy. The captain, who looked to be about twelve years old, insisted on payment up front. Mara smoothly climbed aboard without touching the zipper of her purse and stuck the Russos with the bill. Probably another old habit.

The kid started up the outboard motor—Evinrude, a monopoly in town, I assumed—and it spit a cloud of burnt oil fumes that we passed through on our way out to sea. When the first wave jostled us, I realized I badly had to urinate. With no other options, I stood awkwardly with my back to Mara and sent a stream over the side, praying the wind wouldn't suddenly change direction. The captain, to his credit, slowed to make things easier on all of us, although the judder when he throttled back nearly pitched me into the water with my *polla* hanging out.

"That was class," Mara said when I zipped up and fell back onto the bench. She rolled her eyes in such a way as to imply I was little more than the paid help and should pee on my own time. I certainly felt less in charge of my faculties than I had that morning in Lucía's bed. But maybe that was an illusion too, like all good customer service.

"Look!" Mara's baby blues shot wide open, focused fifty yards out.

"*Ballena*," the kid said with the flat tone of voice that confirmed, from his perspective, a routine sighting.

We watched in awe as the great back of a gray whale crested the ocean surface. It disappeared and breached closer, its plump eye checking us out. Mara, all at once not so jaded, took my hand and squeezed. Despite myself, the excitement sent a surge of adrenaline into my chest too. The whale disappeared again, then resurfaced farther out, showing us its tail. Nearby swam its calf, bigger than our boat.

It went on like that for an hour. When the novelty wore off, Mara let go of my hand. I bought us Coronas from the onboard chest with a handwritten sign that said, "Agua $1 US — Beer $2 US."

"Good to see babies," our young captain said as we turned for shore.

He dropped us in shallow water, and we waded up to the beach and plopped down in the sand, propping ourselves up on our elbows and looking out to sea as shadows lengthened and the legs of my jeans and the hem of her dress dried out.

"You have an instinct for drama," I told Mara.

She trained her big bright eyes on me. "Don't I, though?"

"St. Patrick's of all places."

"That dress cost twelve thousand dollars. If my father could afford you, he'd have sent you to kill me. It's bad enough I converted to Catholicism last year."

"For the Russo kid?"

"Sean, yeah. Poor Sean."

"Is that a commentary on the before or the after?"

She played with some sand. "Both, I guess. We were each in over our heads in different ways. What are you doing here?"

"Earning a living."

"C'mon! I'm being straight with you. It's your turn."

"The old man wants you to speak to your fiancé in the interest of closure."

"Closure!" She laughed. "Some guys can't take a hint."

"Were there any hints? Before the wedding?"

"A thousand."

"Why not end it earlier?"

"It was like I was on a moving train and couldn't get off without breaking my neck."

A beautiful neck it was, too. She opened a few buttons of her dress as the harsh setting sun bit.

"The train came to a screeching halt when I turned the corner and saw everyone in that crowd beaming at me."

"So you didn't plan it—the escape."

She thought for a minute. "I'm bad at telling the difference between plans and dreams." She picked up her mules and knocked out the sand. "How does it work for you, cowboy? Do you get a bonus for finding me, more if Sean gets his closure?"

"Something like that. Can I take your picture, prove that I got half the job done?"

"Sure."

When I raised my phone, she stuck out her tongue. I got the snap, but she jumped up and ran barefoot back to the car, forcing me to give chase.

A few minutes later, she dropped me off where we had started. She flipped the sun visor down, slid the mirror open, and preened her eyelashes.

"Good work, cowboy," she said, and winked at me as I swung the car door closed. She took off without looking back.

Someone had let the air out of the rear tires of my rental car. As I trudged back to the restaurant, it occurred to me that the corridor to the ladies' room led straight outside and Mara had been gone a few moments longer than expected.

The Mayan laughed at me when I came in. He had a rusty compressor I could borrow, which made a racket but got the job done.

"It's not the noise, it's the motion," Lucía had said, when we briefly heard a screamer through the wall.

A few minutes later, I pulled next to Mara's car in the parking lot of a small hotel in town. Finding her again was a cinch—I'd dropped an AirTag on the floor of her back seat.

I slept in my car with the window rolled down and dreamed, improbably, of Lucía. In the dream, we were out to lunch and she wore a colorful, flowing dress that floated in the wind when she twirled. A mariachi band came to serenade us, and her mouth fell open in girlish wonder.

No one bothered me in the car until I heard a rap on the windshield next morning. It was Mara, but as soon as I opened my eyes she walked off. I swept some fingers through my hair, started the engine, and followed her car, having to pee badly again, which I suspected she intuited. As I shifted uncomfortably in my seat, she cruised through town with excruciating slowness and finally worked her way to the outskirts and pulled to a stop along an empty beach.

She had her hair up in a messy bun and wore a tight-fitting navy one-piece bathing suit that I could see through her cover-up when the light hit it right. I danced around by my car as she spread a blanket on the sand and made herself comfortable. Then I hustled behind a tall cactus to relieve myself.

When I sat down beside her, she said, "I feel like you have to go a lot. Maybe you should see someone about that."

"Hardy-har-har."

"Why are you still following me?"

"I'm hoping to collect my bonus from Mr. Russo."

"What if I don't want to cooperate?"

I shrugged. "Why did you let the air out of my tires?"

"Only because you amuse me, cowboy. And I wanted to plumb the depths of further amusement."

"These are Mexican boots. I'm from New York, you know. Like you. No cowboy."

"Gee, who could have guessed that," she said, dripping sarcasm. "Urban cowboy. But that's too much of a mouthful, doesn't exactly trip off the old *lengua*."

She drew out the last word. I couldn't tell whether she was flirting with me or hating on me. She pulled off her coverup and folded it neatly before placing it into the leather-trimmed canvas tote she'd brought for the occasion. "Aren't you hot in those jeans?"

"Not yet."

"You didn't bring swimwear to a beach vacation?"

"What I brought is in the car, but no, I didn't bring swimwear. I'm working."

"Hmm. I get the impression appearances mean a lot to you. Tell me about the birthmark."

"Will you call Sean? All I need is for you to call him. It doesn't matter what you say."

"What's in it for me?"

"Closure."

"I found closure when I stuffed that wedding dress into the trash."

"Twelve K. Poof. Must be nice."

I looked out past the surf. There were whales breaching. We could've stayed on shore yesterday and watched the show and saved the Russos a pot of money.

"What do you plan to do," I asked Mara, "once you quit running?"

"I already stopped running. I'm just on vacation now. Tell me about the face. It must have been hard on you, growing up."

I gritted my teeth and locked my jaw, not cooperating with this inquiry. But once again Mara had transported me back to high school, if only for a fleeting second. That way the popular girls had of condescending to you when they weren't torturing you. The real cruelty came from not knowing their true intentions, not knowing when they'd turn on you and bite, like a coiled rattlesnake. I thought again of Lucía. I imagined her lips didn't fit her face when she was younger—beautiful as she was today. People being people, no matter where they grew up, someone no doubt tortured her for the very thing that would go on to make her a stunner. The port wine stain on my cheek didn't work that way, though. It would never transmogrify. I was stuck—my only strategy was to outgrow the humiliation. And here was Mara attempting to drag me back to that. No, thank you.

"You know," I said, standing up, "you ain't worth the bonus."

She pretended not to care, but she followed me back to the car, walking funny barefoot on the newly hot sand. She shifted her weight from one foot to another as I got in. With the door still open, she reached in and grabbed my arm.

"I'm sorry. It's a bad habit, fending people off by giving them shit. Can you wait?" She ran around and slid into the passenger seat.

Out on the beach, her Birkin bag and fancy tote sat abandoned on the beach towel. People were starting to drift into the area.

"You're gonna lose your stuff," I said, nodding in that direction, "and then what will you do?"

She held out an open palm. "Give me your phone. I'll call Sean right now, I swear."

I selected Sean's number and handed my phone to her, and she was instantly out the door. It crossed my mind that she might have another trick up her sleeve, but she headed straight for the beach towel. The one-piece bathing suit showed a firm ass, and quick-walking through the hot sand gave it a special swing. That might have aroused me yesterday, but no longer. She plopped down on the towel and sat with her legs crossed, phone to her left ear.

The car was getting hot. I stepped out and removed my shirt and sat on the hood watching her with the heels of my boots resting on the fender. My bare chest faced the water, and my bare shoulders were searing with the sun to my back.

Mara's conversation went on for a while, growing more and more animated, free hand gesturing as if Sean was standing right in front of her. She folded her knees to her chest and hugged her free arm around them, and I saw her shoulders rise and fall. She reached back behind her head and released the scrunchie, and her mahogany hair cascaded down, shifting in the sea breeze like sargassum in the tide. Then, suddenly, the conversation ended. She placed the phone on the blanket and sat there, back still to me.

"Everyone knows women don't mind crying in public," Lucía had said when we were down to making small talk. "But tears hide more than they show." She'd been talking about losing her brother to a car accident months ago, and I wondered aloud at the suppression of her emotions.

Now I walked up slowly to Mara but still arrived early enough to see the tears, which she wiped away with both hands.

"That wasn't so hard," she said, laughing at herself and starting to cry again. "Come sit with me, cowboy." She patted the towel.

I picked up the phone and slipped it into my pocket as I sat down. "The good thing about this job is that you get to see that life sucks for everyone from time to time, both the rich and the downtrodden." It was something Lucía had said to me in bed between rounds. She'd added, "And I get to make them forget for a bit," but I didn't repeat that.

"I guess you don't see a lot of people at their best, huh?" Mara said.

She wiped away the last tear and raked her eyes over me from face to waist, her gaze finally coming to rest lustfully on my eyes. "You ever have sex on the beach, Aldo?"

"Not in broad daylight."

"There's a first for everything."

I didn't know where to put my gaze, so I dropped it to one of her scarred knees. "I got a chica in Cabo," I said, surprising myself.

"Gee, a girl can't even get a pity fuck in paradise, huh?" She took my hand and squeezed. "I'm going back to Sean. His father's going to kill him and my mother's going to kill me, because we're eloping."

"No shit, well, that's great," I said, meaning it. A happy ending for one of my clients could only mean more referral business. "Where will you get married?"

"Cabo. Will you and your girlfriend come? We'll need witnesses."

"Temerario!" Lucía cried when I darkened her door again.

She was wearing something more demure than when I'd first met her—a floral dress not unlike the one I saw in my dream. She gave me a perfunctory hug, and when I leaned in for more, she pushed me away.

"I'm late," she said.

"For what?"

Just then I heard footsteps pattering up the stairs. A man stepped into the room, and I felt a pang of jealousy. He looked to be about thirty, full-on well-tanned Mexican, clean-shaven and dressed to the nines with a western floral-print shirt and a bolo tie. He held a cowboy hat in one hand.

"This is my *novio*," Lucía said, and the pang of jealousy became a roar in both ears. "We're off to a fiesta."

They passed together through the door, the *novio* heading for the stairs but Lucía hesitating while I stood inside. She nodded to the doorknob.

"I have to lock up."

I must have looked so forlorn that she took pity on me, reaching up and touching my birthmark, which always flushed hot when I felt embarrassed. Her fingers felt cool.

"I think it's handsome," she said, as I stepped out.

She left me in the hall, my mind turning. Maybe I should have reached into my pocket for cash right away to reestablish the old bond. That might have even pleased the boyfriend, who could have been her pimp, for all I knew, although he didn't give off that vibe.

There was a tequila shop downstairs. I bought a bottle of mezcal and sat in my car caressing it for a while, finally twisting out the cork and taking a couple smokey gulps, enjoying the burn in my throat, wallowing in sudden, unexpected misery as one car after another passed by with its windows open, blasting Latin music.

Two shots more and I'd formulated a course of action that would get me out of Mexico as fast as possible while fulfilling my professional obligations.

Mara and Sean's wedding was slated for the next day at the same hotel where Mara had begun her adventure. I found her and her old new fiancé eating lunch on the patio of the bar restaurant, Mara wearing a different linen dress and Sean in a Hawaiian-style shirt, crisp shorts, and loafers that could only be Tod's because why pay a hundred dollars for shoes when you could drop ten times that and have enough left over to support the staff at your six houses. Yes, I was instantly envious, but only because he had a girl again and I'd lost mine before I even had her in my grasp. Not that I planned to tell these two the truth.

Although we'd never met, Sean jumped up and gave me a man hug as if we were long-lost buddies. He dragged a chair to the table, its feet screeching along the terracotta tiles until a waiter hustled over to help, lifting it into place.

"My hero," Sean said with the kind of pretend innocence that may have charmed some people. He patted me on the back again and poured me a glass of white wine as I sat. When he spoke, he revealed surprisingly crooked teeth, but the rest of his face was handsome enough.

"We on for tomorrow?" I asked.

"Of course," Mara said.

Sean leaned in. "I found a justice of the peace. We'll be married at seven."

"Sunset," Mara said. It came off so flat I concluded right there this marriage wouldn't last five years. Just enough time to drop a couple of kids and extort child support.

The waiter put a menu in front of me.

"I can't stay," I said. "I have errands to run."

Finding a hotel for the next two nights was chief among them. Then a flight out.

"You'll still witness, though, right?" Sean said a little too eagerly, as if my presence was necessary to guarantee Mara's. "And the girlfriend… what's her name?"

"Lucía." I hoped they didn't notice my hesitation. For the life of me, I couldn't come up with an alias in the moment. "I'm not sure she'll make it. Personal matters."

Sean frowned. "She *has* to come. Couple for couple." Whatever the hell that meant. I supposed he considered a stag witness a bad omen.

"I'll do my best," I said, pushing myself away from the table. I wanted to shed my skin. "See you tomorrow."

"Dress nice, cowboy," Mara said.

Cowboy. *Temerario.* Why did all these women want to bestow nicknames on me? I suddenly found it grating.

The doorman called me a cab at the entrance. I'd returned the rental car an hour ago on impulse, one less thing to tie me down. After I made some inquiries, the driver took me to a small hotel in town, just off the main commercial strip. It was noisy—cars honking, music blaring, tourists getting rowdy—but I didn't care about noise. More to the point, the three-quarters of a bottle of mezcal I had left in my sling bag didn't care about noise.

That was my thought when I checked in, but I decided to hit a bar instead. I found one a bit farther from the tourist action, a sleepy place with some kind of Mexican celebration going on in the back room, proof that locals frequented it more than gringos, which suited me just fine. I wasn't interested in idle conversation with compatriots hyped up on sunburns and humid air. There's a kind of magic to these resort towns. They're designed to make you forget your troubles, forget what you left behind, which if you're not careful leads to forgetting who you are. I prided myself on never doing that, yet here I was feeling lovesick over a prostitute, as if I'd ever been a part of her life beyond a brief business transaction.

But of course there's something about sleeping with another person that makes a bit of independence disappear. It happens no matter the relationship—something reptilian in it, back to the days when spreading seed around meant the survival of the species. In the illusion of intimacy, I thought after the third tequila, I'd lost my self-discipline.

Speaking of which, I waved to the bartender for a fourth, trading up to *añejo* as if I was still on the Russo tab. Maybe I should have taken Mara up on her offer on the beach to get the taste of Lucía out of my mouth, but I knew in my heart that would've been useless. I pictured Mara lying under me in the sand like a cold fish. She was more transactional than all the cheap whores in Christendom with little incentive even to fake it—at least not with a hired man.

The bartender produced a fresh glass and poured gently from a nearly full bottle, honoring the old tequila, a rare order on this street. A cheer filtered out of the party in the back room and people started to drift out. I was just lifting the drink to my lips when I spotted Lucía. We both did a double take, and she made straight for my stool, snatched the glass from my hand, and belted it back.

"Ouch. That was *añejo*," I said.

"Is that what he told you?" She started in on the bartender in such rapid-fire Spanish that I couldn't follow a word. Sheepishly, he slid some dinero back in my direction. Then Lucía turned to me. "Did you find the chica?"

"Yeah."

"And you fell in love with her, but she didn't want to have anything to do with you."

"Negative. You're the one—"

She slapped me on the birthmark-free side of my face. Hard. Even the bartender flinched before turning away.

"Don't you dare," she said.

"Dare what?"

But we both knew. If I had a peso for every john who fell in love with a prostitute, I'd be richer than the Russos. And yet here I was. My feelings had deepened every second I was away from her.

I looked around. The last of the guests from the back room were filtering out, among them Lucía's boyfriend, on the arm of a teenager. The party appeared to have been a quinceañera.

I heard the boyfriend say, "Look, it's the dude with the face," and I went to jump from my chair and slug him, but Lucía pinned me down, her breasts in my chest, soft as butter.

"Oh, *Temerario*," she said, "don't be angry. Everyone is imperfect. Some just hide it better."

Yeah, that got to me. I gave up the violence but watched the *novio* with contempt until he'd disappeared into the street. Lucía watched me watching.

"That's my cousin," she said.

You could've blown me away with a wave of the sombrero.

"You're dating your cousin?"

"No, stupid. It's a story I tell." She took my hand and guided me off the stool and out the door and up the street. Her apartment was just two blocks away—I recognized the neighborhood now—but she asked, "You have a hotel room? Yes?"

I told her where it was and we stopped just once along the way for some groceries at a small mercado. She grabbed a few things and stuffed them into a bag, but I was paying no attention. I reached into my pocket to pay, but she shook her head and pulled a credit card from her bra. She didn't carry a purse.

Up in my room, she sat down on the bed fully clothed and emptied the small paper sack. Two bottles of Jarritos Mandarin soda. Four limes. A very red gnarly pepper. I recognized everything well enough. The pepper was a Carolina reaper.

There were two clean glasses in the bathroom. I fetched them and took the bottle of mezcal from my sling bag and poured us moderate helpings.

"*Salud!*" I said, taking a sip. But she didn't touch hers.

"Talk first," she said. "What happened with the woman you were seeking?"

"She passed through right where you said she would. The camels. I found her sometime later. She's getting married tomorrow and you and I are going to be the witnesses."

She threw back her head and laughed. "We? What do you mean, we?"

"If you want to. I can't make you."

"Do you propose to pay me?"

"If I have to. The expense account's run out, though."

"You wasted it whoring around!"

"No." I shook my head. "Just you."

"She was beautiful. Did you sleep with her?"

"You're beautiful. I slept with you."

"But that wasn't real."

"It felt real to me. More real the more I thought about it."

Finally, she took a few sips of the mezcal. I matched hers. She took one more sip and I took another. Mirroring. We laughed together.

She set down her glass and looked at me with penetrating dark eyes. "You don't even know me."

"It's not true."

"Who am I?"

"A kind soul. A stunning—"

"Stop before you get yourself into trouble. I'm twenty three years old and my parents are dead and I'm studying computer science. That—what we did—what I do...pays my tuition. I'm almost finished."

"I didn't judge you. I never judge."

"Shut up. Everyone does. Tell me about the woman you just found. Mara was her name?"

"Yes. A prostitute."

"Don't tease me, *Temerario*."

"She's as much for sale as anyone ever was. She's just more subtle about it."

"And you're going to witness her marriage?"

"Well, what the hell. She's not my problem anymore. We're both witnessing."

"Because they're paying you?"

No. Why had I agreed? I thought about it. "I made a promise, that's all. I keep my promises."

She fell back on the bed, staring at the stained ceiling.

"A little gross. You couldn't find a better place?"

"The place where they're staying has no authenticity. I like to keep it real."

"That sounds like bullshit." Called out twice in one week.

"Okay. The truth is I wanted to be near you."

She looked at me skeptically.

"You only know me as someone who follows people. I do that for a living, but I don't do it other times."

What a lame thing to say, but she gave me the benefit of the doubt.

"I can help you," she said.

"I know that now. Those computer skills can come in handy."

"We could be a regular Mulder and Scully."

"X-Files?" I pretend shivered. "I don't do paranormal."

"Have it your way." She pouted. "Except on *El Día Del Muertos*. Then your soul is mine."

I nodded. "You can scare the pants off me on *El Día Del Muertos*."

"No, it's a happy day." She giggled.

But there was another problem. She wasn't leaving Mexico. Not for me, not for anyone. She had a younger sister to support, living with some relatives who also didn't have two pesos to rub together.

I thought ten seconds about that. I'd grown sick of New York, and I dug the vibe of Cabo for all its tackiness. Behind the facade, the people seemed genuine. Lucía not least of all. Besides, half the Americans who needed running to ground could be found in Mexico. I could specialize.

"It's not too hot for you?"

"No. There's a breeze off the ocean."

"Not too spicy? I like it spicy."

I thought of the hot sauce on the lunch table in Puerto Chale.

Lucía sat up again on the bed and began to undress. When I moved to help, she slapped my hand away. She reached for the pepper, took a bite, and showed me its florid skin on her tongue. The hottest pepper known to man. I was sweating at the sight of it.

"Stand up," she said. And when I did so, she dropped to her knees.

I was still on fire in every orifice when I lifted a slitted eye to see the clock radio glowing six o'clock. Lucía was asleep beside me. On the credenza rested four limes sucked dry, a half-eaten pepper, and two full bottles of Jarritos Mandarin, glowing bright orange in a ray of sunshine. The bottle of mezcal stood empty.

It took me a minute to process the sun shining through the soda bottles. Six in the evening, not morning. We had to make our appearance at Mara and Sean's wedding in one hour.

I shook Lucía awake. "We're late."

She growled and turned over. Her dark hair was a rat's nest.

"You don't have to do this," I said. "You can take everything back if you want."

"Aargh, *Temerario!*" She shot out of bed buck naked and fished around for her clothes. I did the same. "We'll shower at my place." She looked me over. "Oh, Christ. You can't go to a wedding in those jeans and that shirt."

"It's pretty much all I got."

"It's stained with sweat."

In a mad hour we cleaned up and ran to a store and outfitted me like a tourist in linen shorts and shirt, moccasins, even a sharp straw hat. We rolled into the resort with five minutes to spare.

Sean and Mara had someone shooting wedding pictures of them in front of a gaggle of bird-of-paradise plants in the outdoor lobby. When we arrived, they gave us a warm welcome, not at all angry that we cut it so close. The glow of possibilities shone on them. I introduced Lucía, and they insisted we pose for some pictures, too.

The prim hotel manager came out and pressed us toward the beach before the sun would set. He handed Mara a small bouquet of tropical flowers, all white.

The dropping sun touched the horizon when the officiant said to kiss the bride, and the seemingly happy couple went into a genuine show of public affection that might have broken several local laws. Lucía beamed. Mara tossed the bouquet high in the air toward her. My *novia.* I wondered what she would do. She caught it with gusto.

"Now it's our turn," she said, startling me. But I was game. I was hungry to kiss that bride, even though we hadn't been able to take our hands off one another for the past twelve hours. But there was more to it than that. There was her street wisdom and her fluidity—like a pleasant gurgle of cool water—and the way she freed me to shed my thick skin. Yeah, that New York attitude of mine was a posture just like Mara's mean girl act. Lucía's spice came natural. I'd be damned if I'd take a pass on that.

A sliver of russet sun still protruded over the horizon, a brushstroke of tangerine on the still water. We said "I do" exactly as the sun fully disappeared and night fell, walking back up the beach in the glow of torchlight.

Six months later, I read in the rags that Sean and Mara split up. The gossip columnist didn't say who initiated the divorce, but I figured he got his revenge. A man likes to arrive on his own terms, and he sure wants to go out that way.

As for myself, I continued traveling the world tracking down people who didn't want to be found, but I always returned to the Cabo barrio and Lucía's arms.

"A real woman," she said, "knows when to fan the flame and when to bring the fire extinguisher."

She sure did.

The End

ALL FOR THE LOVE

CHARLES SALZBERG

YOU KNOW HE'S TROUBLE. You know it the first time you lay eyes on him. You know this because you've been here before. You know it because all-too familiar bells and whistles and alarms go off in your head and the only way you can silence them, or at least turn down the volume, is to accept the inevitable. You know you're asking for trouble, but you can't help yourself. You know this because you've been down this road before. You know this because you can smell it a mile away. It's a smell no amount of cheap (or expensive) cologne can hide.

So, you ignore those bells and whistles and alarms until they finally fade away. Well, not so much fade away, as they become background noise, adding to the sound-track of your life. Like the incessant hum of traffic if you live near a busy highway. Which eventually reaches the point where the silence is louder than the noise.

After you ignore these warning signs, all you're left with is your own bad judgment. You own it. But that doesn't make things any better.

You meet him at a bar. Where else would you meet someone like him? In church? The library? Volunteering in a soup kitchen? Not that you frequent any of those places, unless maybe you need to get in out of the rain.

It's not raining tonight, so that's not why you're here, at the bar. You're here because the alternatives are too depressing to contemplate. You're not an alcoholic. Not even close. But there are times you need a drink. And you're not the type to drink alone. Never have been, never will be.

They say misery loves company, so when you're in one of these moods, the mood that calls for a drink, where else would you be than a local dive bar, one that's only a block or two from where you live?

Because you're not there to meet anyone—it's the last thing you want—you don't sit at the bar, which is an invitation for someone to sit down next to you and start a conversation. It's not like you're anti-social, it's that you're not there to conversate. You're there to a) get out of the damn apartment, b) have a drink, maybe two— that's your limit—c) have people *around* you but not *with* you.

You have a favorite table. The one in the back, in the corner. Next to the juke box. Most times you don't mind the music, because it cancels out the temptation to take stock of your life, which only leads to reviewing every single mistake you've ever made. And you know this iis an invitation to disaster. This particular bar has a pretty good selection. There's country, but real country, not that fake, packaged stuff piped in from Nashville. And there's your classic rock. Even the occasional classic oldie. But no Taylor Swift. They had her there, but one of the patrons got pissed enough to put two bullets into the juke box. You weren't there when it happened, but you've heard about it plenty. You wish you'd been there because you would have loved to see that. The owner, who understands such things, tacked up a photo of the wounded juke box behind the bar, as well as a blurry photo of the shooter who has taken on legendary status. His name has long been forgotten, but he is a genuine folk hero. At least in this particular bar. Ever since the assault, no Taylor Swift. If you're you a fan and you want to hear her, you go somewhere else. That's just the way it is. And it's fine with you.

So, that's where you are that rainy, cold night in January, a few days after the holidays, when there's nothing to celebrate except the long, cold winter in front of you. It's the kind of night where if it was only a couple degrees colder, that light rain would be snow.

You're sitting at your regular table, minding your own business, nursing a beer, when Gwen, the waitress on that night, sashays over and puts another beer, same brand you're drinking, in front of you.

You're already on your second, your limit, so you look up at Gwen, smile and say, "Thanks, honey, but I've reached my limit for tonight."

"I know," she says. "That's what I told the guy, but he insisted." She sticks her hand in her pocket and pulls out the top of a twenty. Shows it to me, then tucks it back into her pocket.

"Gotcha. Why don't you bring this back to the guy and tell him I said it's much appreciated and thanks but no thanks."

"He don't look like the kinda guy who takes no for an answer," says Gwen.

"Well," you say, "that's his problem. Just tell him I have a hard and fast rule that I never accept drinks from strangers. Oh, and Gwen, you keep that twenty, y'hear? Because you did your part, and my response has nothing to do with you."

"Thanks," she says. "And for the record, Brenda, I think you're making the right decision. This dude gives off a real creepy vibe."

You glance over to the bar and you see exactly what Gwen means. He might as well be wearing a flashing neon sign on his back. Not that it matters. Because you're the kind of self-destructive chick who likes to see things for herself.

You watch as Gwen ambles back to the bar. You watch as she sets the beer in front of your benefactor and says something. You wonder what she's saying. It's times like this you're sorry you can't read lips. You watch as he smiles, gets up from his barstool, and heads in your direction.

There's part of you that says to yourself, 'oh, no. Do I really have to deal with this asshole?' But there's another part of yourself that thinks, 'this might get interesting.'

It doesn't, but you don't know that then. Then, you're intrigued. You think about your life. How boring it is. How nothing interesting ever happens to you. You think, maybe that's true because you don't open yourself up to experience. You think, so what if this guy's an asshole? Maybe that's what you need. Maybe your problem is you're too closed down. Maybe you should be more open to…to assholes.

So, when he comes over and says, "Mind if I join you?" You don't tell him to fuck off. Instead, you don't say a word because somehow that would make you complicit to whatever's going to happen. Instead, you just nod, which is really the same as saying "yes." Because that way sometime down the line, you can exonerate yourself because you never actually said the word.

If you try, you can probably reproduce the conversation, if that's what it was. But why bother? It's not about the conversation, it's about where it leads. So, if someone asks what you spoke about, you might as well say "blah, blah, blah, blah…" Because the actual words, the witty banter, if there was any doesn't matter. Because in the end, it isn't how you got there, but that you got there at all.

In this case, the "there" is that you wind up spending the night with this asshole. At the time, even though you know he's an asshole the minute Gwen shows up with that drink—you tell yourself, you convince yourself, that he's just a guy and maybe "just a guy" is, at that moment, what you need.

It's not. But that's what you tell yourself because at that particular time maybe it is what you need.

So, blah, blah, blah, you wind up taking him back to your place. And when you get back there, he opens up his coat and he's got a half-empty bottle of Jack Daniels tucked into his pants.

When you ask him where he got it because you didn't make a stop between the bar and your apartment, he gives you a shit-eating grin and says, "Borrowed it from the bartender."

You know "borrowed" means stole, but instead of being angry or appalled all you can think about is the logistics. How the hell did he manage to steal a bottle of booze right from underneath the man whose job is to keep an eye on that bottle, because that bottle translates into money for the owner of the bar.

Suddenly, you've got a magician in your apartment. A master of misdirection. When you should be thinking, what kind of low-life, asshole steals a bottle of liquor from a bar, you're thinking with an air of awe, how the hell did he do it?

Maybe there's more to tell about this night together, let's call it a courtship, but not only is it uninteresting, but it's something you can see in pretty much every movie ever made about bad decisions leading to consequences even worse.

The bottom-line is, that night and all the nights that come after it, lead to why you're sitting at the steering wheel of a car you've never been in before while the man who is definitely not the man of your dreams, has gone into a 7-11 outside a town in the middle of nowhere where you've never been before.

"I'll be right back, babe," he says. It's on the tip of your tongue to ask why are you going in there, but you know the answer without asking so why bother? Another thing you know, even without him asking, is to keep the motor running.

So, why don't you just step on the gas and get the hell out of there? It's what you should do. It's what you're tempted to do. In fact, you smile as you imagine him coming out of that 7-11, looking around and not seeing you or the car. You imagine the look on his face, a combination of disbelief, terror and anger. That look alone would be worth whatever he has stuffed into his pockets after he leaves the store.

But you don't take off. Instead, you keep your eyes glued to the front of the 7-11, so you're ready to hit the gas as soon as he opens the passenger door and gets in.

Suddenly, you hear what sounds like a gunshot, and a second later he comes bursting out the door like he's been shot out of a cannon. You try to convince yourself that you didn't hear what you know you did. Or, you try to convince yourself it wasn't a gunshot but a car backfiring. But you know that's not true. You know it is what it was.

Later, when the night is almost over, and you're on the road back to your place, you're only half-listening as he describes the look on the clerk's face when he sees a gun aimed at his head, and how he not only hands over everything in the till, but also reaches into his back pocket, takes out his wallet, and throws his own hard-earned money on the counter, in case what's in the till isn't enough. You're tempted to ask why, if the clerk complied, why didn't you just leave without firing that shot? But you don't. And the reason you don't is because what difference would it make? The better question is, why you did you stick around? Why did you make yourself an accomplice to a crime committed by an asshole? Why are you with this asshole? But no matter how hard you try, you can't come up with an answer. At least not an answer that makes any sense.

The next morning, when you wake up next to the asshole, that same question is still bouncing around your brain. But this time, you have an answer. It might not be the right answer. It might be a ridiculous answer. And, in fact, it's really a question. And the question is, what won't we do for love?

At first, as the word 'love' forms in your brain and forces itself out the brain and then out through your lips, you shudder. How can this be? You just met the guy and this how you feel? What is this connection that seems to come out of nowhere. Why him? Why now? And how much further will you go for him?

It's then that you realize that you hate yourself a little more than you did the day before you met this asshole.

So, this is where it begins. But the real question, the question that will haunt you maybe forever is, where and how will it end?

MIDNIGHT CONFESSION

LAWRENCE KELTER

BILL MORGAN FALLS into a kitchen chair. Not falls but plummets like a sandbag cut free of its mooring high above a stage. Staring out, past his wife Molly, his gaze lands on the kitchen window. Across the alley, lights are out in the old Gustafson place, now leased to the state of Massachusetts as a women's shelter. Indigent women. Victims of circumstance. Substance abusers and other unfortunates sleeping five and six to a bedroom. Against the house, galvanized garbage pails overflowing with refuse wait most of the week for collection. Rain spilling over clogged gutters rat-a-tat-tats on the metal trash can lids like drumsticks rolling on a taut snare.

Molly fights to draw breath, but her lungs have seized. Her heart stumbles, then surges back with a thud. Lightheaded, she somehow manages to exhale, then draws a shallow breath, just enough air to keep going.

She's accustomed to seeing stains on her husband's shirt, congealed yellow egg yolk on his collar, and brown pot roast gravy over his growing belly. She doesn't bat an eyelash when she spot cleans the stains on his laundry before throwing it in the washer. He's the love of her life after all. Her reason for living.

But not blood. Never blood.

Until now.

His shirt is covered in it.

Giant red stains.

Everywhere. Like a butcher's apron after cleaving a side of beef.

Her throat goes dry. Her fingers twitch. Nothing else will move.

His light brown hair is stained crimson. Blood drizzles slowly down his earlobe where it drip-dries thick as house paint. Puddled in his ear canal, it's already coagulating. And there's a haze over his eyes as if there's something in his system that shouldn't be there.

Jagged bolts of lightning rupture the sky. Thunder detonates. She's vaguely aware of the rumbling outside because her mind is logjammed. There's only her loving husband, covered in blood, motionless, frightening her to death.

Molly's heart beats, then doesn't. Can't find its rhythm. The words, *not again*, claw at her heart. Knife-edged talons ripping and shredding. "Bill, what's going on? You're scaring me." Her mouth is so dry it feels as if there are glass shards lodged in her throat. "Have you been next door again?" she implores. Agonizes. "*Bill*, please tell me. Have you...?"

The women housed next door would rather be anywhere else on earth but have little choice. State-funded housing is bleak. Homelessness is tragic. So, here these women live without friends, unwanted by their families. Scorn greets them the moment they step outside the house. They're looked upon as a blight on the neighborhood. They learn to keep their heads down and stay clear of the neighbors. Grow lonesome. Grow still lonelier. As if it's possible. They're ostracized. Shunned. Worse still, ignored. We can't get rid of them so let's pretend they don't exist. Lovely.

Ingrid the local realtor tells Molly the value of their home has dropped thirty percent since the shelter took up residence next door to them and that the company that bought the house and rents to the state is looking for additional properties in the South End. If the state is successful, the Morgans might as well put a match to their home, collect the insurance money, and pray they don't get caught.

Bill's not in great health. He's desperate to retire. Soon. As soon as he can. They bought the house at the peak of the market and are upside-down on their mortgage. They can barely afford to stay and can't afford to sell. And if Bill loses his job as she fears he might… *Dear God*, Molly prays. *I hope a good night's sleep will set him right.* Bill's been demoted and hates going to work. He calls out regularly and has been warned that continued absenteeism might cost him his job. Might as in categorically.

Molly's job doesn't pay enough to carry their expenses. She works as a receptionist for a skinflint doctor. Hourly. No vacation. No medical insurance. She and the physician's assistant come out of pocket for the coffee everyone drinks in the office. He drives a Benz and owns a speedboat that he berths at the Independence Wharf. Brags about the house he bought for his newly married daughter. His investments. Trips to Disneyland. He won't pay for coffee. Supermarket brand. Not Starbucks.

Molly searches Bill's expression hoping to learn something, anything about what's happened. She gets nothing. She hasn't moved in moments but somehow finds the resolve to teeter over to the sink. Wetting a threadbare kitchen towel, she wrings out the excess water before returning to him. Like an artist working in reverse, she removes crimson from his face with precision strokes of the towel, wiping blood from around his eyes until he looks like a panda with light circles in place of dark. She shudders at the sight of him. The bags under his eyes are fleshy white. Unnatural. Ghostly. She cleans the bridge of his nose and the area around his mouth before returning to the sink to rinse the bloody towel, then watches the blood swirl in the sink before going down the drain. Like their lives.

Bill's gut is the diameter of a pickle barrel and each ankle is as thick as the basement sewage line that has leaked since the very first day they took ownership. He's a yeti with hair growing from every pore on his massive body, stiff Brillo-like hair with barbed ends that prick her skin when he lies next to her in bed. Rosebush thorns. No roses.

Doc Showalter tells him to lose weight, lots of it. Again. And again. And yet again. Bill says he'll try but won't. He doesn't. Never has. Not for long. A day or two before falling off the wagon, then back to the snacks, cookies, chips, and beer. Beer is to Bill as methadone is to a heroin addict. The alcohol level in the beer is so low he can't drink enough to get sloshed, to saturate his fat-laden tissues. His gray matter. But he tries. He's in pain and needs to blot out reality. Some way. Somehow. Along with the alcohol come the calories, the cankles, and the pickle barrel gut. He's fat and bloated and probably won't live long, but at least he's not drunk. Drunk is so much worse. Drunk is a disaster. A nightmare from which their marriage can't survive.

When he drinks, he stumbles into the john in the middle of the night and lets fly like a firefighter battling a blaze with a hydrant-pressurized hose and is unable to control the force coming out of the nozzle. He pisses all over the bathroom floor, on the seat, and behind the tank. Splashes the wallpaper. There's a second bathroom on the upper level that Molly uses exclusively. He's too fat to climb the stairs. Thank God.

His blank stare is still focused on the window, fixed on the women's shelter across the way.

"Bill," Molly asks, afraid of what she'll hear, "What happened?" She turns and looks out the window hoping to see something, hear anything that might shed light on what's transpired. *Did something happen next door,* she worries. *To one of those women? Please, God. No.*

A light from one of the upstairs rooms of the women's shelter jabs her eye. She disregards it even though she's heard that the shelter has a strict 10 p.m. lights-out policy. Turning back to her husband, she continues to scrub the blood from his face. "Bill, please talk to me. It'll be okay," she says. "Whatever it is—" But there no weight in her words. Nothing to cling to. How can there be? It's not the first time. Not the second. "Bill, what kind of trouble are we in?" *Should I call the police?* She ponders the suggestion but immediately shakes the idea from her head. The iron-laden stench of freshly moistened blood hits the pit of her stomach, propelling her to the kitchen sink, retching. Moments later, bile chases blood down the drain.

Once waif thin, years of stress have whittled away at Molly's willpower and crushed her vanity, year by year, one unspeakable act at a time. She washes the vomit off her thrift store sweatshirt and returns to him, soaking wet. Searching his eyes imploringly, there's still nothing. Nothing. Not a word nor gesture. Not so much as a troubled sigh.

He's in shock? she realizes. "Let me get that disgusting shirt off of you. Maybe once you're in dry clothes…" Unbuttoning his shirt, she slips it off his arms. Cut up and repurposed, there's enough fabric to fashion a schooner's headsail. She holds the shirt up and examines it. "So much blood. I'll never get it all out." She ponders a moment. "Maybe if I let it soak. I know you like this one. It's one of your favorites. Let's see if I can save it." Holding the blood-soaked shirt with her fingertips, out and away from her body, she carries it over to the kitchen sink. A sudden flash of lightning floods the kitchen with daylight. The strobe of white light turns the bloody shirt into a backlit projector screen with bright red streaks against a stark white background. "That must be close," she says absentmindedly, then turns to Bill as thunder crackles. His freshly scrubbed face looks pale. She wonders if he'll be okay, if he'll make it to work in the morning. The mortgage payment is coming due. *Please, Bill. Pull yourself together.* Once more to the sink, she places the stopper in the drain, fills it with hot water, and pours in a cup of bleach. She drops the big shirt in the solution, then watches as it soaks up the liquid and sinks, immediately imparting a pink hue to the water. "I hope that does the trick."

Bill is still in the chair, unable to move. Catatonic.

Shock, he's definitely in shock. "I'll put on a kettle," she says in an encouraging voice. "A hot cup of tea is what you need. I'll get you a clean dry shirt and you'll be as good as new. Then you can tell me all about it. You poor thing, you're a bundle of nerves." She seems pleased with herself, as if she's arrived at a reasonable course of action. *He'll be okay,* she tells herself. Reassures herself. *He just needs a little time.* Fearing the worst, a drizzle of tears escape. She turns away to hide it from him and dabs it away with her sweatshirt sleeve before filling the kettle. "It'll just be a few minutes, honey." She should've noticed but hadn't, her sweatshirt is not only soaking wet but bloody from cleaning her husband's face. "Look at me. I'm an absolute fright," she says on her way out of the kitchen. "Sit tight. I'll be right—"

Three hard-knuckled raps on the front door halt her dead in her tracks.

She cringes. "Oh shit. Who's that?"

She looks at Bill. He offers no opinion. She rotates toward the door, then back. Tentative. Unsure of what to do. "Shit, Bill what are we going to do?"

His mouth agape, a woosh of air sails past his lips.

"Did you say something?" she asks. Hopeful, imploring him for advice. "I don't know what to do." Her shoulders heave. "Please help me. Tell me what to do." He slouches in the chair—not so much slouches as settles. Her mask slips. "You're so damn useless. Can't you even…?"

She takes a few steps toward the front door, then stops, collects herself, and presses on. Pulling a robe off the coat hook, she covers her bloody, soaking-wet sweatshirt.

A hard-hearted voice booms outside as she inches toward the door. The callous voice stabs her heart with icy spikes. "Boston Police Department."

She puffs rapidly, natural-birth breaths to disperse her panic. Within moments her pulse drops to a steady eighty. Her emotions are veiled, her appearance unassuming. Lightning flashes as she cracks the threshold. No more than a few inches. Just enough to see out. A police officer in raingear stands before her. Her widening eyes express mild surprise.

"Hello, Mrs. Morgan," the officer says with blunt familiarity and a cocked brow. His face is bathed in a shadow that paints him grimly. Rain drips from his plastic-covered hat.

"Officer Quinn, what are you doing out on such a ghastly night? How can I…?"

He stares past her, into the house. "Everything alright in here?"

he asks. He knows something, senses it. He's been on the job long enough to be suspicious when suspicion is warranted, long enough to smell a festering rat.

"Of course. Why wouldn't it be?"

The storm clouds shift. Moonlight flashes into the foyer. No longer than a heartbeat. He scans the interior, left to right, then up and down. His eyes lock onto something, something telling. "I'm coming in," he declares. Without waiting for an invitation, he places his open palms flat against the heavy wooden door. He pushes her and the door aside with a forceful shove. Once inside, his hand travels swiftly to his service weapon.

"Why are you here?" she shouts, chest heaving, eyes wild at the sight of his gun.

"I think you know. Where's your husband? I need to speak with him. Now!"

"Oh, he's..." Her eyes dart back and forth evasively. "He's here."

"Get him!"

"Of course," she says, trembling before turning toward the kitchen. She calls out calmly, "Oh, Bill. Can you come to the door?" She waits patiently for her husband's response. Nothing in her demeanor betrays her intent until she wheels around, slipping a kitchen knife from her housecoat sleeve so fluidly her action appears rehearsed.

"Drop it!" Quinn shouts with his gun leveled at her eyes. "Drop it *now*." His blood runs cold at the sound of her screams as she slashes at him, swinging the large knife like a sickle harvesting stalks of grain. Quinn is a veteran, savvy but no longer quick and certainly not agile. The razor-edged knife cuts his arm, ripping flesh, muscles, and tendons causing his grip to contract reflexively. The gun bucks in his hand.

Quinn's ears are still ringing from the discharged gun. Looks up at a shattered streetlamp lens directly above as an EMS technician works on his arm. He can't release his grip. His fist is locked, his fingertips welded to his palm. The street is dark save for police lights. Otherwise pitch-black.

Meddlesome neighbors congregate in the shadows. They watch from beyond the taped police perimeter as personnel move in and out of the Morgan house. One body has already been carried out encapsulated in a black vinyl body bag. Gossip spreads. It's only the first of two. An old rumor resurfaces and spreads. Molly Morgan has poisoned her husband before. No one has been able to confirm the allegation. They stalk her when she walks down the street, but she's learned to walk staring straight ahead. Avoids probing eyes. Questions. Accusations.

Quinn's pretty sure he knows which kid threw the rock that smashed the streetlamp. Not a bad kid but one who always manages to find trouble. *I'd like to see him on the pitcher's mound over at Moakley Park,* he muses. *With aim like that he'd paint the corners of the strike zone.*

A twinge shoots through Quinn's arm. His eyes flash at the sensation. *That felt weird.* "You almost done?" he asks.

"That should do it," EMS guy says. He applies a final strip of adhesive tape, sealing the bandage wrapped around Quinn's arm. "You're okay for now but you'll need surgery. I'm pretty sure you've got a lacerated nerve. That's why your fingers locked down on the trigger." Rubbing his chin, he muses, "You know, in a way, that crazy woman shot herself."

"It happened so fast. I didn't think I'd fired deliberately, but at a time like that… You know, shit happens. Almost twenty years on the job and I never shot anyone. I wonder if the review board will keep my record intact."

EMS guy shrugs. "How exactly would that work? You *did* pull the *trigga.*"

Quinn rolls his shoulders. "They'd call it accidental discharge. Happens during altercations sometimes."

"Uh-huh," EMS guy says. He's dubious. Purses his lips. Takes a moment to think about what he's heard. Lets it go. "Do you want something for the pain?"

"Got anything stiff? Jack Daniels, maybe?"

"Don't you wish," EMS guy says. "Tylenol with Codeine is about the strongest I carry."

"Nah. I pass kidney stones the size of bowling balls regular as a Swiss clock. This little nick ain't nothing compared with that." Thinks. "I wonder how much downtime I'm looking at?"

"Months. Probably several. Healing time. Physical therapy..."

"I suppose I'll probably have to requalify at the shooting range."

Their heads turn at the sound of a cynical rumble. "Oh, boo-hoo, Quinn," Lieutenant Ryan says as he places a compassionate hand on Quinn's shoulder. "I'm glad you're alright. I watched your body cam feed on the way over. That was a close call, brother."

Quinn reflects. "Luck of the Irish I guess."

"Amen to that." Ryan gazes at Quinn's bandaged arm. "That little scratch might very well push you past the twenty-year mark. If you time it right you might go from disability straight into retirement and not have to tussle with shitheads and wackos anymore."

"I'll be up front if you need me," EMT guy says and moves off. "Let me know if you change your mind on the pain meds, Officer."

Quinn nods. "Hey, LT, you take a look inside yet?" His expression is dire. Paints a picture of the crime scene he encountered after checking Molly Morgan for a pulse and radioing command. He spotted blood spatter on Molly's cheek while standing at the door. Prepared for the worst. The worst is exactly what he saw. Murder victim slouched in a kitchen chair. Shirtless. Upper body bathed in blood. Throat cut. Kitchen linoleum awash in blood. "She hit the carotid artery. Must've blown like a pressure hose."

Ryan retches for effect. "That's fucking vile."

"Oh, come on, LT, I know you've seen worse."

"Yeah, sure I have, but that doesn't mean it gets any easier." Reaches into his pocket for a stick of gum. Unwraps it. Pops it into his mouth. "Want one?" Quinn declines. "I had to jump out of the way to avoid getting clobbered by the fat bastard. He tumbled out of the chair just as I walked into the kitchen. Missed me by an inch." Looks down. His shoes are rain slick, unblemished. There's a streak of blood across his pant leg. "Looks like he got me after all."

Dismayed, Quinn shakes his head. "As I remember, she made a couple of prior attempts on his life."

"That we know of," Ryan interjects. "Trips to the ER that were documented. Poison both times, right?"

"I think so. Swore up and down that they were accidents and I guess he wanted to believe her. I can't see it happening even once. But *twice*? Not a chance in hell. I guess she figured she'd try something new. Three times a charm. Ain't that what they say?" Looks to Ryan for affirmation. Doesn't receive it. "Gave up on rat poison and went at him with a kitchen knife. Cut the poor bastard ear-to-ear."

Ryan listens intently. Chews on Quinn's assessment and the gum simultaneously, his mouth opening and closing like a gasping catfish. The gum is stale. Jawbones jut from his cheeks as he grinds it into pulp.

"All the abuse he must've taken from her over the years—the attempts on his life." Quinn rubs his bandaged arm. Seems concerned. "Boston's a big city, but I've patrolled the South End a long time." Reflects. "I remember when the Morgans first moved in. Used to see Bill jogging through the park now and then. He dressed smart. Held his head high. Got to wonder what the hell happened."

"Sometimes bat shit crazy is all there is." Ryan cracks his neck. "People snap—normal one moment and stark raving nuts the next. I'll make sure the coroner digs into her records for prior psych evaluations."

Quinn spots a kid ducking under the police tape for a closer look. It's the kid he thinks busted the streetlamp. *A-hole kid. We wouldn't have any trouble seeing if the damn streetlight was working.* His cheekbones rise. Refocuses on Ryan. "I know people let themselves go downhill but—" Rattles his head sadly. "God forgive me for saying this, but I think he's better off dead."

Ryan squeezes his eyes shut. Exhales long and low through his nostrils. "And still he stayed."

Quinn echoes, "And still he stayed. That were me, I'd have taken out an order of protection and lit out for parts unknown."

"Probably never thought she'd murder him in cold blood."

"I wonder if maybe she doped him to get the drop on him? Wouldn't be the first time she slipped something into his food," Quinn says. "I imagine switching from rat poison to roofies isn't much of a stretch."

"They're both on their way to the morgue, so what's it really matter?" Ryan looks about. Nothing in particular. "Who called it in?"

Quinn glances at the house next door. "One of the women from the shelter called 911." Movement catches his eye. "Her." Points to a flyspeck of a woman. Her coat swims on her. Hangs down to her knees. Faded jeans. Painfully short. Maybe a kid's hand-me-down. She stares at the house as if waiting for it to reveal its truth, a truth the Morgans have taken to their graves.

"Miss. Oh, Miss," Quinn calls out. "You mind stepping over here for a minute?"

"Me?" she asks. Points to herself.

Quinn waves her over.

It's dark. Hard to see her face. She walks with her head hung low. She knows to be unobtrusive. Invisible.

"You talking to me?" she asks. Makes minimal eye contact. Looks strained. Her expression reads, *make it quick.*

"This is Lieutenant Ryan," Quinn says. "You mind telling him what you told me?" Quinn's memory is good but in all the turmoil has misplaced her name. It's not exactly run of the mill. "... It's Tajana, right?"

She's faceless and nameless to the members of the community. To them, she's part of the mess the state has dumped in their laps. Irritation surfaces. Doesn't bother to confirm her name. "I got to do this again?" Her voice is raspy. A smoker's voice. The voice of a woman with an oxygen tank in her future. "I already told you what I know."

"Thanks for calling 911," Ryan says. Trots out a fatherly smile. Part of his arsenal. Uses it to loosen lips. "A lot of people bury their heads in the sand and wait for someone else to do what needs to be done. So, if you wouldn't mind, I'd like to hear what happened. In your own words."

She looks from one police officer to the other. They both gaze at her expectantly. She's annoyed. Doesn't see that she has a choice. "As I said the first time, I couldn't sleep. Two of the girls in my room snore like water buffalo and I'm a light sleeper." Reaches into one of her oversized pockets. Withdraws a vape. Puts it to her mouth. Takes a long, satisfying drag. "I went to the bathroom, then looked out the window to watch the storm. It was *crazy*. One big lightning bolt came real close and lit up the sky like the 4th of July. I could see right into the kitchen next door and that crazy-ass woman was standing over Bill." Shutters her eyes. "Blood everywhere."

"Bill?" Ryan asks. "You knew the victim?"

"Uh-huh," she says, slow to confess. "He stops by time-to-time to see if we need anything. That man was the only decent soul in the neighborhood. The only one who gave a damn about us women." Another quick drag on the vape. Expels vapor into the night. "Most of the people around here treat us like we don't exist. Like we ain't people."

"I see," Ryan says. "Exactly what did Mr. Morgan do for you ladies?"

"Changed light bulbs. Fixed dripping faucets and what have you. That kind of thing. City services don't do jack shit. Just give us lip service. Say they'll get around to this and that, but no one ever shows up to do the work."

"Mr. Morgan ever talk about his wife?" Quinn asks. "Any problems with his relationship he shared with you?"

"He never talked about his missus, but it wasn't hard to see how unhappy he was. He'd stop by to lend a hand. It was plain to see that he needed comforting. Poor man seemed so lonely." She pouts. "I couldn't hardly bear to see him like that."

Quinn and Ryan lock eyes. "Go on," Ryan says, concealing piqued curiosity.

"The few times I've seen Bill and his missus together it sure didn't look like there was much love in their relationship. Know what I mean? One of them marriages of necessity."

"You see that a lot these days," Ryan says. "Mortgage payments. Car payments. Everything's so damn expensive. You need two oars in the water just to get by." Notices Quinn grimace. Sees the strain on his face. "You hanging in there, brother?"

Quinn's brave face crumbles. "We good for now, LT?" He's not afraid of a little pain. Thought he could handle it. He was wrong. "I need a Cracker Jack surgeon and a shit ton of anesthesia." Sighs heavily. "What time is it anyway."

Ryan checks his watch. "Two minutes till tomorrow. Get going," Ryan says. No hesitation. "Take care of yourself." Waits until Quinn is secured in the ambulance and it pulls away. Turns back to her. "Anything else you can tell me?"

Her gaze drifts. "I'm gonna miss that man. Can't say he was anything to look at, but I tell you what, he was funny as hell." Her shoulders rise, then settle. "Lying on the floor with his big old belly sticking out from under the kitchen cabinet he used to fire off one joke after another. Had me doubled over laughing. Used to be some kind of fancy advertising executive, until…"

"Until?"

"Agency muckety mucks said no one appreciates his brand of humor anymore. Demoted him to some flunky-level position."

"That's too bad. Making people laugh, that's a gift."

"Sure enough is. Most of us gals at the shelter don't have a lot to live for." Raises the vape to her mouth. Pauses. Something's on her mind. "Everyone around here thinks we're all hoes and crack heads. But some of the ladies inside are accomplished. Went to fancy schools and owned businesses. Being down on your luck don't make you a piece of garbage. That man's visits brightened our day and I think spending time with us maybe helped him get through the day."

The rain slows to an intermittent sprinkle. Ryan slides off his hat and shakes off the rain. Runs fingers through his tightly cropped salt and pepper hair. Shrugs. Laments, "Poor SOB. I still don't understand why he stayed with her?"

She scoffs. "Why he what?"

Shrugs. "Why he stayed with his wife. After two near brushes with death, what the hell was he waiting for?"

Tajana's torso is shrouded by the oversized hand-me-down coat. She unbuttons it and affectionately strokes her baby bump. "He didn't stay for that no-good witch he was married to," she declares emphatically. "He stayed for *us*."

THE END

KILLING IN THE NAME OF

SAMANTHA RIPLEY

LENNOX SLID into the dimly lit bar, red hair tucked under a nondescript beanie, her movements fluid yet calculated. The sour stench of spilled beer and unwashed bodies assaulted her nostrils as she claimed a stool in the corner, positioning herself with her back to the wall and a clear sightline to both exits. Perfect. She ordered a vodka she had no intention of drinking and let her gaze drift across the room, cataloging faces against her mental database of targets and threats. The traffickers huddled in the booth by the bathroom looked nervous tonight. Interesting.

The bar sat nestled in the armpit of Eastern Europe, a forgotten place where borders blurred and passports changed hands like playing cards. Low ceiling, lower standards. Smoke hung thick despite laws against it, yellowing the already dingy walls. Men with scars and dead eyes occupied most tables, their conversations a mumble of mixed Slavic tongues punctuated by the occasional harsh laugh.

Her eyes landed on Vasily Karkov, seated in the center booth surrounded by his lieutenants. Mid-fifties, gray at the temples, hands that had strangled more than one uncooperative girl. The Firm's dossier understated his cruelty. She mentally calculated the distance between them—fourteen steps. Six seconds at most.

Not yet. She needed to verify the flash drive was on him first. Her mission parameters required both elimination and retrieval, in that order. The Firm didn't appreciate messy work.

Lennox sipped her water, allowing none of her disgust to reach her face as she observed Karkov laugh, his hand slapping the thigh of a young woman who smiled with empty eyes. Human cargo. The familiar cold rage settled in her chest, a welcome companion. She checked her watch. Twenty minutes until her extraction window closed.

The front door crashed open with such force it splintered against the wall.

A woman stood framed in the doorway, honey-blonde hair catching the dim light like a halo around a face too beautiful for this shithole. Her leather jacket gleamed, her smile wide and wild. In each hand, a pistol.

"Dobryy vecher, mudaki!" she called out cheerfully before firing both guns simultaneously.

Blood sprayed across the bar as the first shots found their targets—two men by the door dropped with perfect holes between their eyes. The room erupted. Men overturned tables, reaching for weapons. Glasses shattered. Women screamed. The bartender ducked.

Fuck. Lennox slipped her hand beneath her jacket, fingers wrapping around her Glock. This wasn't part of the plan. Whoever this psychopath was, she'd just complicated everything. Karkov's bodyguards formed a protective circle, ushering him toward the back exit—the flash drive moving with him.

The blonde woman spun through the chaos like a dancer, each shot purposeful, her movements flowing with a grace that seemed out of place amid the carnage. She laughed as a man charged her, sidestepping at the last moment to trip him face-first into the bar before putting a bullet in the back of his skull.

"Who ordered the brain splatter? Anyone? No?" She kicked a chair into another attacker's path.

Lennox remained still, calculating. The blonde was cutting through Karkov's outer security with disturbing efficiency. Perhaps this unexpected chaos could work to her advantage.

She slid from her stool, staying low as she worked her way around the periphery of the room, keeping her target in sight.

Karkov had almost reached the kitchen door now, two bodyguards remaining. If she timed it right—

A movement caught her eye—one of Karkov's men had positioned himself behind an overturned table, rifle aimed at the blonde's exposed back. Without conscious thought, Lennox raised her weapon and fired. The man's head snapped back, a red mist spraying the wall behind him.

Across the blood-soaked room, sky-blue eyes locked onto hers. The blonde's expression shifted from surprise to something like delight, a smile spreading across her face as she offered Lennox a small nod of acknowledgement.

In that split second of connection, Lennox saw the unmistakable recognition of a fellow professional. Not just any killer, but someone who approached death as an art form. The woman winked at her, then whirled back into the fight.

Karkov had disappeared through the kitchen door. Shit.

Lennox moved toward the same exit, but three men intercepted her, knives drawn. She ducked the first swing, driving the heel of her palm into the attacker's nose with a satisfying crunch. Cartilage gave way beneath bone as she followed through, using his momentum to slam his head against the edge of the bar. He dropped like a stone.

The second man lunged. Lennox sidestepped, grabbing a half-empty beer bottle from the counter and smashing it across his face. Glass shards embedded in his cheek as he howled. She drove her knee up between his legs, then rammed the jagged bottleneck into his throat when he doubled over.

The third attacker hesitated, which was his mistake. Lennox seized a dart from the board on the wall and flicked it into his eye with brutal accuracy. He screamed, hands flying to his face, giving her time to close the distance and snap his neck with a sharp twist.

She turned to find the blonde woman suddenly at her back, facing the opposite direction as another wave of Karkov's men poured in from the front entrance. Without discussion, they positioned themselves back to back, an instinctive formation.

"Friend of Karkov's?" the blonde asked in accented English, shooting a man through the kneecap, then the forehead when he fell.

"Just the opposite," Lennox replied, driving her elbow into an attacker's sternum, then seizing his chin and crown to wrench his head violently to one side.

"Good. I hate to kill the competition, but I will if necessary." The woman spun around Lennox, using her shoulder as a pivot point to kick one man in the chest while shooting another.

Their movements began to synchronize, a deadly dance of give and take. Where Lennox employed ruthless tactics—each strike economical, each bullet finding its mark with minimal fuss—her unexpected ally moved with theatrical flair. The blonde incorporated unnecessary but impressive acrobatics, flipping over the bar to kick the cowering bartender in the face before shooting two men approaching from opposite sides.

"What did these guys do to you?" Lennox asked, grabbing a pool cue to drive it through a man's eye socket. The wet squelch and subsequent collapse brought a grim satisfaction.

"Human trafficking. Sex slaves. You know, the usual scum." The blonde pirouetted—actually pirouetted—around a wild punch, slitting the attacker's throat with a butterfly knife that appeared from nowhere. "Plus they shot my favorite coat last week."

Lennox couldn't tell if she was joking.

A massive man with a shaved head charged toward Lennox just as her magazine emptied. She braced for impact, calculating how to use his weight against him—when a gun skidded across the floor toward her. The blonde had kicked it in her direction while simultaneously breaking a man's arm and forcing him to shoot his own foot.

Lennox snatched the weapon, checked it in one fluid motion, and looked up to meet the blonde's gaze.

"Better than flowers," she deadpanned, then turned and shot the approaching giant twice in the chest without looking. His body crashed into a table, shattering it beneath his dead weight.

The blonde let out a delighted laugh that shouldn't have been so charming in the middle of a massacre. "I like you," she called out, slashing a man's femoral artery with balletic precision. "What's your name, Red?"

"Not the time for introductions," Lennox replied, rolling across the floor to avoid a spray of bullets that splintered the wood where she'd stood. She came up firing, three shots taking down two more attackers.

The blonde pouted theatrically even as she drove her elbow into a man's throat, crushing his windpipe. "No fun."

As the fight continued, Lennox found herself anticipating her companion's movements with increasing accuracy. When the blonde ducked, Lennox fired over her head. When Lennox stepped left, the blonde filled the space she'd vacated, catching a knife meant for Lennox's back and returning it to its owner via his eye socket.

Blood spattered across the wooden bar as they cleared the room methodically. Bodies dropped around them in a choreography of death that might have been beautiful if it weren't so horrific. The blonde hummed what sounded like Swan Lake as she executed a particularly complex combination of moves that ended with three men dead at her feet.

Karkov. Lennox suddenly remembered her primary target. She scanned the room, now littered with bodies and slick with blood. No sign of him.

"Looking for the boss?" the blonde asked, casually reloading her weapon as the last of the attackers bled out at her feet. "He ran out the back about two minutes ago. Heading for the square, if I had to guess."

Lennox swore under her breath. The extraction window was closing fast.

"Don't worry, Red. He won't get far." The blonde grinned, wiping blood from her cheek with the back of her hand, somehow managing to look both terrifying and radiant. "Coming?"

Without waiting for an answer, she headed for the kitchen door, stepping over bodies with the carefree air of someone crossing a puddle. Lennox hesitated only briefly before following. The mission parameters had shifted, but the objective remained. Eliminate Karkov. Retrieve the drive.

And now, apparently, deal with the human hurricane who'd just cut through a room full of traffickers with the same enthusiasm most people reserved for opening birthday presents.

The night air hit Lennox like a slap, biting cold after the stuffy heat of the bar. Snow fell in fat, lazy flakes, already beginning to cover the fresh footprints leading away from the back door. The village square spread before them, a postcard-perfect scene of Eastern European charm with its cobblestones and quaint storefronts, now eerily silent except for distant shouts. Blood dripped from Lennox's fingertips, melting tiny red holes in the pristine white at her feet.

"This way," the blonde said, nodding toward the footprints. "My name is Sasha, by the way. Since we're about to kill more people together, seems rude not to introduce myself."

Lennox didn't respond, scanning the square for movement. The stillness felt wrong. Karkov wouldn't run without backup, and these types of men didn't survive by being predictable.

"You're supposed to tell me your name now," Sasha prompted as she reloaded.

"Lennox," she replied, more out of reflex than desire to share. "And you can drop the friendly act. I'm only following you because my target went this way."

Sasha's smile widened. "Who said it's an act? I'm a delight."

Before Lennox could reply, movement caught her eye. The windows of a building across the square lit up, followed by another, then another. Doors opened, disgorging men with guns.

"Friends of yours?" Sasha asked.

"I don't have friends," Lennox replied, already moving toward the nearest cover—an ornate stone fountain frozen solid in the center of the square.

"That explains so much about your personality," Sasha said

with a theatrical sigh, ducking behind the fountain beside her as bullets shattered the ice sculptures atop it, sending crystalline shards raining down on them.

Lennox assessed the situation with cold calculation. Eight men emerging from the building on the left—a hardware store, if the faded sign was accurate. Five more from what looked like a small hotel on the right. And Karkov, visible through the window of a restaurant across the square, making a phone call. The flash drive glinted on a chain around his neck.

"You crash other people's operations often?" Lennox asked, popping up to fire three precise shots that dropped two attackers.

"Only the interesting ones," Sasha replied with a wink. She rose in a fluid motion, firing both guns in opposite directions. Two men fell. "Though if I'd known you were after Karkov, I might have coordinated. Professional courtesy and all that."

They moved in tandem around the fountain, using it as cover while systematically reducing the opposition. Lennox's style was economical—one shot, one kill, no wasted motion. Sasha, in contrast, treated each exchange like a performance, adding unnecessary but impressive flourishes to her kills.

"There," Lennox nodded toward the restaurant. "Karkov's inside. Cover me."

"Bossy," Sasha said, but she laid down suppressive fire as Lennox sprinted across the square.

A bullet grazed Lennox's arm, tearing through her jacket and leaving a hot line of pain. She ignored it, diving through the restaurant's window in a shower of glass rather than using the door, which would surely be watched.

She rolled to her feet amidst startled screams from the few remaining patrons. The restaurant was small and rustic—wooden tables, checkered tablecloths, the scent of paprika and roasted meat hanging in the air. Karkov stood by the kitchen, bodyguards flanking him.

"Karkov," Lennox said, straightening to her full height. "The Firm sends their regards."

His face went slack with recognition. "Kerr." He spat the word like a curse.

She didn't waste time with banter. Three shots in rapid succession—two bodyguards dropped, and Karkov stumbled back, blood blooming from his shoulder.

The back door of the restaurant burst open, and Sasha tumbled in, laughing as she fired over her shoulder at pursuers outside. "Did I miss the party?" She spotted Karkov. "Ah, there you are, you piece of shit."

Karkov used the distraction to flee through the kitchen, remarkably spry for a wounded man. Lennox cursed and followed, vaulting over the counter.

The kitchen staff cowered against walls as she passed. She caught a glimpse of Karkov's coat disappearing through a service exit. Outside again, into a narrow alley behind the restaurant. More men waited there—reinforcements Karkov must have called.

"Down!" Sasha's voice rang out behind her. Lennox dropped instinctively as a frying pan sailed over her head, striking a man squarely in the face with a dull clang. He crumpled, nose shattered across his features.

Sasha appeared beside her, wielding a kitchen knife in one hand and her gun in the other. "I haven't had this much fun in ages," she said, her blue eyes bright with adrenaline. "You're good luck, Red."

"This isn't my definition of luck," Lennox replied, breaking a man's arm at the elbow and using his body as a shield against incoming fire.

They fought their way through the alley, Sasha grabbing whatever came to hand—a trash can lid became a shield, then a weapon as she frisbeed it into a man's throat. Lennox stayed more conventional but no less lethal.

They emerged into the square again, now littered with bodies. Snow continued to fall, already beginning to cover the dead in a thin white shroud. Karkov was limping toward another building across the square—a long, low structure with fish painted on its sign.

"The market," Sasha said unnecessarily. "Perfect."

They pursued, Lennox's focus narrowing to the flash drive swinging from Karkov's neck as he ran. Almost within reach. The extraction window was nearly closed, but if she could just—

More men spilled from the adjacent buildings, cutting off their direct path. Lennox calculated trajectories, counting bullets and bodies. Too many for a frontal assault.

"This way," she said, veering toward a narrow side street. Sasha followed without question, a surprising display of trust that Lennox filed away for later consideration.

They circled around, approaching the fish market from the rear. The loading dock stood empty in the pre-dawn gloom, the metallic scent of fish blood mixing with gunpowder and the copper tang of human blood that clung to them both.

"After you," Sasha said with an exaggerated bow.

Lennox slipped inside, immediately assaulted by the overpowering smell of fish. The market was cavernous and dark, illuminated only by security lights that cast long shadows between stalls of ice-packed seafood. She spotted Karkov moving between displays, four men with him now.

"Split up," she whispered to Sasha. "I'll circle left."

Sasha nodded, her playful demeanor temporarily subdued as she melted into the shadows to the right.

Lennox moved silently between stalls, the cold seeping through her boots. She selected a filleting knife from a workstation, testing its weight before tucking it into her belt. At a butcher's block, she found an ice pick, its point wickedly sharp. Better.

The first of Karkov's men rounded the corner, and she struck without hesitation, driving the ice pick up through his soft palate and into his brain. She caught him as he fell, lowering his body silently to the floor.

From across the market came a wet thunk followed by a gurgle. Sasha, presumably. Lennox continued her stealthy advance, taking down another guard with the garrote wire she kept in her jacket cuff, pulling it tight until he stopped struggling.

She heard Karkov's ragged breathing before she saw him, the sound of a wounded animal trying to remain silent. He'd taken shelter behind a display of enormous tuna, frozen solid on beds of crushed ice. One guard remained with him, gun drawn and scanning the shadows.

Lennox weighed her options. The angle was wrong for a clean shot with minimal risk. She needed to draw them out or reposition.

A crash from the opposite side of the market solved her dilemma. The guard's head snapped toward the sound, and Lennox used the distraction to her advantage, launching the ice pick with deadly accuracy. It embedded in his temple, and he dropped without a sound.

Karkov panicked, breaking cover to run deeper into the market. Lennox pursued, only to pull up short at the scene before her.

Sasha stood in the middle of the aisle, holding a tiny kitten against her chest. The animal, barely larger than her hand, had gray fur matted with fish scales and what might have been blood. Sasha cradled it with surprising gentleness, her gun temporarily holstered as she stroked its head with one finger.

"Are you serious right now?" Lennox demanded, incredulity momentarily overriding her mission focus.

Sasha looked up, seemingly unsurprised by Lennox's presence. "She was in one of the crates," she said, as if that explained everything. "They were using this place to move more than fish."

Before Lennox could respond, movement caught her eye—Karkov, attempting to circle around them toward the exit. She raised her gun, but Sasha beat her to it, drawing and firing in one smooth motion without disturbing the kitten nestled against her.

The bullet caught Karkov in the knee, and he went down with a scream that echoed through the market. Sasha approached him, still holding the kitten with her left arm, gun trained on him with her right.

"Please," Karkov begged in heavily accented English. "I have money. Whatever they're paying you, I'll double it."

"This isn't about money," Sasha said, voice suddenly devoid of its earlier playfulness.

A man lunged from behind a display of ice-packed cod, knife raised. Without missing a beat, Sasha pivoted, keeping the kitten tucked safely away from the attack as she kicked the man's legs out from under him. He fell face-first onto the counter. Sasha grabbed a nearby fillet knife and drove it into the back of his skull with her free hand, never jostling the tiny animal in her arm.

"She doesn't deserve this life," Sasha said softly, stroking the kitten's head while blood from the knife dripped down her wrist. The creature mewed and nuzzled into her jacket, apparently unfazed by the violence surrounding it.

Lennox stared, momentarily forgetting the mission, the extraction window, everything but the surreal image before her—this deadly woman covered in blood and brain matter, tenderly protecting a stray kitten in the midst of a massacre.

The contrast struck something deep in Lennox's chest. Not just the violence and tenderness existing in the same body—she'd seen that before, even in herself—but the unself-consciousness of it. Sasha made no apologies, offered no explanation beyond the simple statement that the kitten deserved better. As if saving it were as natural and necessary as the killing that surrounded them.

"Your target," Sasha said, nodding toward Karkov who was attempting to crawl away, leaving a trail of blood on the icy floor. "Don't let me interrupt."

Lennox blinked, snapping back to the moment. "Right."

She strode toward Karkov, who looked up at her with terror in his eyes. "Please," he whimpered.

Lennox crouched beside him, drawing the filleting knife from her belt. "The flash drive," she said, indicating the chain around his neck.

With trembling fingers, he removed it and held it out. Lennox took it, verifying the serial number embossed on its casing before pocketing it.

"The Firm thanks you for your cooperation," she said, then drew the blade across his throat in one clean motion. Blood sprayed across the ice, startlingly vivid against the white. Karkov made a wet, gurgling sound as he clutched futilely at his neck, then went still.

Mission accomplished. Extraction window officially missed, but the primary objective achieved. Lennox wiped the blade on Karkov's coat before standing.

Sasha watched her with an unreadable expression, the kitten now purring audibly in her arms. "Efficient," she said approvingly. "I like that in a woman."

Before Lennox could formulate a response, shouts echoed from the front of the market. More of Karkov's men, coming to investigate the gunshots.

"Time to go," Lennox said, already calculating escape routes.

Sasha nodded, tucking the kitten inside her jacket where it disappeared from view, leaving only a small bulge. "After you, Red. You seem to know what you're doing."

They burst through the market's rear exit as gunshots peppered the metal door behind them. The alley stretched dark and narrow before them, snow now falling in earnest, obscuring visibility beyond twenty feet. Distant sirens wailed—apparently someone in this godforsaken village had finally called the police. Lennox did a quick inventory: two magazines left, knife, garrote wire, various cuts and bruises that registered as background noise to her adrenaline-soaked system. The flash drive sat heavy in her pocket. Mission accomplished, extraction compromised. Time to improvise.

"We need a vehicle," she said, already moving down the alley toward the street beyond.

"Lead the way, Red." Sasha fell into step beside her, one hand inside her jacket, presumably steadying the kitten. "Though I hope your getaway driving is better than your extraction planning."

Lennox shot her a cool glance. "My extraction was perfect until someone decided to shoot up the bar."

"You're welcome," Sasha replied with a grin.

The alley opened onto a quiet residential street lined with parked cars half-buried in snow. Lennox scanned them quickly, looking for the sweet spot between inconspicuous and functional. Her eyes landed on an ancient Lada, boxy and rusted but with decent tires.

"Cover me," she said, approaching the car.

Sasha took position at the corner of the building, guns drawn and focused back the way they'd come. The kitten's head poked from her jacket, tiny eyes wide but surprisingly calm.

Lennox crouched by the driver's door, pulled a thin metal tool from her boot, and went to work on the lock. The mechanism was laughably simple—Cold War era engineering at its finest. The door popped open within seconds.

Gunfire erupted from the alley. Sasha returned fire with one hand, the other still cradling the kitten inside her jacket. "Time to go, Red! Company's coming!"

Lennox slid into the driver's seat and attacked the ignition, quickly stripping wires. Bullets shattered the back window, sending glass fragments across the worn upholstery. She twisted the wires together, and the engine coughed to life with a sound like an asthmatic chainsaw.

"Sasha!" she called.

The blonde backed toward the car, still firing down the alley. She ducked into the passenger seat just as a black SUV skidded around the corner, men with automatic weapons leaning from the windows.

"Drive!" Sasha shouted, pulling the kitten fully inside her jacket as she twisted to fire through the broken back window.

Lennox stomped on the gas pedal. The Lada lurched forward, tires spinning on ice before finding purchase. They fishtailed down the street as bullets pinged off the metal frame and punched new holes in the bodywork.

"Your friends are persistent," Lennox said, wrestling the wheel through a sharp turn that sent them sliding across the intersection.

"Not my friends," Sasha replied, ejecting an empty magazine and slapping in a fresh one. "More of Karkov's crew. He had operations across three countries. These guys look Chechen."

The SUV stayed on their tail, joined by a second vehicle that roared out from a side street. Lennox pushed the Lada to its limits, the old engine protesting as they careened through the sleeping village.

Snow-covered streets made conventional driving impossible. Lennox used it to her advantage, intentionally inducing controlled slides around corners, using momentum rather than braking. The pursuing vehicles, heavier and less maneuverable, struggled to match her technique.

Sasha leaned out the window, honey-blonde hair whipping in the wind as she took careful aim at the lead SUV's front tire. The shot connected, and the vehicle swerved violently before smashing into a lamppost.

"One down," she called over the wind noise, sliding back into her seat. The kitten mewed in protest at the commotion, its tiny head poking out to glare accusingly at Lennox.

"Where did you learn to drive like this?" Sasha asked, genuine admiration in her voice as Lennox executed a perfect drift around a tight corner, the Lada's back end swinging within inches of a stone wall before straightening out.

"Scotland. Spent my teens joyriding on icy mountain roads," Lennox replied, downshifting to climb a steep hill. The engine whined in protest. "You?"

"Moscow Ballet Academy, until I was sixteen," Sasha said, reloading again. "Then FSB special program. Less dancing, more killing. Though the footwork transferred nicely."

The second SUV gained on them as they crested the hill. Lennox's eyes narrowed as she spotted a market stall ahead, abandoned for the night but laden with wooden crates.

"Hold on," she said, accelerating directly toward it.

"What are you—" Sasha began, but cut off as Lennox yanked the handbrake and spun the wheel.

The Lada rotated 180 degrees in a spray of snow, now facing back down the hill directly toward the pursuing SUV. Lennox released the brake and hit the gas, playing chicken with the much larger vehicle. At the last possible second, she swerved right, clipping the SUV's fender and sending it into an uncontrolled slide. It plowed into the market stall, wood splintering and crates exploding on impact.

"Blyat!" Sasha exclaimed, her face split in a wild grin. "You're insane!"

"Says the woman who shot up a bar full of traffickers while rescuing a kitten," Lennox replied, unable to suppress a small smile of her own as she navigated back toward the outskirts of the village.

The kitten in question poked its head from Sasha's jacket again, apparently deciding the worst was over. It had bright green eyes that seemed oversized for its tiny gray face, and it meowed with surprising authority for such a small creature.

"She's hungry," Sasha said, stroking its head with one finger.

"She's lucky to be alive," Lennox replied, checking the rearview mirror. No pursuit visible. "Like the rest of us."

They drove in companionable silence for several minutes, the village receding behind them as they followed a winding road through pine forests heavy with snow. The adrenaline began to ebb from Lennox's system, allowing the various injuries she'd accumulated to make themselves known—the bullet graze on her arm stung, and a deep cut on her hand throbbed in time with her heartbeat.

"There's a turnoff up ahead," she said finally. "Unmarked road. Leads to a safehouse."

Sasha raised an eyebrow. "Your safehouse or The Firm's?"

"Mine," Lennox replied. "The Firm doesn't know about it."

Sasha nodded, understanding the significance of that admission without need for elaboration. In their line of work, personal safehouses were valuable secrets, shared only out of necessity or trust.

The unmarked road was barely more than a track through the trees, untouched snow indicating no recent traffic. The Lada's tires crunched through the fresh powder as they climbed a gentle slope to a small clearing. A cabin stood dark and silent, its wooden exterior weathered gray by seasons of snow and sun.

Lennox parked beside the cabin and killed the engine. "Home sweet home. Temporarily."

Inside, the cabin was sparse but functional—one main room serving as kitchen, dining, and living area, with a small bedroom visible through a doorway. A woodstove squatted in one corner, cold but ready for use.

Sasha set the kitten down on a worn sofa, where it immediately began exploring its new surroundings. "Cozy," she said, eyes scanning the space with professional assessment. "Defensible. Good sightlines."

Lennox nodded, moving to the woodstove. Within minutes, she had a fire going, warmth beginning to push back the chill. She found her emergency kit under a floorboard—medical supplies, cash in various currencies, spare ammunition, and a satellite phone.

"Hungry?" she asked, tossing Sasha a burner phone from the kit.

"Starving," Sasha replied. She examined the phone. "There's delivery out here?"

"One place. Number's saved in contacts. They don't ask questions." Lennox began checking the cabin's perimeter, securing doors and windows.

Twenty minutes later, a bewildered delivery driver stood on the porch, staring wide-eyed at the blood-spattered women who answered his knock. The kitten, now named Koshka according to Sasha, peered curiously from behind Lennox's legs.

"Food," the driver said weakly, holding out a bag.

Sasha smiled brightly, which seemed to terrify him further.

"Spasiba," she said, handing him far too much money before taking the bag.

The driver backed away slowly, nearly falling down the porch steps in his haste to retreat. They watched him slip and slide back to his car, engine roaring as he sped away down the track.

"I think we scared him," Sasha said, closing the door against the cold.

"Can't imagine why," Lennox replied dryly, gesturing to their blood-soaked clothing and various visible wounds.

They ate ravenously—some kind of meat-filled pastries and a container of hearty stew—before turning attention to their injuries. Lennox laid out the medical supplies on the small kitchen table, methodically cataloging what they had to work with.

"Let me see your arm," Sasha said, her playful demeanor subdued by exhaustion and pain. A deep gash ran across her left shoulder, visible now that she'd removed her ruined jacket.

Lennox hesitated, then sat on a kitchen chair and extended her injured arm. The bullet graze wasn't serious, but it was deep enough to require cleaning and bandaging. Sasha worked with surprising gentleness, her fingers efficient yet careful as she cleaned the wound with antiseptic.

"Not my first bullet hole," Lennox said when Sasha paused, noticing the collection of scars visible on Lennox's exposed skin.

"I'd be worried if it was," Sasha replied, applying a bandage with professional precision. "There. Your turn."

Lennox examined the cut on Sasha's shoulder, which gaped open to reveal muscle tissue beneath. Blood still seeped from it, turning Sasha's skin into a macabre canvas of red rivulets against pale flesh.

"You need stitches," Lennox said, gathering suture materials from the kit.

"No, they say women enjoy scars," Sasha dismissed with a shrug, then winced as the movement pulled at the wound.

"Hold still," Lennox ordered, cleaning the area thoroughly. "This will hurt."

"I've had worse," Sasha replied, but she grabbed the edge of the table as Lennox began to stitch, her knuckles whitening.

Lennox worked methodically, each stitch neat and even. She found herself acutely aware of Sasha's skin beneath her fingers—smooth despite the collection of scars that told stories of past violence. The intimacy of the moment wasn't lost on her, this tending of wounds between killers who had been strangers hours ago.

When she finished, Sasha exhaled a breath she'd apparently been holding. "Thanks, Red," she said softly.

They moved to the couch, Koshka immediately claiming Sasha's lap. Lennox produced a bottle of whiskey from a cabinet, uncapped it, and took a long swallow before passing it to Sasha.

"To unexpected alliances," Sasha said, raising the bottle in a toast before drinking.

The whiskey burned pleasantly, warming Lennox from within as the woodstove heated the cabin around them. Outside, snow continued to fall, insulating them from the world beyond.

"So, The Firm," Sasha said, passing the bottle back. "European intelligence?"

Lennox nodded. "Officially doesn't exist. Unofficially has fingers in every major conflict since the Cold War."

"And you're their cleaner," Sasha said. Not a question.

"Among other things," Lennox replied. "You? Freelance now, I'm guessing."

Sasha stroked Koshka's fur, the kitten purring loudly in the quiet cabin. "After Moscow, yes. The FSB and I had a... philosophical disagreement."

"About?"

"Who I should kill." Sasha's voice remained light, but something dark flickered behind her eyes. "Turns out I'm selective. They wanted someone who wasn't."

Lennox nodded, understanding. Even in her line of work, lines existed. Different for each operative, perhaps, but present nonetheless.

"I grew up in Moscow," Sasha continued, gaze distant. "Trained as a ballerina from age five. Was on track for Bolshoi when the program recruited me. They liked dancers—discipline, pain tolerance, body awareness."

"Makes sense," Lennox said. She hesitated, then offered: "Scotland for me. Highlands. Father was military, mother died young. I was stealing cars by twelve, running jobs for local crime bosses by fifteen."

"How'd The Firm find you?"

"I stole the wrong car," Lennox said with a small smile. "Belonged to an operative. He was impressed that a teenage girl managed it."

They passed the bottle back and forth, trading fragments of their histories as the night deepened around them. Lennox found herself sharing more than she intended, drawn out by Sasha's genuine interest and surprising insights.

The kitten eventually fell asleep, curled into a tiny gray ball on the cushion between them. Sasha watched it with a tenderness that seemed at odds with the violence she'd displayed earlier, yet somehow perfectly aligned with the complex woman Lennox was coming to know.

As dawn approached, the tension between them reached a breaking point. Their conversation faltered, giving way to charged silence. Lennox found her gaze repeatedly drawn to Sasha's mouth —lips surprisingly full and soft-looking for someone so deadly.

The whiskey bottle stood nearly empty on the table before them. Lennox wasn't drunk—she never allowed herself to be—but the alcohol had softened the edges of her usual reserve.

Sasha looked up, catching Lennox's gaze. Something shifted in her expression, playfulness giving way to something more genuine, more vulnerable.

Lennox leaned forward first, or maybe Sasha did—neither would remember later who moved first. Their lips met in an awkward but passionate kiss that tasted of blood and whiskey and unspoken understanding.

Sasha's hand came up to cup Lennox's jaw, careful of her injuries. Lennox found her fingers tangled in honey-blonde hair, softer than it had any right to be after the night they'd had.

They pulled apart, both surprised by the intensity. Lennox stared into sky-blue eyes that reflected the same wonder she felt—the unexpected connection formed in blood and chaos.

"Well," Sasha said, a smile tugging at the corner of her mouth. "That was worth getting shot at."

Morning light flooded the cabin as they prepared to leave, gathering weapons and supplies. The Lada wouldn't get them far —too damaged and too recognizable now. Lennox had cash for train tickets, enough to get them across at least one border.

Sasha cradled Koshka, who now sported an improvised collar made from a leather bootlace. The kitten looked marginally cleaner after a makeshift bath, revealing silver-gray fur with subtle stripes.

Lennox checked her gun before holstering it, the flash drive secure in an inside pocket. The Firm would be looking for her by now, wondering why she'd missed extraction. She should contact them, explain the situation, arrange a new pickup point.

She said nothing, watching as Sasha cooed softly to the kitten in Russian.

"Where to now?" Sasha asked, looking up to meet Lennox's gaze.

Lennox felt a smile tug at her lips—not her usual sardonic half-smile, but something more genuine. "Wherever they're not expecting us," she replied, decision made.

The Firm could wait. The mission was accomplished. What she did next was her choice—and for the first time in years, she found herself wanting to choose something unexpected.

Sasha grinned, understanding what remained unsaid. "Lead the way, Red," she said, falling into step beside Lennox as they headed out into the snow-covered morning, three predators now hunting together.

THE END

RED ESPERANTO

PAUL D. BRAZILL

THE WINTER NIGHT had draped itself over Warsaw like a shroud, and a sharp sliver of moon sliced the death black sky. I was in the depths of a crawling hangover and feeling more than a little claustrophobic in Olena's cramped, deodorant-soaked apartment. I poked my trembling fingers through a crack in the dusty slat blinds and gazed out at the constellation of neon signs that lined the bustling avenue.

Sex shops, peep shows, twenty-four-hour bars, booze shops, and kebab shops were pretty much the only buildings that I could see, apart from The Westin Hotel, with its vertigo-inducing glass elevator. Looking at it made my stomach lurch a little. I fought back the acrid bile that burned my throat as I watched a black taxi jump a red light and cut across the road, narrowly missing a rattling tram. A police car's siren wailed and pierced my pounding head like a stiletto. Another cop car joined the chase, quickly overtook the cab, swerved, and screeched to a halt in front of it. The taxi driver tried to stop but the taxi skidded back across the icy road, just missing another tram before stopping on the pavement outside a garishly painted peepshow. A tall blonde dressed only in red high heels and suspenders looked out of its front door, saw the police cars, and went back inside, slamming the door behind her.

A massive, bull-necked man with a bald head wearing a black leather jacket raced from the taxi towards the front of Olena's apartment block but, before he could get close to the front door, a swarm of policemen swiftly surrounded him and dragged him down onto the snowy ground, attacking him with truncheons before handcuffing him and hurling him into the back of a police van, giving him the occasional kick. I turned back towards Olena. She handed me a glass of bourbon. The smell made my stomach roll. I took a furtive sip and balked.

"So, you are not a Maker's Mark fan?" she said.

"I prefer Jack Daniels," I said. "And usually with cola. Though, to be honest, I usually only drink whisky when I'm so drunk I shouldn't be drinking anything at all. When I've drunk the pint of no return."

I winked and Olena grinned as I persevered. After a while, the burning sensation was cleansing. I turned back towards the window. A mob of English football fans staggered down the street singing loudly,

Olena came up behind me.

"When the Pope—the Polish one—died, the whole of the street was lined with multi-coloured candles, in tribute," she said, looking almost tearful.

Her English was perfect, but her Ukrainian accent was as dark and as bitter as the Galois cigarette that she deeply inhaled. "It was a thing of rare beauty," she continued, a halo of smoke floating above her, though she was no angel. She'd previously worked for my sister in London, doing a bit of pickpocketing, shoplifting, and lord knows what else.

She switched off the flickering light and switched on a small lamp with a dusty red bulb. My mouth was dry, and I felt as if my heart was caged tightly within my chest and ready to burst free. Olena finished her drink and carefully placed the glass on the rickety bedside table. She handed me a bunch of keys and I gave her a wad of notes of mixed denominations.

"Are you ready?" she said.

"Yes, let's skedaddle," I said.

I could hear the thump of a bass line coming from one of the pubs across the road and for a moment I wished I was there. There was loud banging on the door.

"Who the bloody hell is ...?"

Olena put a finger to her lips.

"Quiet. It's only Bronek. Wait," she whispered.

"Who?"

"Oh, he's just a customer who has problems separating business from pleasure."

The banging continued. And then the shouting began. Well, it was more like the cry of a wounded animal. Repeating Olena's name over and over again. She shook her head and leaned close to me.

"Wait until he has gone, eh?" she said.

She kissed my cheek and poured the last of the bourbon into my glass. She held up a finger and stepped into the bathroom.

Olena showered and dressed in a black polo-necked sweater and leather skirt. She cracked open another bottle of bourbon, sat next to me and we slowly drank in silence until, just before midnight, the noise stopped.

"I think you can go now," said Olena, standing, stretching, and yawning.

"Are you sure? Is it safe?" I said.

"Yes. He will be at mass now and then he'll return home to his wife and children, full of guilt."

I stood up, a little unsteady. Olena produced a handful of business cards from her bag and sifted through them.

"Maybe we can get a taxi together?" she said.

"Safety in numbers, eh?" I said, and I forced a smile which Olena didn't return.

"Oh, I think we're outnumbered where Bronek is concerned," she said, with the hint of a smile.

I took the last of my notes from my wallet and stuffed them into the taxi driver's sweaty paw while Olena wiped the white powder from her nose and pulled a Zippo from the pocket of her black

PVC raincoat. She lit another French cigarette, dissolving into the darkness as the flame flickered out.

"We made it in one piece, then," she said.

"Just about," I said. My nerves were shot.

Before I'd come to Warsaw, I'd heard stories about "The Night Drivers." Legend had it that they were a group of amphetamine pumped young men who, each midnight, tied fishing wire around their necks, and the cars' brakes, and then raced each other from one end of the city to the next.

So, when I saw the cut-marks on the taxi driver's neck and his red, red eyes, I didn't exactly have the Colgate ring of confidence.

I was relieved minutes later when we pulled up outside The Palace of Culture and Science, Josef Stalin's unwanted Neo-classical gift to the people of Warsaw, which loomed over the city like a gigantic gargoyle keeping evil at bay. A large red banner stretched across its entrance advertising an avant-garde jazz concert.

"So, see you next month, then?" she said.

"Yes, why not," I replied, to the fading sound of her high heels click-clicking on the palace's wet concrete steps.

I waited a moment until she was inside and then rushed across the road into Rory's Irish Pub. I headed straight into the putrid smelling toilets to puke.

"Out with the old, in with the new," said a familiar, well-spoken, sandblasted voice from the next cubicle.

I wiped my mouth with toilet paper, flushed, and walked up to the basin. As I splashed my face with water, Sean Bradley stumbled out of the cubicle.

"We are all in the gutter but some of us are looking at it through the bottom of a rather nice glass of gin and tonic, eh?" he said.

He swayed as he zipped up his fly, waved to me and walked out the door.

Sir Arthur Conan Doyle once described London as being a "great cesspool into which the flotsam and jetsam of life are inevitably drawn" and the same thing might reasonably be said of the world of TEFL teaching. A Teacher Of English as a Foreign Language can usually be described as either flotsam—perhaps a fresh-faced young thing taking a break from university -or jetsam —the middle-aged man with the inevitable drinking problem and enough skeletons in his closet to keep a palaeontologist happy for months. And, I'll make no bones about it, Sean fit rather snugly into the latter category. I literally stumbled into him the first week I arrived in Warsaw. After that, we seemed to orbit each other more than somewhat. Sean was a permanently drunk, dapper, nicotine-stained example of jetsam, who supplemented his teaching income by chess hustling.

I walked into the half-empty bar, ordered a beer and a shot of vodka to cleanse my palate.

"Oh, bollocks," I said, as I realised I had no more folding money left.

"Can I pay by credit card?" I said.

"Yes, of course," said Blanka, the tiny barmaid with the statuesque, purple Mohican haircut. "But there's a minimum amount you have to spend."

"Fair enough," I said. "I'll run up a tab."

And then I headed towards oblivion like rainwater down a storm-drain. I sat at a chequerboard table with Sean and watched Andy -a big, dumb-looking American I'd seen shuffling around the ex-pat pub circuit -play pool with Rory, the owner. Rory was a pallid, ghostly, prune-faced old man with all the charm of a pit bull.

"Evening gents," I shouted.

Rory glanced up, irritated.

"For fuck's sake," he grunted by way of a greeting.

Like I said, he wasn't well known for his charm. But, in his favour, he was equally ignorant of the smoking ban that had been introduced in Poland's bars and restaurants. The air in the bar was as thick as pea soup. Little blue clouds of cigarette smoke hung below the green lamps that dangled from the low ceiling.

A Stone Roses song crept out of crackly speakers as a smoke-smudged TV screen showed an episode of *Friends*. Andy sat opposite Sean, sipping a Diet Coke, and keeping an eye on the door.

"The thing is, some people absolutely loathe the place," said Sean, jabbing a yellow finger at a postcard of The Palace of Culture and Science that Andy had been using as a beermat. "The locals call it the Russian Wedding Cake, you know? And, indeed, that's what it looks like: a wedding cake plonked in the middle of the road."

"I see what you mean," said Andy, who quite clearly didn't.

The night staggered on. Andy bailed out pretty quickly and then the cloak-room attendant left. Sean and I were soon in our pots, sat at the end of the bar smoking cigarettes and drinking whisky, watching the ice cubes glimmering and shimmering in the wan light. Blanka had gone home, too, and Rory clearly wasn't enjoying Sean and I exploiting the Polish tradition that a bar can only close when the last customer has gone. I was about to order another round of drinks when I heard a loud bang that seemed to send seismic tremors through the pub.

I turned and saw a stunningly beautiful blonde woman burst through the frosted glass door and rush into the bar bringing a trail of snow behind her. Her wet hair hung down like party streamers. Even in my drunken stupor, just looking at her was like lightning hitting a plane. She was tall, with long blonde hair and a slash of red lipstick across her full lips. She was wearing a long black raincoat which flapped in the breeze behind her.

"Ding dong," I said "Who's that?"

"Oh. That's C.J. Crazy Jola. Better watch out for her," said Sean. "She's eaten more men than Hannibal Lecter."

"Looks like a pretty tasty morsel, herself," I said.

"No, really, she's trouble. She's a married woman, for a start," said Sean.

I shrugged.

"That's not the greatest of sins."

"Yes, but she's married to Robert Novak. You do know who he is?"

I shook my head.

"He's a twat, that's who he is," said Rory, as he went over to Jola's table.

"He's a mid-level gangster who owns a lot of property in the area. He's also a second-hand clothes Baron," said Sean.

"Who and a what?" I said.

Sean finished the last of his drink and shuffled off the bar stool. He staggered close to me. Even as drunk as I was, he still stank of booze. I recoiled.

"He's a mid-level gangster, basically," said Sean.

"Yes, you've already said that."

Sean tried to gather his thoughts.

"He owns a couple of bars. Peep shows. And another one of his business enterprises is to get Poles that live abroad to collect donated clothes that's been left outside charity shops overnight in, say, London or Dublin, and ship them back to Poland to sell in second-hand shops. You can get some damn good stuff, actually," said Sean, pointing to the Hugo Boss label on his shirt.

"The only crime is getting caught," I said, shrugging.

"Yes, but if a butterfly beats its wings in the forest, a one-handed man claps, and a tree falls down," said Sean, and he stumbled off in the direction of the toilets.

I ignored him and tried to catch Jola's eye. Rory was placing a drink in front of her. She said something to him and, for the first time since I'd known him, I actually saw him laugh. Though when he turned back to me, he had the same grimace he always wore.

Jola took out her mobile phone and began sending a text message. Fuelled by Scotch courage, I walked over.

"Would you like another drink?" I said, swaying a little.

Jola looked up and tried to focus on me, as if she were attempting to take in a magic eye painting.

She sipped her drink and shook her head.

"Well, I would, but I really shouldn't," she said, with a fake-sounding transatlantic accent. "I should go home and hit the sack. I've hit the bottle enough for one night."

"Maybe one for the, er, *Ulica*?" I said.

She laughed.

"Oh, what a fantastic use of Polish. You're a regular polyglot. I'm guessing you're an English teacher?"

"Surprisingly not," I said. "Do I look like one?"

"Well," she took in my worn leather jacket, scuffed Dr Marten boots and frayed jeans, "you certainly don't look like a businessman."

"Which means?"

"Hack?"

"Bingo!"

"So, do you work for one of those shitty rags that dig out all the sleazy tales about Poland and sell them to the English tabloids for shock horror stories?"

"No," I said. Although, I did do that sometimes. "I'm freelance but mostly I work for *EuroBuilder Magazine*."

I gave her a sweaty business card.

"Have you heard of it?" I said.

"Yes, of course. My asshole husband has a lot of property in this city, so he buys it and reads all of those fascinating articles about warehouses and shopping malls."

"It's all my own work," I said. "Well, some of it. Well … a bit."

Jola stared blankly at me.

"Never mind. So?" I said, gesturing towards the bar.

"Oh, why the hell not?"

I ordered another whisky for me and a gin and tonic for Jola.

"Gin makes you sin," I said as I put the drinks on the table.

"Oh, I don't need a drink for sinning," she said.

Sean had disappeared and we were the only customers in the bar.

I put some money in the ancient jukebox. Thin Lizzy sang about someone with a "Bad Reputation." Something that always attracted me to a woman, of course.

Jola sipped her drink and seemed to hold on to the table to steady herself.

"Where is your hometown?" I said.

"Well," she said. She knocked back her drink in one and her words staggered out like drunks at closing time. Disorderly and unruly.

"I'm from the industrial wastelands of the east," she said, playing with a cigarette lighter with a picture of a matador on it. "Bialystok. Have you heard of it?"

"Amazingly, I have."

She looked as if she didn't believe me.

"It's true. I had a friend from there. He showed me a photograph of a big Soviet tank in the town centre that was painted a very camp pink."

"That's the place," she said. "It's not the most exciting place. A real 'one-whore-town,' as they say. So, as soon as I could, I got out of there fast."

"And, so you came here to Warsaw?"

She shook her head.

"No. First, I headed off to Chicago for a couple of years. And then to London. Which is where I met my wonderful husband."

"Where in London?"

"West Ealing? Do you know it?"

"Yes," I said. "I even worked there for six months back in the eighties, looking for the streets that were paved with gold. I'm still looking, mind you."

"Well, there's a golden shopping mall here in Warsaw, as I'm sure you know, but the streets are as grey and cold as anywhere else."

Jola took out a Marlborough from a battered pack and lit it.

"What line of work are you in?" I said.

"I manage a bar. Robert, my husband, is the owner. The Emerald Isle. It's over on Esperanto Street. Do you know it?" said Jola.

I nodded.

"Yes, it's another one of Poland's authentically Irish pubs," I said.

Jola laughed. "Well, there are pubs in Ireland selling Polish beer and food, so, why not?"

"Why not, indeed."

I shifted in my chair.

"Is it fun?" I asked.

"The pub or the marriage?"

"Both. Either …"

"They serve their purpose."

"Which is?"

She rubbed her fingers and thumb together.

"I suppose marriage to Robert was what you would call a marriage of convenience," said Jola. "Though it's not so convenient, these days."

"It's better to regret something you've done than something you haven't," I said.

"Indeed."

Leaning close to me, Jola put a hand on my shoulder and looked me up and down, like she was deciding on whether or not to buy a second-hand car.

"You'll do," she said, and stood up, dragging me out of the bar by my tie and through a metal door marked "Private".

I looked over at Rory, who was lighting a cigar. He took a glance and ignored us. I got the impression that he'd seen this sort of thing many times before.

Jola locked the door behind her and switched on a strip light that flickered and buzzed before it blanched the tiny room, which was stacked with crates of Peter Walker and metal beer barrels. On the wall was a dartboard with a poster of David Beckham hanging over it. Three darts perfectly placed between his eyes. I sat down on one of the crates.

"Won't Rory mind?" I said, as Jola took off her black leather skirt.

"Not a chance," she said. "Robert ripped him off in a big

business deal a while back. He despises my husband so much he lets me get away with murder."

"Really?"

"Well, everything but that," she gasped. "So far."

At some point during the night, I woke up in my own bed, soaked in a cold sweat, with no recollection of getting there. Jola, naked, was smoking and gazing out of the bedroom window. The tip of her cigarette glowed bright red and then quickly faded to black. I closed my eyes and let the sea of sleep enfold me.

In the morning, slivers of sun sliced through the blinds and slashed across my eyes, stinging like a knife blade. After a moment, I focused and looked around the room. Jola was gone.

The days bled into weeks and then months. I visited the usual watering hole with the same regularity but increasingly less enthusiasm. I guess the novelty had worn off. Sometimes I met up with Olena, and we just talked until the early hours. She told me of her lesbian lover with the violent husband, and how they were saving enough money to get out of Warsaw.

A warm spring dusk was struggling to break free of winter as I left my apartment block in a daze which, for once, wasn't due to the booze. I'd been drifting through the weeks like a phantom, with thoughts of Jola haunting me. For whatever reason, I couldn't get her out of my mind. I knew I had to see her again. I really should have known better but I rarely did.

As I walked along the deserted street, a massive figure suddenly stepped out of the shadows and in front of me. He was a real behemoth, with a shaved head and a black leather jacket. His gigantic fist grasped a knuckle-duster that slammed into me and sent me sprawling backwards until I smashed into a kebab shop window, setting off the burglar alarm.

I sunk to the ground, blood oozing from my burst lip, as the giant shouted and screamed at me. My head was spinning, and my limited Polish was never too good, but I recognised one word that he said before storming off down the street. Olena.

A small group of old women wearing mohair berets surrounded me, speaking too quickly for me to understand. I struggled to my feet and did the best thing I could think of to do. I went to The Emerald Isle.

Nursing a beer and a shot of vodka, I phoned Olena and explained my predicament.

"Yes, you're right. It's Bronek," she said. "My former client. He's getting crazier. He started following me. Watching me and my friends. He's got it into his head that you are going to marry me and take me away to England."

I drifted out of her conversation and thought that maybe it was better to be hung for a sheep than a lamb. Hanging up, I ordered another shot of vodka. The Emerald Isle was far from emerald. For a start, the walls were painted garishly red. The furniture was pitch black. The atmosphere was grim and grey.

Portishead's "Glory Box" whispered through the sound system as Robert Nowak, well-dressed and overweight, with what seemed like a constantly constipated expression, drank whisky and played chess with a statuesque Indian girl.

A small group of fashion students sat sharing two beers, occasionally topping the glasses up with the contents of a bottle of supermarket vodka, while keeping a furtive eye on Robert.

I sat by the window, drinking my second glass of beer. I briefly turned my gaze outside, to where the morning rain poured down in sheets and the wet pavement reflected a nearby kebab shop's flickering neon sign. Police sirens screeched through the roaring wind.

Jola came down a staircase at the side of the bar and briefly paused when she saw me. She helped herself to a drink and headed outside with a pack of cigarettes in her hand. She stood under a grubby umbrella smoking as if it was the last cigarette on earth. I waited a few moments and joined her. Turning my collar up against the rain, I sat in a grubby white plastic chair and sipped my drink.

"You shouldn't have come here, you know? Robert is a very jealous man," she said, lighting a second cigarette, not looking at me.

"Does he know about us? About that night?"

"Of course not. But he has his suspicions. All sorts of suspicions. Especially when he's snorting cocaine from morning to night."

"I...just wanted to see you again. I thought you might want to go out somewhere, sometime."

She turned slightly and looked at me. Closed her eyes. Smiled.

"Oh, why the hell not?" she said.

I grinned like a schoolboy. "When?"

"We can meet tomorrow night if you want. Somewhere out of the way, though?"

I thought for a moment.

"What about my place?"

"Cut to the chase, eh?"

I smiled.

"In for a penny, in for a pound," I said.

The night was like a thunderstorm of drinking, smoking, sex, and conversation. In the early hours, we lay on my bed in the wan light listening to an old mix tape that Jola had brought with her. Elton John's 'Tiny Dancer,' eased into a Fleetwood Mac song, and Jola turned and looked me in the eye.

"You know," she said. "Life with Robert is like a living death these days. I really do want to get away. Escape. I've managed to save some money but it's not enough. Anyway..."

And in the space of that short pause, the thought of running away with Jola was like the lone, beautiful whore in a rundown brothel, teasing and tempting.

I said, "Can't you divorce him?"

"Ha! He's a Catholic. He'd never let me divorce him. He'd never let me leave," she said, stroking the bruises on her neck. As a mild spring trudged on into a scalding hot summer, our meetings became more frequent and dangerous thoughts hovered over us like a hawk ready to strike its prey.

And before long, thought congealed into action.

The plan was simple enough. We were to wait until New Year's Eve and when Robert was drunk, Jola would drug his drink with some cheap cocaine and take him to bed when he passed out. Then, after clearing the safe at The Emerald Isle, and Robert's bank account. Jola and I would head off out of Poland, towards Spain or who knows where.

The hope was that during New Year's Day, people would think that Robert would be sleeping off the previous night's indulgence, giving us plenty of time to head out of the country. Simple? As simple as Chinese algebra.

It started to snow, and fireworks filled the sky as I headed through an alleyway and into The Emerald Isle. The place was stuffed with drunken, overdressed people celebrating the New Year. Robert was drunk already, holding court to a group of no-necked skinheads. Jola was already on her way upstairs to the safe.

The fire exit was propped open with a fire extinguisher, and I eased my way through. Feeling all too confident.

Then a familiar looking behemoth stood in front of me. And this time, he seemed to growl. And the growl turned into a roar.

Robert indifferently smoked a large cigar, his bleary eyes glaring at me.

"So, you are the one Bronek was telling me about, eh? The Englishman that is stealing little Olena from him. Eh?"

Robert and Bronek stood either side of me. Grinning. Putting on knuckle dusters.

"My brother Bronek can be very protective about our property," said Bronek, "and he has taken far too much interest in little Olena. But that is his right as my brother. So, it really wouldn't do for us to let you take her away, would it?" I couldn't agree or disagree. I couldn't say a thing and I couldn't move. I'd taken a beating and I was slumped in the oak and leather armchair like an insect trapped in amber. It was all I could do to try and wipe the glass from my eyes and ignore the burning before the brothers raised their fists and the world turned red.

The hospital was migraine bright and stank of antiseptic. Not that it bothered me that much. The morphine was working, and the last few days I'd been feeling stronger. Able to move around. And to check my emails on my iPhone. The usual crap, of course. Gifs. Memes. Jokes.

And there was an email from Olena, a photo of her on a beach in Spain was attached. She was with Jola. And there a message thanking me for creating a diversion and allowing them to get away, and hoping that I get well soon.

I lay back on the small bed, closed my eyes and let the sea of self-loathing enfold me until the day melted away just like cold breath on a windowpane.

THE SEVEN OF HEARTS

TROY LAMBERT

I hope you're happy
I hope you're good
I hope you get what you wish for
And you're well understood

—*Blue October, "I Hope You're Happy"*

"COUNT BACKWARD FROM ONE-HUNDRED," a female voice said.

The practice was something Jack had become quite familiar with in his several surgeries. He always tried to think of something to count.

Most of the time they were positive things. He reached down to scratch Boris' head. The dog wasn't there, of course. Not in an operating room, not even in pre-op as much as he tried to convince them the dog didn't shed, and he was cleaner than some of the humans in the room.

Comfort and friendship were absent.

"Ninety-nine," he said. He thought of the Queen, her final bullying of him, and her death at his hands.

Of Brandon, another man sent to kill him and his final words. "I think I'm in love."

That stirred something in Jack, and he felt the corner of his mouth turn up in a smile.

"Ninety-eight," he said. The vision in his one good eye blurred. He wondered if he would ever use the other one again.

He tried, struggled really, to picture her in his mind. But her smell. He could remember that, even if the name of her perfume escaped him.

Ninety-sheeve-e-en," he heard his own words slur, and felt his eye close. His head would not turn—it was held motionless, prepared for the surgeon's skilled, knife wielding hand.

His eye closed, and he fled into darkness.

His eyes were closed, but the scent of summer was replaced by—Chanel, Something-or-Other. He couldn't remember the name, although he was sure he'd purchased her most recent bottle the previous Valentine's Day.

Jack remembered walking up to the counter holding a crumpled piece of paper. "One of these, please," he'd asked the clerk. She'd presented it, and he'd proudly paid with his credit card, his first, the kind nearly every young person gets to start their credit off on the right foot.

Beside the pool, he opened his eyes. She stood there, his crush, his love, Katie. He looked up at her, starting with her well-tanned legs, toned and thin but not overly muscular. The bottom of her robin's egg blue two piece suit were modest, the waist resting just under her navel. Her wide-strapped top fully covered her breasts and draped over her petite shoulders. A thin gold chain holding a hummingbird hung around her thin but not overly long neck.

Her rounded chin, full lips and button nose…

Jack laughed. He couldn't help himself. Her sunglasses, which must have been recently purchased, were ridiculous. Green plastic frames, shaped like stars, contained red-tinted lenses that hid her eyes. Her shoulder-length, golden hair was visible under a large, straw sun hat that matched her suit exactly.

"Hi," she said, pushing her lips out in a much-too-cute pout. "Would monsieur like a drink?"

The French accent was not hers, but a veteran of high school and some college theater, she had a knack for it, and others. Acting was her dream, her pursuit of an accounting degree likely her reality.

Jack loved her either way.

"Monsieur would indeed," he said. It was only then he notice her arms were held wide, containing two large drinks with umbrellas stuck in them.

She handed him one of them, and then gracefully spun to sit next to him.

"You weren't sleeping were you?"

"Not at all."

"Are you ready to go back to school?"

"No," he said frankly. "And yes."

"What do you mean by that?"

Jack's father was in real estate now, but Jack Jr. was not naive about what his father actually did. He had connections, and some of his deals were much sweeter than they should have been just because of who was behind them and the reasons they wanted certain commercial properties. His dad was a go-to-guy because he got things done.

He wanted Jack to have a degree, to pursue his own interests, but Jack wanted to be like his dad. No, he wanted to be his dad, and he didn't need a degree for that. He already had his father's tongue and penchant for persuasiveness.

"I kind of just want to get to work, you know. I'm not sure a degree is for me, but it is important to dad. "

"I get that," she said. "You're smart, Jack. Your dad knows it and so do I. You'll do well no matter what you do."

"Glad you believe in me," he said. "You will, too, you know."

"Well, when you are a big business giant like your dad, you'll need an accountant," she said, sliding the glassed down on her nose.

Jack laughed again. He couldn't help himself. The "star" glasses looked even funnier pushed down. Only a tiny portion of the end of it peeked out from between the lenses.

"Do you want to go inside?" she asked. "We could get changed, and gamble a bit after dinner?"

"Sure," he said. "I would love that."

She slurped the last of her drink through her straw. "We could have dessert first, and then shower—"

He loved that about her. How playful she was, and how much she adored the same things he did.

They walked in through the back doors of the casino, a place his father told him he didn't "own" per se. It's just a place I've invested in. You and Katie can certainly stay there though. I'll get you a room."

Room was an understatement. They were put up in a suite, one with a large bathroom and one of the jetted tubs big enough for four people. We only used half of the king sized bed, never turned on the large TV, although it promised "more cable channels than we could possibly watch" in the brochure. There was a mini-bar, but even though his father was buying, Jack feared what the little bottles inside would cost, so he left them alone.

The showered was luxurious, and we explored the variety of settings while we also explored each other. It was an afternoon of kisses, laughter and lovemaking.

The west facing window lit up as the sun set, and he discovered he was hungry.

"Are you ready for dinner," he asked her.

"Of course," Katie told him. "You have helped me work up quite the appetite."

Jack put on a custom-tailored suit, one his father had purchased for him. He wore a white shirt, blue tie, and a silver tie pin with matching cufflinks.

Katie walked from the bathroom, her dress and gown exquisite, the hem toying with her knees. She spun, and the sunlight and shadows from the window against the sequins sewn into the dress sent sparkles into every corner of the room. The short sleeves puffed at the shoulders. Her hair, free of her beach hat, cascaded over her shoulders, honey mixing with the caramel of her tan.

She reached for him, wrapping her hands around his neck, pulling his lips to hers. "I love you, Jack Bardlow," she said before they kissed.

Jack held her tightly against them, and only stopped kissing her when he ran out of oxygen. He suddenly wants to cancel the whole night.

Forget dinner. Forget gambling. Forget dancing to big band music in the high ceilinged ballroom with the giant disco globe hanging overhead.

He wanted nothing more than to stay in her arms, at this moment, in this place right here. "I love you, too, Katie."

As he said the words, she broke from the kiss, broke from the embrace, and shattered his daydream of the evening. The pieces of it flew off of them, darting their sharpness into reality. She'd had enough of their time in this room.

Katie wanted him to take her out, show her the town.

"Shall we, m'lady?" Jack said, gallantly offering her his elbow.

"That is so sexist," she said, and took it anyway, her delicate hand wrapping around his arm.

The memory of that moment would stay with him forever. He just knew it.

Jack locked the hotel door behind them, pocketing the key attached to a giant plastic fob with their room number on it.

She stumbled once as they walked to the elevator, adjusting to her evening footwear no doubt.

They kissed for the first part of the trip down, until a couple joined them when the elevator stopped at the third floor. The older couple stood apart, not touching each other. The man smiled at them, his wife scowled her scorn for young and foolish love.

Jack wondered if he and Katie would ever be like that. He nearly laughed out loud at the very idea of her scowling.

The woman must have seen his smile, because she huffed,

sounding disgusted, and turned to face forward. Out of her view, her husband winked at Jack.

He winked back. Katie saw, and stifled a giggle.

When they all departed the elevator, she and Jack couldn't contain themselves any longer.

The laughter exploded, and they were so loud, others turned to stare. Katie teared up, then bemoaned that she would destroy her makeup. Jack stood guard while she found a ladies room and fixed it.

The entrance to the restaurant was just ahead, and as soon as Katie "felt presentable again" the pair headed that way, narrowly avoiding laughter when they saw the elevator couple ahead of them. The woman seemed angry at her husband for not making a reservation, and her eyes threw sharp darts made of ice their direction when Jack announced both his name and the time of their reservation.

Katie looked at her and stared, until the woman dropped her gaze, but Jack swore he could still feel the darts entering his back as they were escorted by a smiling host wearing a vest and a bow tie to a booth near the back of the dining area.

Although the benches of the booth were covered in what would be considered luxurious leather, the table itself seemed to be made of cheap formica. In the center, a red dollar-store candle flickered in a small jar decorated with fake gold.

Jack sat down, and Katie slid in beside him on the same side. He rested his hand on her thigh, and they pushed aside the second menu they'd been offered, sharing one instead.

"Should we have an appetizer?" Katie asked.

After some quick calculations regarding the balance left on his credit card, Jack nodded. "Certainly. Dessert too, if you wish."

Katie smiled, and selected a shrimp cocktail.

"Drinks?" the waiter said when he returned.

They ordered a bottle of wine, Jack grimacing slightly at the price. Perhaps a shared dessert would be best.

"So, what next, Jack?"

"What next?" he answered. "In what way?"

"When I graduate next year, and you the year after. What next?"

They'd talked about their future before, usually in jest. Never this seriously.

"We should get married, I suppose."

"You suppose?" she said, elbowing him.

"Well, when I graduate and can go to work. I want to make a good living and be able to support you."

"We don't have to wait, you know."

Jack had been thinking the same thing, but his father thought otherwise, even though his parents had married much younger than he was now.

"I know," he said. "I just want to be sure."

"You're not sure? About what?"

"I didn't mean it that way," Jack said. He was interrupted by the arrival of the wine.

When both of their glasses were full, she turned to stare at him.

"In what way did you mean, then?"

"I—I want to be sure—you're really out of my league."

"You want to be sure I'm committed?"

Jack stared at the table, and folded and unfolded his hands there. Any answer he gave at this point would not be the right one.

"I--yes. I do."

Katie turned to face him. She pulled his hands from the table and into the tiny space between them. "I won't ever leave you, Jack. No matter what. I've grown to love you, and I know whatever comes next we can work it out, together."

They leaned together, their lips meant, and at that moment Jack knew this was the woman he would spend the rest of his life with.

Next the appetizer arrived, and they fed each other shrimp. He felt her tiny fingers brush against his lips and then his teeth. He gently took the offered bite. It was the freshest he'd ever tasted. It melted in his mouth.

A sip of wine followed. The waiter popped by, asking about an order. They both ordered seafood: Jack went for the salmon, Katie the rockfish.

Both disappeared quickly, shared bites and snippets of conversation aside.

They talked about how many kids they wanted, him two, her three. Maybe four if they had twins.

She wanted a house in the suburbs. He wanted a flat in the city. They settled on the fact that they'd live in the suburbs, as long as he could have a dog. She agreed, provided she could have a cat, and the dog would tolerate it.

They hashed it all out: hardwood floors with rugs vs. carpeting; granite vs. marble counters; dark cupboards vs. light ones; split-level vs. single story. By the time the dessert arrived, was set on fire, extinguished, and then consumed, their future lives together were planned, pending a ring and a proposal, which Jack promised soon.

He even got on one knee, and anointed her finger with the wooden ring that had been around the cloth napkin.

She used that napkin to dab away happy tears.

Then the manager came to their table, not with the check but with an urgent message.

There was a call for Katie. She must come up front at once.

"What is it?" Jack asked, following her.

"I don't know. The only one who knew I was here was my mother."

"Okay," he said. "Let's find out together."

The waiter appeared with the check as they walked, looking apologetic, and Jack gave him his credit card and dismissed him with a wave.

When Katie picked up the phone, her face changed. It fell from happiness, thudding into first sadness and then sobs in an instant.

"Jack, I have to go. My father…" It was all she could say.

"Do you want me to come?" The words stumbled from his mouth, landing in a heap at his feet.

For a moment it looked like she was considering it. Then her face folded again.

"No, Jack. I'll call you. I'll be back as soon as I can."

"Promise?" he asked. He felt something ominous waiting outside the doors of the casino. Something watching, preparing, taunting.

"I promise," she said.

He took her into his arms, and she sobbed on his shoulder, the kind of sobs that shake and exhaust your entire body. By the time she stopped and they parted, the manager told them the cab she'd ordered had arrived.

Jack followed her, and helped her into the cab. She rolled down the window, and as she did, his vision blurred, first at the edges, and moving toward the center.

He focused on her face, trying to see, trying to remember. He tried to hold that moment in his mind.

But the blurriness was replaced by blinding light.

Jack blinked, but the light remained. He lifted his eyelids.

Katie?

No. That had been a dream. The kind he called a memory dream, where he was sure his mind didn't have quite all the facts straight, but the feelings? They were as real as he'd felt them the first time.

That night had been the last night he'd seen Katie. Ever.

There was an accident, he was told. A fire. Everything was destroyed. There was no body to view. Nothing but photos to offer at the service.

When his heart broke, Jack heard it like the snap of a twig tromped on by a clumsy lumberjack stumbling through the woods he called life.

It had never healed.

"Mr. Bardlow?" A voice brought him back to reality. "Mr. Bardlow, can you hear me?"

Something felt—different. But Jack nodded. And as he did, he realized something.

For the first time in years, he could see something out of his right eye. It was just light for now, but if he focused, really tried, he could see the pattern of gauze.

He felt a tear roll down his left cheek.

"It's okay, Mr. Bardlow. It will be a while before you can see, but this kind of reaction is perfectly normal."

Then he felt something else. A tear rolling down his right cheek. It felt—odd, but he had tears on his right side. And a tiny bit of vision.

Jack cried. Not because he was overwhelmed with emotion the apparent surgical success, but because he had no one to share it with.

A hand appeared, covered in a green glove. It gripped his left shoulder, what he still considered to be his good one.

"I'll have Doctor Larry come in and let you know exactly how things went and what's next," the voice said. "But for now, get some rest."

Jack closed his eyes and searched for Katie's face, and for some way to enter his dream where he'd left it, to resume where he'd been pulled away. If he could warn her, if he could let her know, maybe he could save her.

But he couldn't. Jack drifted in a bank of empty loneliness, a blurry recollection of Katie's face leading him. In his mind, he called out to her.

But she was nowhere to be found.

THE END

THE BUYOUT

SCOTT KIKKAWA

I WAS DOWN to my last cigarette with a near-empty flask on the ewa side of River Street again. Honolulu's Japantown. Sakura Lounge. Home of the Tokyo Revue showgirls and one-dollar rye. I wasn't at a stage-side table. I was in the piss-smelling alley outside the stage door issuing a "warning" to some pomade-headed racketeer's flunky.

September 1952. I had just been promoted to Detective after a mere three years in Patrol thanks to an Ivy League sheepskin courtesy of the G.I. Bill and the ability to speak Japanese passably courtesy of my parents and the compulsory lessons they forced me to take as a kid. I thought making dick was an opportunity to exercise the gray matter between my ears, but so far, I hadn't smelled any casework. Since Day 1 in plainclothes it was strictly strongarm shit on the Vice Detail.

Detective Sergeant Francis H. Yoshikawa had a nice ring to it, but three months with the title and I was nothing more than a goon beating the motivation to do business in the Japantown cabarets out of pimps who routinely crossed the Nuuanu Stream from neighboring Chinatown in search of liquored-up customers with their balls in an uproar from the floor show and the kimonoed hostesses. Most were working for a lowlife racketeer named Jack Takano, who owned a couple of teahouses and had arrangements with the Chinatown brothels for a cut of the clients out of Japantown his boys sent their way.

The cabarets weren't very happy about Takano's parasites luring away their customers. The mama-sans preferred their payday victims to stay in the club and blow the entirety of their paychecks right in the cabaret, investing in a "relationship" with a hostess of their choice, rather than run across the stream to a brothel. That's why they made the complaint to the brass, and the brass sent in the cavalry. Us. We had instructions not to arrest, but to "persuade".

Honolulu had seen an influx of pretty, powdered faces from Japan after the immigration ban was lifted earlier in the year. These women were creatures we plantation-bred nisei were unaccustomed to. Bar hostesses. Showgirls. War widows. Second-string geisha. They were city girls. Pale and slim and elegant with their noses in the air, a far cry from our sun-browned, calloused-handed sisters and cousins who cooked rice in the sweltering kitchens of Waipahu and yelled at us to wash up before dinner.

The showgirls came by the boatload, or even by airplane if they could hustle enough drinks in the red-light districts of Tokyo and Osaka to purchase the tickets. The women in our own families talked about the new imports like they were pure poison. Money grubbers. Shameless. Disrespectful leeches who preferred to earn their living on their backs instead of on their feet. They were all wrapped up in pricey silk. Pretentious. Incapable of putting a decent meal on the table or keeping a house clean.

This was the indictment I'd heard ad nauseum out of the mouths of my gossip-addicted older sisters and the Kakaako matrons at the Hongwanji bake sales. My sisters knew that I had encountered these women at work and prodded me for details at dinners at my mother's house on Kawaiahao Street. When they asked me how they were, I'd just shrug and say I couldn't really tell them. I didn't talk to these women. Not in a real sense. They were the same to me as the paper folding screens and noh masks hanging on the walls of the Sakura Lounge. Decoration.

That was, until Yuki.

The cabarets of Japantown attracted nisei working stiffs like flies, and where they bled their paychecks, the racketeers followed, especially Jack Takano's errand boys. He sent his pimps in to arrange for liaisons across the Nuuanu Stream Bridge in Chinatown, in the old "hotels" of Hotel Street. For them, gathering their marks was shooting fish in a barrel. They were drunk and worked up by the burlesque on stage and the kimono girl sitting next to them, holding their sweaty hands and making them feel like nobility. They were ready to have their itches scratched.

Our job was to yank the pimps off the floor and drag them out to the alley in the back where we read them the riot act on violation of solicitation ordinances. Often, the "reading" included some well-placed blows, sometimes with a sap or brass knuckles for the more obstinate operators. New dicks like me got to deliver the beatings. The old-timers did all the talking; they complained about how the task of administering the physical warning aggravated their bad backs, and how close they were to collecting their pensions.

Naturally, the mama-sans were grateful for our efforts. Keeping the customers in their clubs meant more drinks purchased for the hostesses and under-the-table gratuities for under-the-table services instead of the money going to a Chinatown brothel with a cut to Jack Takano and his lapdogs. They were vultures who cut into their profits.

Naturally, we needed a break from our "warning" sessions every now and then. Intimidation is thirsty work. So, when we needed to rest our weary arms from too many uppercuts to the face and jabs to the midsection thrown, our drinks were on the house. So was a steak dinner if we wanted one, and the steak naturally came with company.

One night, after administering a vigorous "warning", I felt that a little sustenance wasn't a bad idea. It was the first time I had availed myself of the offer of a steak, though I had knocked back countless one-dollar ryes, gratis. The medium-rare teriyaki T-bone was brought to me on a sizzling cast iron platter by a hostess in a kimono. I'd seen dozens of women do the same with my house rye, but instead of just placing my order down on the table followed by a polite bow and taking tiny, shuffling steps away from the table, this one had a seat next to me.

Like all of them, she was fair and graceful and smelled nice. They were all desirable, though almost uniformly so. I often had trouble distinguishing one form another for that reason, but it was also because I usually paid these women little attention. They were just a part of the scenery of a place I went to work.

This one was a curious blend of old country and new. Her kimono was traditional, though bright, in sky blue adorned with pink and red plum blossoms and green sparrows, cinched up with a bright yellow obi. Her hair was something out of Hollywood, coiffed like a red-carpet starlet's and accented with an elaborate gold pin. Her makeup was pure silver screen, modern and expensive.

"Good evening, okyaku-sama. I am Yuki." It came out of her painted lips soft and demure and only audible because she leaned in close enough for me to catch a whiff of her Chanel No. 5.

"You don't have to address me like I'm one of the moneybags in here who actually pays for his drinks," I said. "I'm just a guy enjoying the generosity of the house between giving beatings."

"Any man I am directed to sit with is a valued customer. May I know your name?"

I laughed, and not without real amusement. Sometimes you've got to laugh when things turn out to be exactly as you expect them to be. Sakura lounge was one of those places where surprises were in short supply. The pretty little fixture's schtick was so far predictable. "You were directed to sit with me, huh? I'll try to make this painless for you. I'm Yoshikawa. Detective Sergeant, Honolulu Police Department." I took a swallow of my free rye and added, "Hajimemashite. Yoroshiku Onegaishimasu." I bowed slightly.

"Your Japanese is beautiful," she said. She couldn't contain the astonished look on her face.

"You mean for one of us crude nisei yokels. You can thank my parents for that. They insisted on sending me to Japanese school after regular school. It's a miracle that I had any time to learn the game of baseball. I'll tell my mother that you were impressed. She'll be thrilled that all those whacks with a ruler I got from the old lady sensei in the gray dress paid off."

"Oh," she said. I thought I caught a hint of a flush under her face powder. "I meant you no insult. I meant only to compliment your speech. I am sorry."

"Don't be. Most folks don't expect a thug with a badge to do anything more than grunt. I'm used to shocking people when I talk."

Yuki picked up the fork and knife next to the platter and started cutting up the steak for me. The last woman to do this for me was my mother, and she only did it because I was to small to use a knife myself. I watched her carve the T-bone up into slender, bite-sized pieces. She made it look like a real skill.

When she was done with her expert table knife work, she laid the fork and knife back on the table and produced a pair of hashi from her kimono sleeve. They were fancy, mother-of pearl inlaid lacquer chopsticks. She used them to pick up an nice piece from the filet side of the T-bone and moved it toward my mouth, her free hand cupped under the piece of beef to catch any drips.

"Open your mouth, please, Detective."

"I can feed myself, you know. I'm a full-grown, taxpaying adult. Somewhere along the way I learned how to do this."

"I know that you are capable of doing this, but I am here to provide you with this service. Does your wife not do this for you?"

"If I had one, I don't think she would."

I saw a suggestion of a smile, so subtle it almost wasn't there. She may have blushed, too, but it was hard to tell in the dim lighting of the place.

"Open your mouth, please."

"You don't have to do this."

"Open your mouth, please. Your steak is getting cold."

What the hell. I rolled my eyes and opened my mouth. Yuki placed the piece of steak dead center on my tongue. I closed my lips around the hashi and she withdrew them slowly, allowing me to clean them. I chewed the piece of filet. Warm and juicy. Done just right. I hadn't even eaten a steak until I enlisted with the 442nd, and at that it was some kind of tough chuck at the Camp Shelby mess hall. I thought it was the food of the gods. This T-bone made that basic training steak taste like a boiled boot. Was it really that good? I hated to admit it, but being fed by a fragrant, pretty girl in a kimono probably enhanced my enjoyment of the meat.

"Does it not taste better this way, Detective?" she asked. Mind reader. I came to regard women who did this as dangerous, though it was hard as hell to look away from the carnival act.

"It's a nifty little trick," I said. I picked up my glass and swallowed some rye.

"Yes, I suppose it is. You look like you are relaxing now. Open your mouth, please."

I let her feed me. It didn't last long. The steak had disappeared before my drink did. But it was nice in a way that I never thought it would be, having a woman treat me like an infant.

When she was done feeding me, she took up a linen napkin from the table which was done up in some origami fold and gently shook it open. She used it to dap my lips and face clean. Again, this was something that hadn't been done for me by someone else since I could talk and protest, but this, too, was strangely satisfying. And cute as hell.

I glanced at my wristwatch. I had spent nearly fifteen minutes sucking a couple of cigarettes and a glass of rye and getting the mommy treatment from Yuki with a T-bone steak.

"Thanks for the dinner service, Mom. Goshisama deshita. But there's a pimp in the alley out back waiting to be convinced to hit the road. Duty calls."

She stood up as I stood, pulled my chair out to ease my exit from the table and bowed deeply. She stayed bent in her bow until I was several steps away. I remember feeling I could get used to this and feeling irritated with myself for feeling that way.

The next few nights on the persuasion detail pretty much went the same way, I got into the habit of asking for a complimentary steak on my break every evening, just like the old-timers. Tey gave me shit for not having done it sooner. Annoyingly, I realized that my dinner habit wasn't so much about the steak as it was about Yuki. She had gotten into the habit of having a conversation with me while she fed me. She'd ask a question, wait until I was finished chewing, dab my mouth clean with a napkin, then rest her chin on the heel of her hand fetchingly while she listened to my answer.

"Where is your family from?"

"Hiroshima," I said between bites. "Out in the sticks to a Tokyo girl like you."

"I am not originally from Tokyo. I was born inn Aomori, in Tohoku."

"Up north."

"Do you know it?"

"Only from maps. I've never actually been to Japan. My mother had a couple of wooden dolls that were made there, so I looked it up."

"Kokeshi."

"Yeah, that's what she said they were called. Sticks for bodies, balls for heads. Hand painted."

"Yes," said Yuki. She looked wistful, eyes soft and moist. "You know so much about them. Listening to you talk about them makes me miss my home."

Our conversations went this way. She asked about my birth in Waipahu and growing up in Kakaako, about my playing baseball in high school, for the 442nd in basic, in college and currently in the Honolulu Japanese League. She asked about my time in college at Columbia University on the G.I. Bill and why I chose to study medieval and renaissance literature. She asked me why I became a cop. She responded to all my answers with: "You are a most interesting man."

Those words are the most intoxicating thing a man can hear from a woman. Forget that they're attracted to you or impressed by you. Men who think they want to feel important are missing the point. What men really want to be to women is interesting. What made Yuki so damn good at her job is that she knew how to make me feel interesting. The world was full of handsome, rich and powerful men. To be told you're interesting, though, is to be told you're unique. One-of-a-kind in a sea of posers who routinely bought influence, friendship and love because it was the only way they could get them.

This is what made Yuki dangerous. I was finding it harder to keep myself in check around her. I wanted to let go of my skepticism and believe she really found me fascinating.

So, I did the only thing I could do to save myself. I deflected. I turned the tables on her and asked her to talk about herself. I asked all the questions, one after the other, like I did in all my "soft" interrogations.

And damn if she wasn't interesting, too.

Yuki's story was a short, sad affair. The war had visited all kinds of bad shit upon Japan. Death. Destruction. Hunger. Poverty, Disease. You name it, they had it. It's what happens when your rulers wage a war they can't win and don't acknowledge the fact until they can no longer operate in denial. Most men who weren't too old, too young or too crippled were claimed by the war. It was largely women and children who lived and died with the war's consequences on Japanese home soil.

Yuki was one who realized she had one lone great asset that wasn't taken by the ruin: her body. Many women used theirs to pick cotton, smelt ore or mine coal in Japan's great postwar economic recovery effort. She used hers to greater effect on occupying U.S. forces and extracted ten times the money from them than her salt mine counterparts made breaking their backs.

Yuki married a young haole G.I. who had frequented the Tokyo club she solicited high-priced drinks in. There was talk of the immigration restrictions on Japanese people being lifted, and she paid this G.I. a hundred bucks to marry her and file an immigration petition for her. The newlyweds on paper came to

Honolulu on military transport and got themselves a quickie divorce before he skipped back stateside a month later.

Mission accomplished. She had made it to the Territory of Hawaii where a lucrative job at the Sakura Lounge awaited her and had the legal status to work there. Of course, she had to enter an indentured contract with an establishment that operated under the table like places in the old country: until she worked off the amount, the place practically owned her. It wasn't legal by our standards, but there was no way we could prove it.

Asking her questions didn't make her back off. It drew her closer.

Eventually, it wasn't just about feeding me or listening to me talk about myself or telling me about her life. She started massaging my shoulders and arms, aching from the regular beatings I delivered. She cleaned and bandaged the cuts on my fingers made by the brass knuckles. She even placed a soft kiss on the bandages, marking them with her red lipstick. Yuki started to hold my tired hand under the table and lean up against me while I finished my rye and cigarettes. I didn't stop her.

The mama-san, once a dainty geisha who had seen too many bottles of beer and bowls of rice, thanked us nightly at the end of our "conversations" with the pimps and racketeers. One night as I was leaving, she grabbed my sleeve.

"You like our Yuki-chan, do you not?" she asked. She smiled obscurely.

"Sure. She knows how to cut a steak. What's not to like?"

"She likes you, too."

"Of course, she does. You've directed her to sit with me. That makes me a valued customer, and she likes valued customers. I guess you might say that means you've directed her to like me. Why not? I eliminate your competition nightly. That assures your livelihood. And hers."

"I am grateful."

"Sure, you are."

I went home each night at the end of my shift with pain in my shoulder and the delicate scent of Yuki in my head. About three weeks into the knuckles detail, it happened.

As I was about to grab my hat from the coat check counter, Yuki wrapped her arms around one of mine.

"Will you stay for a short while with me before you leave?"

"Why? Is there a stray T-bone that needs to be fed to someone?"

"Please."

I shrugged and let her lead me to a door beyond the stage that led to a hallway and another door that led to a small, dark room with a futon on the floor. The space was illuminated by an old-country-style paper lamp.

Yuki shut the door behind me and threw the brass bolt into place. Then she flung her silk-clad arms around my neck and drew me close.

"Hey," I said. "What the hell is this?"

She looked up at me with soft, hot eyes.

"I want to be with you."

I sneered and laughed.

"I appreciate the thought, but I don't get paid until next week and that check is already spoken for by my landlord."

"I do not want your money."

"You're kidding."

She pressed her mouth on mine. Hot and wet, like a home-brewed head cold remedy, but better tasting. The heat spread from my tongue to my brain and all points south. It was a straight bourbon drunk in an intense concentration. She was feather-light and pulsated luxuriously in my arms.

I understood in that moment why men burned their paychecks for this. I was ready to burn my pension for it.

We went down to the futon in a tangled mess, hot and wet and sloppy.

When it was over, she insisted on dressing me, including tying my necktie. She did it in a four-in-hand, the way I like it, without being told. She was an observant one. Like being fed, the last woman to dress me was my mother. And like being fed, being dressed by Yuki was something I was convinced she did better than I could for myself.

After three nights in a row with her at the end of her shift, I was convinced that I wasn't just another asset to be bled. Our short conversations during my breaks and on the futon became more personal, more intimate. Yuki became a habit, and I didn't care. She was the one thing that made me momentarily forget how shitty my professional existence really was.

After we finished one night in the paper lamp room, I asked, "Why the hell are you doing this with me?"

"I want to make you happy."

"Sure."

She gave me a look of genuine hurt.

"Hey," I said. "Whatever you say."

Did she make me happy? I don't know. She made me addicted, and I was sure about that.

Every night was wonderful with her. Until the night when it wasn't. That night, she clung to me but she was distracted. Stiff. Even our conversations felt disjointed.

"What's wrong?" I asked. I stuck a cigarette in my mouth and she was quick with her S.T. DuPont lighter as always.

"I was told by mama-san that my contract will be bought out."

"Oh, yeah? What does that mean?"

"It means that I will not be working here anymore."

"Correct me if I'm wrong, but that means no more obligation to this slave shop of a club, right? You'd be free to decide your own future. Free to do whatever you want with your life."

Yuki hung her head.

"No, I would not. I would belong to the man who bought my contract out."

"That's crazy. We don't do that here. Just who the hell is buying out your contract?"

"His name is Takano."

Jack Takano. The mama-san's nemesis. The man whose pimps

and errand boys we'd been beating the shit out of night after night to keep them away. Takano owned a couple of teahouses, pathetic little shitholes that were set up to lose money but make it on paper. Laundering fronts for his real money, cash from prostitution and gambling referrals of Japanese clients to Chinatown along with a cut from heroin dealers on the harbor side who sold to Japanese middleman peddlers in Aala. A real parasite, even in the criminal world.

Takano was also a sick son of a bitch. He had a thing about "marking" the women he'd been with, like a dog peeing on a fire hydrant. He would mutilate ex-mistresses with a barber's razor, cut their faces or other body parts before discarding them so they would never be desirable to another man. These women never pressed charges out of fear that they'd lose a lor more than their beauty. It wasn't that Takano got some kind of perverted pleasure out of hurting them. It was more an affirmation of his status as a man important enough to get short use out of a woman and spoil her for all other men. In a way, it was more deranged than being a mere sadist.

I wasn't going to let him do that to Yuki.

I took a draw off my cigarette, then held it out to Yuki. She grasped my hand with her two small hands and pulled it down toward her face. She took her own drag, staining the cigarette with her lipstick.

"How much is your contract?" I asked.

"A thousand dollars. I had been trying to work off the amount on my own, so I can keep what I earn from my drinks, but I have only been able to pay off two hundred dollars since I started."

"Mama-san won't give you the time to work it off?"

"If an offer comes in to buy out a contract, she will always take it. It is faster than letting us work off our own contracts. I came here because she bought my contract from the bar in Tokyo I was working in. Not every girl gets this kind of buyout offer, so mama-san takes it whenever it comes."

"When is he coming to buy out your contract."

"Next week."

Those words hung in the stale air of the little back room and drifted slowly downward toward the futon where they dissipated. Yuki and I just stood there looking at each other.

"This has been nice," she said. "This, with you. I wish for it to be nice for the next few days, until the end."

"You think so? Maybe it's not the end."

"How can that be?"

"What if someone else buys out your contract?"

"Who would do that?"

"Someone like me."

The thick silence returned. Yuki cast her eyes downward, then she looked up to her left. Her eyes were moist and would not meet mine.

"How could you do it? It is a lot of money."

"I have ways."

Her eyes moved again, avoiding me. This time she looked down at the futon.

"I have been owned by men before I came to Hawaii. I was bought and sold by two men and three bars, including this one. Would you want a woman who had been owned by so many others?'

I took a drag off the cigarette and blew smoke over her head toward the ceiling. I placed a finger under her chin and lifted it gently, so she was looking at me at last. I gave her a smirk.

"You've been owned by two men and three bars? I've been owned by a lot more than that. My entire chain of command treats me like a slave. I'm a harness bull who takes orders from his betters. Orders to knock a pimp's teeth out of his mouth to keep him out of a club that pays for our services. And if you count every taxpayer in this territory who thinks he gets to tell me what to do, I'm owned by a hundred thousand men. Two doesn't seem like a hell of a lot. Not to me."

"But you can get someone else. Someone who has not done the things I have done."

"Do you want me to do this, or don't you?"

She threw her arms around me and sobbed into my Arrow shirt.

"I'll take that as a yes."

The following night when break time rolled around the mama-san asked me if I'd like the "usual' for my break.

"You better enjoy while you can," she said. "Yuki-chan is gone next week." She laughed obscenely, genuinely amused by her own sick comment.

"When's Yuki's buyer coming?"

"Next Friday. Eight o'clock."

"Paying in cash?"

"I don't do credit here."

On the next Friday night, I waited out in front of the club for Jack Takano. He showed up in a rayon aloha shirt printed with Japanese cranes and pine trees with his hair slicked back. He had a dark sportscoat on over the shirt that barely concealed a pearl-handled automatic stuck in his waistband.

Predictable. Tacky. Just how I liked them.

I grabbed him by the arm.

"Hey! What gives? Better take your hand off me before you lose it!"

"Shut up. I'm a police detective. Want to see the badge?"

"No need." He sneered and spit at my feet, narrowly missing my wingtips. "You look like you can't be anything else."

"Good. Then come along."

I pulled him around the building into the alley.

"What the fuck is this?"

"Shut the fuck up, criminal. You're in no position to ask questions."

I threw him against the wall. The old-timers were inside, taking a steak break. I was all alone with Jack Takano.

"You're going to buy a girl tonight. Is that right?"

"Fuck off, cop."

I drew my arm back and slapped his pockmarked face with an open hand, hard and loud. He reached for his waistband and tugged his automatic free.

A shot split the rank, still air of the alley.

Jack Tsakano crumpled and fell face first into a puddle of something foul.

I holstered my .38. He wasn't fast enough. When I had seen him go for his nickel-plated toy, I drew from my shoulder holster as I has dozens of times in qualification rounds. Practice makes perfect, I guess.

I crouched down and stuck two fingers on his neck. Dead.

I fished a wad of cash from his pocket and withdrew ten hundred-dollar bills, no more, no less, then stuck the stack back in his pocket. I put the thousand in mine. The old-timers came into the alley just as I stood up.

"What the fuck happened here?"

"Can you believe this pimp tried to shoot me?"

They looked at each other and shrugged.

"Not so smart," said one.

"Not so smart at all," said the other.

Sakura Lounge was crawling with patrolmen in a few minutes. The mama-san was forced to shut down for the evening. It was near dawn when we were finally able to call it a night.

Before I left, I dropped the thousand dollars on the table in front of the mama-san, who sat nursing a glass of gin.

"What's this?" she asked.

"It's for Yuki's contract. I'm buying it out."

She collected up the bills and stuffed them in her kimono sleeve, cackling.

The next night, I got an extra-large T-bone and a slice of chocolate cake from Yuki.

"I heard about what happened," she said.

"I did it. You're free."

"I know. I am grateful."

She grasped my hand on the tablecloth and gave it an ardent squeeze.

"I will be leaving early this evening, if you do not mind," she said.

"That's nice. But you don't need my permission."

"You bought out my contract. I am yours."

"Didn't you hear me? You're free. Nobody's going to cut up your pretty face when he's all done using you. You don't belong to me. I bought your freedom, not you."

She fed me in silence, then bowed deeply and left the club.

When I got to my little apartment in Kaimuki, I saw Yuki sitting on the floor outside my front door. She was in a western dress with her hair down, every bit as appealing as she was in a kimono.

"I went shopping," she said. "That is why I left early."

"Breakfast. I am guessing that you do not have anything in your icebox."

What the hell.

It was nice.

Even if it didn't last past breakfast.

THE MAN WHO PRAYED FOR THE END OF THE WORLD

VINCENT ZANDRI

"It's not fair... that's not fair at all... there was time now!"

--The Twilight Zone, "Time Enough At Last."

1

BESTSELLING AUTHOR, Lynn Meredith, hated people. Rather, hate might be too strong a word for it. He had fans after all. Fans who read his stories strictly online. And when you think about it, fans were people too.

His two ex-wives were people, even if they were still running away from him years after their respective divorces. Lynn's adult daughter living in California whom he never saw was people and he had the opposite of hate for her. Heck, even the short, stocky, salt and pepper-haired Lynn was a people (if you pardon the grammar). Technically speaking, that is.

For certain, Lynn hated other writers and writers were people too. In fact, he recalled the old days when he was just a young man starting out in the publishing industry with his first big sci fi book, *The Beast that Devoured Manhattan*, how his editor pulled him aside during a lunch they were engaged in at a restaurant down in the Bowery.

"Let me tell you something, Lynn," he said, "writers are assholes."

Lynn recalls smiling and lighting a cigarette. While he smoked, his editor's words sank in. He thought about all the times he rejected his then wife's pleas for a little attention, love, and understanding for the sake of keeping their marriage intact.

"I need to write," he'd tell her. "I never have time enough to write because too many people want too many things from me."

And then he'd lock himself in his Lower East Side writing studio for hours at a time. By the time he'd return, it would be the middle of the night and his wife would be fast asleep, dreaming of the day she could finally leave him.

"Writers really are assholes," Lynn had whispered to himself. "I should know."

2

Now, twenty-plus years later, Lynn Meredith has left the confines of New York City where he would no longer have to deal with publishers, agents, bookstore owners, fellow writers, enemies, or friends he no longer had. He moved up north, beyond the Adirondack Mountains to a secluded, remote piece of mountaintop wilderness property not far from the Canadian border where the deer and moose far outnumbered human beings. It was a place that had electricity and (badly needed) internet, but in terms of all mod cons, that was about the extent of it.

His water came from a well, his natural gas from refillable tanks, and his toilet flushed into a septic system. His wooded property was situated approximately 3,500 feet above sea level, and it measured about 50 square miles. But since it abutted the far upper Adirondack Park wilderness, it actually measured more like tens of thousands of square acres.

That said, the parcel he owned was surrounded by a chain link fence that was topped with razor wire. The single gate that accessed the place via a two-track extended three miles to the nearest state road, the Shun Pike, was secured with a heavy chain and a padlock. A metal sign bolted to the gate read, KEEP OUT! TRESSPASSERS WILL BE EXECUTED!

Lynn always grinned at the use of the word "executed" since it conjured images of him tying a wayward trespasser to a wood pole, blind-folding him, and asking him if he had any final words prior to his putting a .223 round from a AR-15 into his head.

Speaking of weaponry, Lynn, the writer was also a man of guns. Inside his single story, two bedroom, one and a half-bath log cabin, he kept and maintained a .45 caliber Kimber model 1911 semi-automatic pistol, a 9mm Glock, two twelve gauge pump-action shotguns, and an AR-15 that had a laser site mounted to its utility wrack. He was also in the possession of a World War Two .30 caliber air-cooled, tripod mounted machinegun. Finally, much of the fence's front perimeter (the portion closest to the cabin) was mined with Vietnam War era bouncing betties that he purchased on dark-web from a military surplus outfit located in Thailand.

Taken altogether, Lynn Meredith's property was a killing field which made him proud. If a trespasser was intent on invading is land, chances are, said trespasser would not only die trying, but he would die without his legs intact.

3

The Adirondack snows were just beginning to thaw when, one early morning just after dawn, he hopped into his ten year old Ford F-150 and made the drive through his gate (he made sure to throw the truck in park, get out and lockup the gate before proceeding), over the three mile stretch of two-track to the Shun Pike.

It was a long downhill run with the winding road flanked by tall pines, oaks, and birch trees. When finally, he came to the small town of Wilsboro, he pulled into the Clarkson Market. In reality, the market was a rundown, combination gas station, grocery store and diner. Since it was the only place in town for coffee (no McDonalds or Dunkin Donut way up there), it was a meeting place for some of the old men who still lived in town, living on social security and cheap beer until the night came when they'd go to sleep and not wake up the next morning.

Lynn couldn't wait for that to happen to all of them. If he had his way, he'd get the market all to himself when he came in most mornings for a large coffee, a ham and egg sandwich, and a lottery ticket. This morning, per usual, he poured himself a coffee, put a little milk in it, then grabbed one of the premade egg sandwiches, and made his way to the counter.

A couple of old farts were seated at one of the four booths attached to the window wall. They were old before their years and dressed in heavy Carhartt overalls, snow boots, and wool caps. Lynn could feel their stares digging into his backside like daggers while he approached the counter. He secretly hoped they'd choke on something tonight, or perhaps die of heart attacks.

A young man who bore a thick black beard was standing behind the counter. He was tall and wiry and was the spitting image of his dad who was about Lynn's own age. He was wearing a tan work shirt that had a rectangular green patch stitched on the pocket over his heart that said Clarkson's in white letters.

Standing behind him while stocking some shelves, was an

attractive young, brunette woman who was also wearing a matching Clarkson's shirt. She was the young man's new wife.

"Your paperbacks are selling out, Mr. Meredith," the young man said, trying his best to workup and maintain a smile in front of the crotchety writer.

"Yes, Mr. Meredith," the young woman said, glancing over her shoulder. "They are very popular." She said it with a sweet smile. A smile that even Lynn couldn't help but admire.

But that didn't prevent him from taking on a scowl.

"People should read on their phones," he said. "That way I don't have to bother with asking the publisher to tell the distributer to tell their printers to tell the truckers to deliver more damn books." Then, his eyes glued to the quickdraw machine. "Give me a ticket with my usual numbers, would you, Timmy?"

"I understand," Timmy said. "About the books, I mean. I always read on my phone. Guys and gals my age never don't read paperbacks that much."

"Good for you," Lynn said. "Now please give me my ticket and cash me out. I've got writing to do."

"Right away, Mr. Meredith," Tim said while typing Lynn's usual numbers into the quickdraw.

While Lynn waited, the door to the market opened, and the bells attached to the door chimed. In walked a woman. She was an attractive, sandy blonde-haired forty-something woman. Small, thin, maybe a marathon runner. Or so Lynn thought as he glanced at her over his shoulder. As she closed the door behind her, and the bells chimed once more, the writer noticed she was wearing a vest that bore thin red, electrically lit tubes of light, as if the vest had been plugged in and charged overnight, which is exactly how her expensive, high-tech vest operated.

Lynn had seen expensive vests like this before on some of the tourists who were passing through, north-bound, on their way to the Canadian border, or south-bound to Lake Placid for the skiing.

"Here you go, Mr. Meredith," young Timmy said, breaking the writer out of his spell.

"Oh, yes, Timmy," Lynn said as he reached into his pocket, pulled out a twenty dollar bill and slapped it on the counter.

While he waited for his change, Lynn refocused on the woman as she stepped up to the coffee klatch and began filling a large cup with steaming black coffee. Mounted to the wall above the klatch was a flat-screen TV. CNN was broadcasting news of the Russian-Ukraine war. The carnage was horrible, with women and little kids being mowed down by machinegun bullets that were mounted to heavy-duty tanks. Buildings were being shelled and blown to bits. Vehicles were on fire in the streets. It was a virtual hell on earth.

"Here you go, Mr. Meredith," Young Timmy said.

Lynn scooped the change and his lottery ticket off the counter and shoved it all into his jean's pocket.

"Thanks," he mumbled. "I'll get the publisher to send more books."

"Gee," Timmy said with a broad smile. "That would be great, Mr. Meredith. You have lots of fans in Wilsboro."

Lynn waved the kid off like he was an annoying insect.

"Yeah, yeah, yeah," he said. "I just wish they'd go online and read my books and leave me alone. I hate dealing with the people at my publishing house. They're just a bunch of snot nosed, woke kids."

"Well," Timmy said, "I guess some people—Boomers mostly--still love the feel and smell of real paper books."

"They should get with the twenty-first century," Lynn said.

He walked away from the counter and stood near the exit. He eyed the woman as she watched the carnage displayed on the T.V. He also glanced at the two old farts. Rather, he glared at them.

The woman stole a sip of her still too-hot coffee.

"If this gets any worse," she said aloud to herself, "it will turn into a nuclear war. Millions upon millions of innocent people will die."

Lynn couldn't help but feel himself grin.

"Good," he said.

The woman about-faced quickly.

"How can you say that?" she said, obviously horrified.

"The planet's overpopulated," Lynn said, one hand on the doorknob, the other balancing his coffee and egg sandwich. "It's time we had a culling, don't you think?"

The woman just stood there stunned, her lower jaw having dropped to the floor. The two old farts were gazing at him with scrunched brows and wide, bloodshot eyes.

"You all have a nice day now, ya here?" Lynn said, as he opened the door, and stepped out into the cold air.

He couldn't wait to get home and be all alone again.

4

Pulling up to the fence gate, Lynn threw the pickup into park, opened the door and got out. He unlocked the gate, then got back in the truck and pulled forward. When he was through the opening, he put the truck in park once more, and got out and relocked the gate. He would not be going out again for the rest of the day or night. Just the thought of not having to see people, made his lungs expand, and his body feel lighter than air. People wasted your time, and he needed time to write.

Of course, Lynn Meredith depended on people to buy his books, but that didn't mean he had to like them.

"People suck," he whispered as he got back in the truck and pulled forward along the heavily wooded two-track. "To hell with them."

5

Back at the house, Lynn took his coffee and sandwich with him to his writing desk. The desk was located in a small room beside the kitchen. The space wasn't much bigger than his bedroom, but had just enough room for his floor-to-ceiling mounted bookshelves and his desk. It overlooked the back lawn, which he kept trimmed, and a big pond that was situated maybe two hundred feet in the distance. Beyond that was thick woods that extended for miles and miles.

His desk was covered with various books, some of them his and others he needed for research, like the The Writers Guide to Weapons, by Ben Sobieck, for instance. Mounted to the wall beside the big picture window was a bulletin board that contained all sorts of memorabilia he'd collected back when he was still married and living in the suburbs. The memorabilia came mostly from his travels. Back when he was still young and during a time when average folks, both friends and professional acquaintances alike, might have referred to Lynn Meredith as a "people person."

There was a wooden mask he acquired in Sub-Saharan Africa while working as a freelance foreign correspondent for a Russian, English speaking breaking news outlet. There were photos of he and his first two wives snapped in Rome, Paris, Venice, California, New York City, and other hotspots. The faces in the photos were shiny happy and oh so *fucking young*. Or so thought Lynn while he unwrapped the tinfoil from his sandwich and took his first bite.

While he ate and drank his coffee, he thought about his wives, and how much they hated him now. He remembered how both of them were so in love with him at first and how supportive they were of his career. Until something snapped inside them, and they couldn't stand him anymore. It was a bizarre if not perplexing thing to witness for the writer.

Had it been the booze that got to them? His bouts of drinking that always ended up in a heated argument over the littlest thing? Was it the endless nights of writing till dawn, only to sleep all day, not wanting to be disturbed. No, that's not right. More like, you would face his wrath if he was disturbed from his slumber. Because a rested brain was a brain that could put together words. A disturbed brain was a blocked brain that stared at the blank paper for hours and hours and hours.

Or maybe it was the suicide attempts. It wasn't like he had any real reason to take his life. His books were selling, and contracts were coming through from not just one publisher but several. Maybe he wasn't making a boatload of cash like some more popular fantasy and sci-fi authors, but he was holding his own financially.

Be that as it may, not one but both wives had caught him with the barrel of his .45 semi-automatic tonsils deep in his mouth. Both of them screamed at him at tops of their lungs, "Don't you fucking do it!"

Of course, in the end, he didn't do it. But the temptation was always there back when he was married.

However, something curious happened when he was finally alone up on the mountain. He no longer felt like killing himself. He no longer drank himself into oblivion. He was no longer made to feel badly about writing all night and sleeping all day. He no longer snapped at anyone for waking him out of a sound sleep. No one was around anymore to walk on the eggshells he'd personally planted in and outside the bedroom.

In a word, now that Lynn Meredith was alone, he was at peace.

Nowadays, he kept lever-action .30-30 leaning against his writing desk, easy access. Like all the weaponry and explosives at his disposal, it guaranteed the writer's peace. If intruders and trespassers were to infiltrate his property, he wouldn't hesitate to shoot to kill. It was his private property after all, and his time was his and his alone. Selfish? Maybe. But that's the way the writer wanted it.

But there was one person...one special person...who Lynn truly liked or maybe even loved. One person who made him feel good inside. One person whose company he enjoyed, even if the only time he engaged with her was online. Her name was Tara, and she was long, sandy blonde-haired beauty who lived down in Albany. She was married but they had struck up a sort of secret relationship that happened very much by accident.

Left to his own devices, Lynn would never belong to a social media platform like Facebook or Instagram. The only thing worse than being around people was having to put up with their posts that boasted pictures of their dinner or their lunch, or what they were watching on Netflix, or of the kid's soccer match, or worst of all, fellow writers who just had to brag about their new publishing and movie deals. The latter type of post especially rubbed Lynn the wrong way. Why? Because he didn't give a fuck about anybody's success other than his own.

And yet his publishers made him contractually agree to actively participate on social media. In that manner, Lynn had no choice but to glance at his Facebook account a couple times per day, and to post about his books in the hopes that some of his so-called friends might actually part with a couple of bucks and purchase one of his close to 100 eBooks and/or paperbacks.

But it was while he was posting one day, he noticed a personal message that came through from a woman named Tara. Before even reading the message, he went to her profile only to find out what a stunningly beautiful woman she was. When moments later, she sent him a request to be his friend, he not only immediately accepted, he felt his heart pumping wildly against his sternum. His stomach went tight, and his mouth went dry while he clicked on Tara's personal message.

"Hi Lynn," she wrote. "You might not remember me, but we attended grammar school together. It came as a wonderful surprise for me to see that you've become a famous writer. How wonderful! Now I can say I knew you when. Well, I've become quite a fan over the years. I've read everything. I especially love the Harry Jones, PI series. Rumors have been spreading that it's going to be a Netflix show soon. Maybe one day soon we can get together and have a drink. That is, you still live in Albany, New York area. I hope you have time to write me back."

Lynn did write her back, telling her how great it was to get reacquainted, even if only over the internet. He was so happy to hear from her, in fact, he sent her the raw manuscript version of the latest Harry Jones PI book, The Murderers, which she read in a single sitting. Or she claimed in a follow-up Facebook message.

That was three years ago, and while Lynn had never met Tara in the flesh, no matter how many times she begged for permission to come visit him at his home in the Upstate wilderness, he refused to divulge his address.

"You wouldn't like me after a while," he wrote her. "After a while, they all run away from me."

Tara tried to convince Lynn Meredith that she'd be different. She would be the one who would stick it out, through thick and thin. She would leave her husband for him. That's how much she wanted to be together.

"I love you," the teary-eyed Lynn wrote in response.

"I love you so very much too," Tara said. "Now then, can I see you for real? In the flesh."

"No," Lynn said. "That's just the way it has to be."

After that, he never heard from Tara again. And while they were still Facebook friends, she no longer returned his messages or commented on his posts. It had become as if Lynn dropped off the face of the earth and forgot all about the love she claimed to have had for him in her heart.

6

Lynn worked on his newest Henry Jones PI novel for most of the morning, until he got up from his desk and stretched out. It felt good to have the time and isolation to write when he wanted for as long as he wanted. He was getting hungry again, and he contemplated some lunch. But first, he exited his writing studio, and entered into the kitchen where he kept a bottle of whisky. Pouring himself a generous shot into a coffee mug, he carried it with him into the living area where a big stone fireplace provided enough heat to keep the entire cabin comfortable even on the mountaintop's coldest winter days.

He went to the fireplace and added a couple of logs. He then approached the big wood coffee table and snatched the TV remote off of it. Turning on the TV, he channel-surfed until he came to FOX News. The video footage that was already being broadcast was not pretty. It showed refugees running from missiles and bombs exploding all around them. People were lying in the road, bloodied and missing limps. Babies dressed in winter coats and little boots were lying face down in the street. Cars burned while Russian tanks ran over them. It was a grisly scene.

A worried looking reporter spoke into a hand-held mic. He was wearing a military grade helmet and black flak jacket that said, PRESS in big white letters across the chest.

"World War Three has officially escalated now that both Poland and Germany have been invaded by the Putin's army," he said, in a tight-as-a-tick voice. "Rumors abound that the dictator wants nothing less than total global war. That said, the Russian Army is said to be considering the use of tactical nuclear weapons to destroy NATO troops while they are exposed and on the defensive. And if that happens, NATO and the U.S. will have no choice but to retaliate with their own nuclear strikes." He stared into the camera like he was looking directly into Lynn Meredith's brown eyes. "I, for one, pray that this is not the end of the world."

The writer sipped his drink and clicked the television off.

"Maybe we should pray that it is," he said. But then, as soon as he said it, "Or maybe not."

At one time, Lynn might experience a wave of happiness wash over him when he considered the end of humanity. But this time, he didn't feel happy. He had a daughter out there somewhere. Not that he'd laid eyes on her in years, but he loved her to death. Now that the end of times seemed more and more like a real possibility if not inevitability, he felt almost sad that this what his entire life and life of everyone else on the planet was leading up to. To be evaporated or burned to death. He knew that he was probably safe all the way up here in the mountaintop wilderness and that more than likely he'd survive a nuclear exchange between Russian and the Americans. But he wondered about his ex-wives and his daughter. Did they still live in a city which would surely be targeted if the Russians quickly escalated from tactical nukes to the heavy-duty thermonuclear variety? He wished he had some way of getting in touch with them. Of warning them, of insisting they come live with him for a while even if they no longer wanted anything to do with him.

He also wondered about Tara.

He sipped his drink and he thought about the pretty face and the clean, lush, sandy blonde hair that appeared for him on Facebook in the Facebook messages and live chats that used to have not all that long ago. He thought about the way her hair draped her shoulders. He saw her blue eyes and her smooth skin and he suddenly felt the need to touch it for real. Maybe he'd been making a mistake when he insisted she cannot see him in the flesh at his wilderness home. Maybe, if there was going to be a nuclear exchange, he should at least try and save one life.

He drank the rest of his whiskey and set the glass on the wood counter in the kitchen. He wasn't feeling very hungry anymore. Making his way back into his writing room, he sat down at his desk, went on to Facebook and typed Tara's full name into the search engine. He clicked Enter. He fully expected to see her beautiful face. But something else happened instead. She didn't show up.

"What the hell," Lynn said aloud. "Did I spell her name wrong?"

He typed the name into the search engine once more. He clicked Enter again. Same deal. Tara's page didn't come up. He tried a third and fourth time. Nothing doing. Sitting back in his swivel chair, he rubbed both his hands over his scruffy round face. He wondered if it was possible Tara was no longer on Facebook. No sooner had the thought entered his head, when he felt his stomach tighten and the adrenaline fill his brain.

"Has she blocked me?" he said aloud, as if speaking of his being blocked made it seem all the more real. "Had she fucking blocked me like my daughter and my two ex-wives have?"

Acting on instinct, he picked up his smartphone. But he quickly realized that he didn't have her phone number, much less any other way to contact her other than Facebook. But what if she was on the other social media platforms?

He set the phone down again and went on to Instagram. He typed Tara's full name into the search engine. Just like Facebook, he got nothing. He went to Twitter and TikTok and LinkedIn. Nothing. Finally, he simply Googled her name. He did it out of desperation. Again, nothing.

It was like Tara no longer existed. Rather, she no longer existed for him, and the feeling was no less painful than having been kicked in the stomach. He stared out the window and noticed a gathering of deer down by the pond. For a time, he just sat there watching them, wishing Tara, his love, was watching them along with him.

His eyes filling with tears, Lynn got up from the desk and slowly, lumberingly made his was out into the kitchen. He went into the living area and headed for the front door where he pulled his old, somewhat tattered Carhartt coat off the wall-mounted rack and put it on. He grabbed an old baseball hat that had the letters

NYSP on the brim or New York State Police, and he made his way out the door and into the cool if not cold Adirondack afternoon.

Making his way around the log cabin, he went to one of the two stand-alone sheds that occupied the property, opened the door and stepped inside. Careful not disturb any of the spiders that were spending their winter months wrapped in their webs in the shed's rafters, he grabbed a Maxwell House Coffee can off the shelf and carried it outside with him.

Making his way slowly down toward the pond, he stopped a few feet away from the deer. Under normal circumstances, they might have scattered into the woods by now, but they were used to seeing Lynn. As much as Lynn wanted to be alone, and for all his weaponry, he did not take any enjoyment in shooting deer, neither for sport or food. He knew that if worse came to worse, he would have no choice but to shoot one for meat to survive on. But until that day arrived, Lynn would rather call the deer his friends. The only friends he had on the planet.

Opening the lid on the can, he grabbed a fist-full of the dry food and scattered it onto the ground, as if they were seeds he was planting in a field. The deer hesitated at first, until the alpha male approached some of the food and started to eat. The rest followed, while Lynn spread out a few more fistfuls of food.

Turning, he was heading back up the hill in the direction of the shed, when he heard something that can only be described as hell on earth.

7

A bright white light emerged from out of the south. Correction, it wasn't a light so much as a flash. Then began the unearthly rumble that quickly grew into a loud concussive explosion. The earth shook beneath Lynn's feet and the now frightened deer scattered around the pond and back into the relative safety of the wilderness.

The writer rubbed his wet, tired eyes, and he focused his gaze in a southerly direction. What he witnessed both fascinated and repulsed him. It was a mushroom cloud that rose up from the earth like a giant two or three-mile-high monster made of fire and brimstone. It rose so high it disappeared into the atmosphere.

Then came two more flashes that for a split second, blinded Lynn. He made out the explosions and again the earth moved beneath his booted feet. Two more mushroom clouds rose up menacingly into the sky. He thought for certain that would be the extent of the nuclear detonations.

"The Russians must have targeted Albany and New York City," he said to himself. "It must be all gone now. Oh my God, my little girl…"

He also thought of Tara. He realized that she had to be dead now. If only he'd been man enough to let her come to him, she would be alive right now instead of evaporated or worse, burned alive inside her own home.

Then came another flash of searing bright white light and another explosion. Louder and more intense this time. It hadn't come from out of the south but instead, out of the north. The earth trembled so badly he nearly lost his balance. The can of deer food slipped out of his hand and dropped to the frozen ground, the food spilling out of it.

"The fuckers have destroyed Montreal," he whispered in a dry, hoarse voice.

Never, ever, had he contemplated the peaceful quaint city of Montreal, Canada as being in the crosshairs of the mighty, angry

Russian Bear's army. But the hot mushroom cloud that was now rising up into the blue sky no more than seventy-five miles away was proof positive that Montreal was gone, and along with it most, if not all its inhabitants.

Yet one more flash of light coming from out of the south-west and another massive explosion followed by the trembling of the earth told the writer Quebec was now obliterated too. He was surrounded by nature's beauty, but he was also surrounded by mankind's hatred and destruction. He also realized that no matter how far he was from civilization, there was no way he was about to outrun the radiation that was sure to come from these five nuclear blasts.

Lynn realized then that the end of the world was upon him. That it was quite possible he would die, perhaps even as early as today or tonight. Surely, if the radiation didn't get to him, the shock waves from the blasts would destroy everything around him.

All this destruction...It's what he had prayed for. To be left entirely alone.

It was the worst mistake he could have ever made.

8

But Lynn did not die. At least not right away. While he fully expected the shock waves to plow the forest down and his cabin along with them, they never came. He didn't know why they never came, but he must have somehow been protected by the mountain his property was constructed upon. The higher the elevation, the more protection, or so he deduced.

Running back into the cabin, he snatched the remote off the coffee table. He was surprised to see that he still had power, much less a picture on the TV. However, the picture was coming and going, as if it was about to die at any moment. He could barely make out the same CNN reporter he'd been watching before. The anxious one wearing the military-grade helmet and the flak jacket with the word PRESS printed on it.

The picture was fuzzy and distorted. It was coming and going, but one thing was for certain, the reporter's face was bloody, and it looked like he was missing an eye since there was a thick, bloody patch that covered it. The darkness that surrounded him was broken only by the flashing blue and white lights on the many police and EMT vans that were scooting and shooting all around him. Smoking rubble was all that remained of the Ukrainian street he'd been standing on earlier. A tear was falling from his one good eye.

"Paris, Berlin, Warsaw, Kiev," he said, "they're all gone now. As are London, New York, Los Angeles, Chicago, Lincoln, Denver, Montreal, and so many, many more. Initial death toll is estimated to be close to five hundred million and climbing. Despite the crippling effects of the first strike, we fully expect a retaliatory strike on behalf of all the NATO nations, including the US and the UK, any minute now. We also..."

The picture cut out then, and so did the television. Lynn pressed the green power button several times, but it was no use. Setting down the remote, he shifted himself toward the end table that was positioned beside the leather couch. He tried to turn on the lamp. It didn't work.

"The power is cut," he whispered.

Just to make certain that was the case, he made his way into the kitchen and opened the door that accessed the basement. His natural instinct was to turn on the overhead light that illuminated the staircase, which is what he did. But the light didn't come on. About facing, he walked back into the kitchen and grabbed one of the flashlights he stored in a drawer.

He flicked the flashlight on, and then made his way down the basement stairs. Like the entire cabin, the basement was new. It wasn't constructed of concrete block, but the more sturdy poured and formed, reinforced concrete. He had to pay a lot extra for it, but it was worth it. He made his way past stacks of emergency food stores like cases of pasta, freeze-dried meals, canned and potted vegetables and meats, plus boxes of snacks, cereals, cake mixes, powdered eggs, milk, coffee, medicines, and so much more.

He made it past the gallons upon gallons of fresh water (enough to last three years), and past the cases of beer and bottles of whiskey (enough to last a year), and past his heavy-duty Black and Decker hybrid generator that ran on both gasoline (which he had stored in fifty gallon drums in a second shed located only a few feet away from the one where kept the deer food), and solar sunlight (the cabin's cathedral roof was covered in solar panels), until he made it to the breaker box.

Shining the flashlight onto it, he saw that the breakers hadn't engaged.

"Power's out," he whispered. "I wonder if it will ever come back on."

Lynn went to the generator and shined the light on it. He started it by yanking on the lawnmower-like starter. When it came to life, the lights in the cabin came back on. He checked the gas level and saw that it was full. Or perhaps the machine was running on stored solar power at present. He didn't really care what it was running on so long as it was running.

Turning off the flashlight, he shoved it into his belt, then grabbed one of the ten-gallon jugs of spring water and set it onto his shoulder. He made his way back across the basement floor and started making his way up the wood staircase.

He heard the noise then. The higher he climbed, the louder it became. Making it to the top of the stairs, Lynn set the water bottle down, and this time made his way out the back door off the kitchen. He stood on the long back deck in the chill of the afternoon and looked up at the sky. The mushroom clouds were still there, but something else was visible too. Missiles. Rather, outbound missiles.

"We launched our arsenal," Lynn said to himself.

As a writer who researched all sorts of weapons for his books, he remembered that both the Russians and the U.S. alike had hypersonic missiles which could be armed with nuclear warheads. It told him that the first nukes had already been detonated over Russian soil. More than likely, Moscow was already gone along with some other key Russian cities. If only he could get a report from his television.

That's when he thought about his smartphone. Heading back into the house, he picked the mobile phone up off the counter. He brought up the Google search engine and typed the letters CNN into them. While Google was able to give him a page of results, when he tapped on the cable news network's main page, all he got was a page that said the site could no longer be reached.

He went back to the search engine and typed in Fox News. Clicking on the site's main link, he got more of the same. The site could no longer be reached. He checked all the mainstream networks and none of them were operation. He even checked local news stations, and they were down too. Of course, all this made sense if New York City no longer existed. It's where most of the mainstream media was located.

If he were writing this plot for a book, Lynn figured two things were at play. The Russians had launched not only a strategic nuclear attack on the West's major and medium sized cities, but also a crippling international cyberattack. Or, the nuclear attack was enough to demolish both the electrical and internet superstructure to the extent that they were now unusable.

His phone in hand, Lynn went back inside his writing space and sat down at his laptop. He stared at the black words on the white screen, and he grinned. But it wasn't a happy grin. Because that's when he knew for certain that without the internet and without electricity, he was pretty much out of a job and a career. How much had he sacrificed for his career?

"Everything," he said. "I prayed for the end of the world, and I got it."

As he got up from his desk, Lynn slowly made his way back out into the kitchen where he replaced the empty water bottle with the new one in its dispenser. He then entered into the living area and went to the vestibule. Without thinking about it, he grabbed his coat and his baseball hat and put them on. He also grabbed his truck keys. As he placed his hand on the doorknob, he also remembered something else.

Turning back around, he made his way back into the writing studio and grabbed his .45 semi-automatic off the writing desk. Spotting a leather holster that hung from a six-penny nail embedded into the log wall, he wrapped both ends around his waist, and buckled it tightly. He then stored the gun in the holster. Since the holster already housed two additional nine round magazines, he didn't feel the need to grab any additional ammo.

Making his way back to the front door, Lynn Meredith, exited the home and started for his pickup truck. He was about to get a first-hand observation of humanity. That is, the humanity that was left.

9

He made his way back out the gate, making sure to lock the padlock behind him. He then negotiated the two-track out to the main road. As far as he was concerned, everything looked perfectly normal. If anything, the sunny afternoon made the thick tall trees appear magnificent and timeless. As if God had designed them to be impervious to destruction, no matter what variety of nuclear violence mankind could throw at them.

But then, Lynn also knew this. Radiation was a silent killer. It was as invisible as it was tasteless and odorless. He wasn't ignorant of the fact that the radiation could be bombarding his system right this very minute. It could be that he was being invaded by massive doses of radiation. It was invading his liver, his lungs, his heart, and his brain.

What was left of the entire world...the unlucky survivors... would be experiencing the same thing. Radiation poisoning on a colossal level. It made him wonder what was the point of using nukes when by their very nature, they destroyed the spoils of war. And wasn't that the point of all wars? The spoils going to the victor?

As he drove, he began to feel a little sick to his stomach. Perhaps it was the shot of whiskey he drank earlier on an empty belly, or maybe it was the power of suggestion...just the thought of all that radiation bombarding his fragile system. If he was, in fact, being bombarded with radiation, how long did he have to live? A month? A week? A day?

He continued down the mountain, tapping the brakes as he went so that the truck didn't lose control on the steeper drops. The more he continued downhill, the more something became evident. The thick stands of trees that flanked the narrow, winding road, were damaged. The more altitude he lost, the more damage he could see. Eventually, Lynn came upon entire swaths of giant oaks, pines, and birch trees that had been blown over like they were matchsticks.

"The blast wave," Lynn whispered as he glanced out both his passenger and driver's side windows.

The fact that he could see for miles meant that hundreds of thousands if not millions of trees had been destroyed, the landscape entirely flattened. He felt a lump in his throat, as Wilsboro came into view. Or what should have been Wilsboro. Every building that had occupied the small town was obliterated. The homes, the businesses, the general store…they were all gone. Cars and trucks were tipped on their sides or on their roofs. Charred bodies littered the roads. Some of the bodies had been blown part and only a naked torso remained.

As he slowly negotiated the town's road, careful not to run over the dead, he couldn't help but see that two bodies were lying in the road not far from where the general store had stood. One body still had its arms and legs, but it had no head. The other body was just a torso. Judging by their clothing, Lynn deduced that the mangled bodies belonged to the two old guys who drank their coffee in the store every morning and who always glared at him when he came in for his breakfast and lottery ticket.

"For the love of God," Lynn said, as he came to the end of the road and made a three-point turn.

Driving back through the town, doing only ten miles per hours, he opened his window, and stuck his head out.

"Is anyone alive?" he shouted. "Is anybody still alive? Does anyone need help?"

He stopped the truck near a pickup truck that was flipped over onto its back, its front wheels spinning fast, as if the driver still had his foot on the gas pedal. He listened intently for anything. He heard nothing. The only sounds came from the spinning truck tires, and the snap, crackle and pop from the flames that consumed what was left of the general store.

Tapping the gas, Lynn pulled the truck forward. As he left the town behind him, he didn't bother with peering into the rearview mirror. What was the point? He was alone now.

All alone with all the time in the world to write whatever he chose.

Just the way he'd wanted it.

10

The writer might have headed back up the mountain where it was safe. Or, relatively safe anyway. But for how long, was anybody's guess. Instead, he headed along the road that led to New York Highway 87, the north-south highway that connected the Adirondack wilderness with the city of Albany and its surrounding suburbs and towns like Saratoga Springs and Clifton Park.

He gazed at the gas gauge. He had a full tank since he'd filled up just a couple of days back. He was aware that if he drove all that way into Albany, he might not have enough fuel left to make it back home. But maybe if he drove to Saratoga, he'd have plenty of gas for the return trip. If not, he'd have to find a way to syphon the gas out of a dead man's car or truck.

He turned onto the highway and gazed straight ahead. Majestic tall peaks surrounded him on both sides. But most of the trees had been felled. Only the mountain summits still contained upright trees. Or so it appeared from all the way down on the highway. He noticed another strange occurrence. The little lakes and ponds that littered the landscape...all of them were dry now, as if the poison wind that followed the nuclear blasts had literally blown the water away. Or maybe the heat from the detonations vaporized the liquid.

When he passed by the great Lake Champlain, he could see that the big inland sea was still there, and it filled him with at least a ray of optimism. But the optimism was short-lived as he began to notice the many semis, cars, pickup trucks, Jeeps, panel trucks and more that were either tipped on their sides, turned completely over, or just plain stopped in the middle of the roadbed. As he passed them by, he noticed that in almost all cases, the front windshield had been blown in. As he slowed and crawled past one black Mercedes Benz sedan, he saw that not only had the windshield been blown away, but the car's driver was missing his head and both his arms.

Lynn drove another twenty miles, southbound. Soon the many vehicles that occupied the road showed signs of being battered and burned. It looked like each one of them had been hit with a missile. Some were mangled beyond recognition, while others were entirely flattened like a giant foot had crushed them, and still others were aflame. It looked like a war zone because it was a war zone.

"A nuclear war zone," Lynn spoke aloud.

He drove further. In just twenty more miles he would reach the town of Saratoga Springs where the horses raced every summer and where all kind of folks shopped in the town's many high-end stores, and where they ate and drank in its many bars, restaurants, and pubs. Students who attended the prestigious college located on the northern end of the town would get drunk and stupid on the weekends and stumble back to their dorms, happy and horny. In the summer, the street might be closed off entirely so that people could spill out of the bars and party on the sidewalks and in the middle of the road while bandstands were set up on both ends of the town. It was a magical place to be alive.

But now, as the writer entered the burning and entirely flattened town of Saratoga Springs, he witnessed nothing but death in its purest most gruesome form. The fires were so hot, he could feel them through the closed windows on the pickup. He didn't dare drive into the center of the destroyed town. Everything was on fire. The exposed building foundations, the stumps that used to be the old oak trees that bloomed along the sidewalks, the many vehicles, even the road itself was burning.

As Lynn threw the transmission into reverse, he saw something he never would have believed possible. It was a man. He was running into the middle of the burning road. Lynn wanted to get out and help him, but the tall man's entire body was on fire. The writer's eyes entirely focused on the burning man, he watched him drop face first into the hell-on-earth fire, his heart having finally given out. How had he survived this long? The only thing Lynn could surmise was that he'd been underground for the entire attack, perhaps even inside a bomb shelter that had been constructed in the 1950s.

Backing up, Lynn drove away from the town. But rather than get back on the highway, he took the road that ran perpendicular to the main road and that accessed the Saratoga racetrack and its surrounding paddocks where the thoroughbred horses lived. Like everything else in the town, the racetrack's century and a half old grandstand, which was made of wood, was not only entirely leveled, but the wood fragments that were left over were still burning. The track itself, which was gravel, had been charred and blackened and the grass track located inside the gravel ovel was blacked and still smoldering too.

Lynn gazed out the driver's side window and what he witnessed shook him to the core. It was the many corpses of the horses, all of them either still burning, some smoldering, others having roasted to the bones so that all you could make out was a skeleton. You could smell the meat cooking even from inside the truck.

Ever the creative writer living inside his imagination, Lynn pictured the scene. Just this morning, the horses were being fed hay. They were being groomed and trained on the track, even in late winter. No one would have guessed that someone very far away would have had the balls to actually push the button that would annihilate the whole world. The button that ushered in the end of the world.

For a brief second or two, Lynn felt my his fill with sad tears. But just as quickly, he felt the rage enter into his bloodstream like an injection of gasoline. He could only hope that the enemy had gotten it as bad as the U.S. had, or worse. Making a fist, he slammed it on the dash.

"I wanted the end of the world," he reminded myself. "Now I'm the only one left alive."

Turning the truck around, he headed for the highway. The

nausea he'd been experiencing on the way down here was getting worse. His best guess was, it wouldn't take him long to join all the dead horses.

11

Lynn didn't care about obeying the speed limit. What was the point now that there were no more cops alive to pull him over to issue a ticket? When the speedometer hit 100mph, he punched the pedal even harder until he got to 125mph. If the truck went out of control and flipped, so be it. He was a dead man anyway. As if to remind him of this, he wasn't halfway home, when he felt his stomach turn over.

Hitting the brakes, he pulled over onto the soft shoulder, the all-terrain tires skidding against the gravel. He threw the stick in park, opened the door, and puked his guts out. The violent heaving felt like his stomach was about to emerge out of his mouth. His chest felt like it was splitting in two at the sternum. His insides and mouth burned from the bile. Maybe dying now wouldn't be such a bad thing anyway, he thought. Death by radiation poisoning was like dying by a thousand cuts. But then, he couldn't be entirely certain he was suffering from radiation poisoning. It was possible he was just in shock, and the vomiting was merely a symptom of it.

When he was empty and could breathe normally again, Lynn wiped his mouth with the back of his hand, and pulled away from the soft shoulder, the tires spitting gravel until they connected with the highway blacktop. The farther north he got, the less destroyed cars and trucks that littered the highway. The late afternoon was sunny, with a blue sky that seemed infinite. But it soon dawned on the writer that within a matter of hours, the sky would turn dark, and not because of the sunset. Instead, it would turn dark and stay that way due to a thick cover of debris, dust, sand and ash. Debris kicked up by the massive nuclear explosions.

What did they call this effect when he was a kid growing up during the Cold War?

"Nuclear Winter," he whispered, answering his own question.

Soon, daylight would be a rare commodity, while the winter

would settle in perpetually. Even if he stayed alive long enough to see the summer months, he would be plowing himself out of a radioactive-tainted snow that would cover every square piece of real estate from Portland, Maine to Portland, Oregon. If the radiation currently cruising invisibly through the air while he drove, invading his white and red blood cells, didn't kill him first, the Nuclear Winter would surely get him. It would be a slow, painful, excruciating death.

"A death by one thousand cuts," he repeated to himself.

The thought of dying weighed so heavily on his mind after he got off the highway and started the climb up his mountain to his wilderness writing retreat, that the man who once prayed for the end of the world, fell into a great and heavily weighted despair. Turning onto the two-track that led to his cabin, his eyes once more filled with tears.

When he came to the padlocked gate, he stopped the truck and put it into park. He stared at the words printed on the gate-mounted sign. KEEP OUT! TRESSPASSERS WILL BE EXECUTED!

"Nobody left to execute," he whispered.

Getting out of the truck, he went to the gate, and unlocked it. But that's not before the key slipped from his trembling fingers and dropped onto the gravel covered track. When he bent over to pick the key up, he suddenly felt the full two and a half pound weight of the .45 resting against his ribcage, and beyond that, his heart.

Pushing the gate wide open, he slipped back behind the truck's wheel and stared forlornly onto the nothing that lie ahead of him. That's when he lost all control of his actions. Something else, far more powerful seemed to be commanding him. So, when he pulled the gun out of its holster, and pulled back on the slide, loading a live round into the chamber, it wasn't him performing the action, but someone or something else entirely.

He swallowed the metal barrel and pressed his finger on the trigger. He was dying anyway and all alone in the world, so what difference did it make if he died right now, right this very second? He'd be doing himself a great favor.

That's when something caught his attention in the rearview. Something that told him he wasn't all alone after all. It was a woman, and she was running away from him along the fence line.

12

Without thinking about it, Lynn knew that it was the woman he saw this morning at the general store. The attractive, long sandy blonde-haired, blue-eyed one with the electrified vest. She was still wearing the vest and it gave her identity away. Pulling the gun out of his mouth, Lynn felt a sudden rise in blood pressure. He felt a jolt of happiness.

"I'm not alone," he said aloud. "I'm fucking not alone."

If he didn't know any better, he was sporting a grin. But then he thought about the landmines he'd planted along the fence-line and panic filled his veins. Slapping the gun onto the passenger seat, Lynn threw open the door and jumped out.

"Hey, wait!" he shouted. "Stop!"

He spotted her moving along the fence-line, the heavy woods shading her from a sun that would soon be mostly blocked with radioactive ash. She stopped, and slowly turned around. She eyed Lynn, her eyes big and wide and unblinking.

"Don't take another step," he said.

"Why?" she said.

"The place is mined," he said.

"Mined?" she said, disbelief tainting her voice. "But why?"

He moved quickly along the fence line, fully aware of the location of each and every mine. After all, he personally planted them.

"To ward off intruders," he said.

She did something strange then. She worked up a smile.

"I can assure you, Mr. Meredith," she said, "there are no more intruders."

He came within a foot or two of her.

"You know my name," he said.

"Everybody knows your name," she said. "You're famous."

"For my books?" he said.

"For your books," she said. "And also for being kind of an asshole."

Now Lynn couldn't help but grin.

"I guess you have every right to call me that," he said. Then, "Come with me. It's not safe out here."

He took a chance and grabbed hold of her hand.

"Is there anyplace safe anymore?" she said.

He turned away from her and chose not to answer her question.

13

Lynn came around the truck and opened the passenger side door.

"After you, mam," he said, graciously.

"Why thank you," she said.

It was such a courteous exchange, it was like the end of the world was just a whole bunch of fake news. The woman got in and Lynn closed the door. He then came back around truck. He didn't need to open the driver's side door since it was already open, the built-in alarm that was engineered to alert him to that fact, pinging annoyingly. He got back behind the wheel, slammed the door closed, and pulled forward. When he was through the gate, he stopped the truck and went to get out so he could lock the gate behind him.

"That's not necessary," the woman said, anticipating his action.

"Not necessary," he said like a question.

"They're all dead," she said. "And I mean all of them."

He stared out the windshield for a long beat and thought about everything he'd witnessed over the past few hours. He relived the terrible sight of the burned and mangled people lying in the road. He saw the burning and demolished vehicles, the leveled towns, the mountains with their many trees felled or stripped from the earth at their mighty roots.

He saw the mushroom clouds and felt the white-hot flash of their detonations burn his retinas (he would likely pay for looking directly into the flashes tomorrow morning, if he lived that long). He saw America's own nuclear arsenal on its way to Russia. He knew that most of the world was indeed dead or dying now. For certain, he and this woman could be among the dead in a matter of days.

To think this is what I wanted, he thought. *To think this is how badly I wanted to be left alone. I deserve to die.*

"I guess you're right," he said.

Throwing the transmission in drive, he pulled forward and drove the two-track until his cabin came into view.

"You live here all alone?" the woman said.

He glanced at her.

"That was supposed to be the point," he said. "Live alone in solitude so that my world would be just me, my words, and my books."

"Don't you like people?" she said.

He pulled up to the gravel turn-around outside the cabin's front porch and came to a stop. He put the transmission in park and killed the motor. Silence filled the cab interior. It wasn't a good silence.

"I didn't know how much I liked them until now," he said. His daughter came to mind, and his throat closed up on itself.

"Until they were all dead," she said.

He nodded and felt his chest grow tight and his mouth go dry. If he wasn't in the presence of a beautiful woman, he might have burst out in tears. He drove the one hundred or so feet up to the cabin graven turn-around, and killed the engine. He opened his door and so did the woman. They both got out. Something dawned on him as he once more came around the front of the truck.

"Tell me something," he said.

The woman was already climbing the four wood steps up to the porch. She turned and gazed at him.

"What is it?" she said.

"How did you manage to survive?" he asked.

She looked at him for a long time. Or so it seemed. It was one of those laserbeam gazes that bore into you rather than simply viewed you.

"I'm not sure," she said. Then, smiling wryly. "They say that only insects and rats will survive a nuclear Armageddon. Maybe that's what we are, rats."

"Or cockroaches," Lynn said. "But you do realize we're dying now from radiation."

"It crossed my mind," she said. "How long do you think we

have before our blood starts squirting out of our pores and the boils and pustules cover our entire bodies?"

"A few days maybe," he said. "Maybe never."

She grinned again.

"Do I detect a hint of optimism in the face of certain doom and gloom, Mr. Meredith?" she asked.

"I've never been known as the optimistic type," he said.

"Yes, old and crotchety. I believe was the way the boy behind the counter described you after you left the store this morning."

"Oh, he did, did he?"

She nodded, turned and climbed the final step onto the porch.

"Would you like a drink?" Lynn barked.

"I'd like to get fucking plastered," she said as she helped herself to opening the front door.

"For tomorrow we most definitely die," Lynn said to himself.

He wanted to ask the woman her name, but she was already inside the cabin.

14

Once inside, Lynn took off his coat and hung it up on the rack. He also took off his holster and the pistol it housed and hung that up too. Just like locking the gate that protected his property, he wasn't entirely sure he needed the firepower anymore. But then, if the woman who was presently standing inside his kitchen was still alive, there was bound to be others. It dawned on him that maybe he should go back and lock the gate. For certain, he would do it before nightfall.

In the meantime, he went to the fire, stoked it, and put on a couple of fresh logs. He then made his way to fridge in the small galley kitchen and pulled out two beers.

"Hope you like cheap domestic beer," he said. "I guess it's entirely impractical to head down the mountain and drive the sixty miles to Plattsburgh for some craft beer."

She took the beer in her hand and popped the tab.

"Plattsburgh doesn't exist," she said. "It's that close to Montreal, which also doesn't exist anymore."

She took a deep drink of the beer. It was the kind of long swig you might expect of a man. A big, lumbering, construction worker type of man. But who could blame her? It had been one hell of a day, or so Lynn thought. A day for the ages. A day that ushered in the end of the world as they knew it.

The author pulled two clear drinking glasses from out of the cabinet over the gas stove. He set them on the butcher block counter and grabbed the bottle of Irish whiskey that was stored there. He poured two generous shots. Raising his glass, he looked the woman in the eyes. There was something about the eyes and the pretty face that went with it. Something about her sandy blond hair and the way it was neatly parted on the side. How clean and lush it was.

That's when it hit him that she looked a lot like Tara. Of course, he'd never met Tara in the flesh. He'd never heard her voice or seen even so much as a video of her. The photos on her Facebook page were mostly five or even ten years old, so he couldn't even be sure what she looked like today. But he felt he knew her. Knew her inside and out. He also felt like he was in love with her, if such a thing were even possible.

"Here's to your health, Tara," he said.

"What did you call me?" she said, raising her glass.

"Tara," he said. "That is your name isn't it?"

But she didn't answer him. Instead, they both drank the shots down in one swift swallow. The woman slapped her empty glass on the counter.

"Hit me again," she said.

Lynn poured them both another generous shot. This time they didn't bother with a silly toast about life or even the prospect of a future. They just drank.

"Again," the woman repeated.

And again, Lynn filled both their glasses. But this time, they didn't shoot the whiskey. Instead, without saying a word to one another, they automatically gravitated into the living area with their drinks in hand and sat down beside each other on the leather couch that faced the roaring fire burning in the big stone fireplace.

"You know what?" the woman said after a long beat.

"Radiation hasn't gotten to my ears," Lynn said.

"If I didn't know the whole world was either dead or dying, we could be on vacation." Sitting up, she peered over both shoulders. "This is really a beautiful little spot you've managed to carve our for yourself, Mr. Meredith."

Of course, she knew his name. He was famous after all. Well, sort of famous anyway. The most famous writer in Wilsboro, God rest its soul.

He stared into the fire. "I just wanted to be alone, Tara."

The woman stood up and sipped her drink.

"Why do you keep calling me that?" she asked.

"I already told you," Lynn said. "That's your name."

"Okay," she said. "That's my name."

Lynn stared not at her, but into her.

"Tara," he said, "how did you survive the blasts?"
She drank the test of her whiskey and smiled warmly at Lynn.
"Mr. Meredith," she said. "Will you do me a favor?"
"Anything, Tara," he said.
"Will you make love to me?" she said.

15

Without another word, they retired to the cabin's one bedroom. Slowly undressing one another, Lynn gazed at her body and was amazed at how beautiful she was. Her breasts were firm, her nipples erect. They fit into his hand when he cupped them. Her belly was also firm but smooth and her ass was round and pert.

They lie on the bed, and he ran his hands through her hair, and they kissed passionately. When he entered her, he felt her wet warmth and her tightness. He moved slowly, and she moved with him, in synch with his every thrust. He could feel the sweat building on his brow, and he felt his heart pounding against his sternum, and he quickly felt himself coming to that special place. He knew she was coming close to that very special place too because now she was moaning and whispering, "Don't stop. Please don't stop."

Her eyes were closed and her mouth slightly ajar, her hair veiling her face like an angel.

"I love you, Tara," Lynn said as he released inside her. "I've always dreamed we'd be together like this."

"I love you, Lynn," she said, as she released at the same time.

When they were emptied, they held one another as tightly as they could without breaking bones. Until finally, they released one another and lie on their backs, the sweat glistening off their naked bodies in the firelight that leaked in through the open bedroom door.

"That's the one," she said after a time.

"That's the what, angel?" he said.

"That's the one," she said. "Our making love. That's the one that will give me…give *us*…a child."

He turned over onto his side and he ran his fingers through her hair.

"How do you know?" he said not without a grin. "It's only been a couple of minutes."

She glanced at him.

"A girl knows," she said.

He thought about it for a long beat.

"Hell of a time for us to be having a baby," he said. "The world is coming to an end if you hadn't noticed."

She looked him in the eyes.

"What if we're immune to it all," she said. "What if up here on this mountaintop, we're protected from everything? The blasts, the radiation, the destruction…what if we're immune to the end of the world?" Suddenly, she sat up and placed her open hand on her flat belly. "What if this is the birth of a new world for us, Lynn. We just might be the new Adam and Eve."

He sat up too. He found himself smiling. It was a smile so big, he thought his face might crack. He was no longer the middle-aged, crotchety writer who lived in the wilderness so he could write his stories and books in peace. He no longer hated humanity so much that he prayed for the end of the world. If what Tara said was true (and he had no reason not to believe her), he was going to be a new dad in nine month's time. He would be raising a brand new child in a brand new world.

How odd that he had never been happier in his life?

"Hungry, Tara?" he said.

"Starving," she said.

Together, the two slipped out of bed and got dressed. Rather, Lynn put his jeans and boots back on, along with a red LL Bean pullover. He collected some sweatpants and a second pullover for Lynn. The clothing was floating on her, but she looked beautiful anyway. He also found her some thick wool socks so her feet didn't get cold on the wood plank floor.

"Another drink, honey?" he asked.

"I'd better not," she said, once more gently placing her hand on her belly. "I've got to start thinking about the little one. Have you thought about a name yet?"

Lynn pulled down a box of dry spaghetti from the shelf over the sink. He also pulled a pot off one of the hangers that was mounted to the adjacent wall. He began to fill the pot not with tap water, but spring water from the dispenser. When the pot was full, he set it on the burner and turned on the gas.

Still have gas, he thought. *Miracle of miracles.*

He opened a beer for himself, and he looked at Tara while she warmed herself by the fire. Her back was to him and when he looked at her, he thought he'd never been so in love with a woman in his entire life.

"We only just made love, babe," he said. "Let's make sure you're really pregnant first."

She turned and smiled at him like she was filled with sunlight.

"I told you," she said. "I know my body."

Again, she placed her hand on her belly.

"Well then," he said, pouring some spaghetti sauce into a smaller pot, "if it's a girl, I like Sarah. If it's a boy, maybe we can name him Lynn Junior. What do you think, babe?"

"I love it," she said. "Sarah if we have a girl and Lynn Junior if it's a boy."

Lynn went through his beer while he cooked the spaghetti and then he opened another while they sat down at the counter to eat. It was the first time since he'd escaped the city and moved up here to the mountaintop wilderness to be alone with his laptop and his books, that he shared a meal with someone. He never realized what he'd been missing. Sure, he would speak to Tara online on Facebook, but it wasn't nearly the same as having her around in person, in real-time, in real love.

When they were through, Lynn made a coffee with the Keurig for himself, which he sweetened with some Irish whiskey. For Tara, he made some tea. They sat on the couch, their bodies pressed up against one another, sipping their beverages. They watched the fire, not saying much of anything, because when you're that much in love you don't need to speak to one another. Just being together is enough.

Once their drinks were done, and they both started yawning, Lynn got up.

"It's been a day for the ages, baby," he said. "How about we hit the hay."

Tara slowly rose from the couch, stretched her arms over her head and let loose with another long yawn.

"Mind if I use your toothbrush, lover?" she said. "I forgot to bring mine."

"Mi toothbrush," the writer said, "su toothbrush."

Tara giggled and headed toward the bedroom and the bathroom that was connected to it. Lynn tossed another couple of logs on the fire and began to lock up the cabin. For a split second, he thought about heading down to the gate and locking it. But a little voice inside his head told him not to. If there was somebody out there who needed help, he was willing and able to assist them. That is, anybody was still alive out there. It was certainly a possibility. If Tara had survived the thermonuclear onslaught, certainly there could be others.

With that clearly in mind, he wanted his property to be a refuge, a shelter from the storm, so to speak. Not a place where people were told to Go Away. He did, however, lock the front and back doors. He also brought his semi-automatic with him to the bedroom where he set it on the nightstand. If people were still alive, there could be some bad actors out there, and he had a family to protect now.

As promised, Tara used his toothbrush and then got in the bed, snuggling herself under the covers. Lynn also got in bed and spooned into her.

"I love you, Tara," he whispered, placing his hand over her hand which again was pressed against her belly. "I love you to death."

"I love you too, Lynn," she said. "I love you and our baby."

Closing his eyes, Lynn felt entirely at peace. He fell to sleep with the satisfaction of knowing his future was bright.

16

The next morning, Lynn was wakened by a strange tapping on the tin roof. His eyes didn't open like they normally would. That's because a strange kind of discharge had formed a crust that sealed his eyelids shut. When he finally managed to open his eyes, he felt them burning. It was like he'd looked directly into a white-hot weld without the protection of a welder's mask, and now he was paying the price.

But then he remembered the white flash that accompanied the nuclear detonations that occurred less than twenty-four hours ago, and his burning eyes suddenly made sense. For almost the entirety of the previous night, he'd almost forgotten about the deadly nuclear exchange between America and Russia. He'd almost forgotten about the devastation, about the end of the world he once prayed for. He was so happy being with Tara and making love to her, that their world had become a heaven on earth. A heaven surrounded by hell.

"The reaction must have been delayed," he whispered to himself out of a desert-sand-dry mouth. "I should have never looked into the light."

He slowly sat up and slipped out of bed. His bones and flesh pained him so badly, it was like he'd aged thirty years overnight. How could that be? He'd gone to bed feeling so good, and so young. But now, he was so out of balance, he had to extend his arm and plant his hand against the log wall.

Walking slowly, achingly into the bathroom, Lynn noticed that he left the seat up. He'd have to get used to putting it down after using the toilet from now on. There was a woman in the house, after al. He stood over the bowel and began to drain his bladder. He couldn't help but notice the streaks of blood in his yellow urine. It might have alarmed him if he weren't still so exhausted, and if his bones, muscles, and ligaments were aching so much.

"Maybe I'm coming down with something," he whispered. "Got to take better care of myself if I'm going to be a new dad."

Flushing the toilet, he shifted to the sink. He turned on the hot water and waited a long beat for it to heat up. He used the time to glance into the medicine cabinet mirror. What he saw shocked him. His hair which had been thick and salt-and-pepper colored, seemed thinner somehow, as if he lost a whole bunch of it overnight. It had also turned gray-white. His skin was pale and his cheeks gaunt. He appeared far older than the viral man who made love to Tara last evening. Or perhaps he was just imagining the rapid aging. He stared up at the exposed ceiling-mounted lightbulb.

"Maybe it's the lighting in here," he whispered. "Better get a new fixture now that there's a lady around. Tara will want to make herself look beautiful for me everyday."

When the water felt warm enough, he trapped some into his cupped hands and he splashed his face with it. He then pulled his toothbrush from holder mounted to the wall. He put some toothpaste on it. As he brushed, he felt pain in his gums, and his teeth felt loose. Sticking his index finger into his mouth, he felt a loose molar all the way in back. He pushed and pulled on the molar until he felt a snap. Reaching in with two fingers, he pulled the broken molar out.

He stared at the gray, brown, and black molar.

"I'll be dipped," he said. "Maybe it's time to see a dentist before they all fall out."

Tossing the tooth into the garbage, he rinsed his mouth and spit a combination blood and mucous into the sink. He watched the sickly mixture circle the drain until it disappeared. He then dried his face with a towel that hung on the back of the door. Opening the door, he stepped back into the bedroom and saw that his love was still sleeping on her side, the covers concealing her from head to toe entirely.

He grinned at her.

"New momma needs her rest," he silently whispered to himself.

Slipping into his jeans and boots, he also put on his work-shirt and then the red LL Bean pullover. He went to the window on the far wall near the bathroom, pulled up some of the slats on the Venetian blind. What he saw made his heart sink. The sky was raining ash. No, that's not right. It was snowing ash.

"Fall out," he whispered, the reality of the previous day's nuclear exchange bearing down on his shoulders like thousand-pound weights.

Several inches must have accumulated overnight. Something else occupied the grounds. There were at least six or seven dead deer lying on their sides. A couple of them were bucks with impressive eight and ten-point racks. He also noticed a whole bunch of birds that had fallen from the sky to their deaths. Some geese, some blackbirds, a few robins, and even a hawk.

"Damn shame," he said. "I hope this ash thing doesn't last too long, or all the animals will die."

He closed the blinds before Tara woke up and looked out the window. He didn't want to see her so disturbed so early in the morning. Tip-toeing around the bed, he glanced at his love once more. He knew he shouldn't risk waking her, but he couldn't help himself when he went to her and pulled down the blanket just enough to give her a gentle kiss on the cheek.

"Sleep well, darling," he whispered, pulling the comforter back to its original position.

Turning, he made his way into the living area, where he stoked the now smoldering fire. He also put a couple of fresh logs into it. The dry wood took immediately and began to burn. For a time, Lynn stood in front of the fire and allowed its heat to soothe his tired bones.

As the temperature in the cabin elevated, he went to the front door, and put on his Carhartt coat. He unlocked the door and made his way out into the cold morning. Descending the porch steps, he felt the ash fall onto his head and he couldn't help but notice how much it felt like real snow. Maybe it was real snow combined with ash. It was certainly cold enough.

A strange worm smell had tainted the air, like after it rains all day and the worms come out of their drenched underground holes. He examined the front turn-around and saw the bodies. A man and a woman. They must have come through the open gate overnight. He could see from where he was standing that they were dead. Their blue, swelled faces, wide open, unblinking eyes, and ajar mouths were a dead give-away.

"Pardon the pun," he whispered.

He also thought of something Hemingway had said about the dead many years ago during his reporting on the Spanish Civil War. "The dead look really dead when they're dead."

He knew both of the dead from the general store. It was Timmy Clarkson and his young wife.

"Nice kids," he said, his throat closing up on itself and his stomach turning over. "I should have been nicer to them. Tara's gonna be so sad when she hears about this."

He turned around and started for the house again, but he didn't make it to the steps until he doubled over and started heaving the bile that was stored in his gut. His throat and mouth burned, and his stomach felt like it had been pounded with a sledgehammer.

Lynn stared at the puddle of bloody mucous on the hard, ash-covered ground.

"Pepto," he whispered. "Pepto-Bismol will do the trick."

He struggled to make it up the steps. But when he finally made it, he crossed over the porch floor, opened the door, went inside and closed the door behind him. He removed his coat and hung it on the rack. Inhaling a deep breath, he got his bearings. He also glanced at his watch. Eight A.M. on Friday morning. Or was it a Sunday morning? He had no idea.

Under normal circumstances, he might drive into town for an egg sandwich, a large coffee, and a lottery ticket. It would be his only brush with humanity for the day. But this morning was different. He had his family home with him. That meant a home-cooked breakfast.

"Up yet, babe?" he said in a voice that was both loud but

somehow weak. "How about some scrambled eggs and toast? Our little boy, Junior, needs his nourishment, don't forget. You need it too."

"What do you mean little boy, silly?" Tara said from the bedroom. "We could very well be having a little girl."

Lynn grinned and felt that now familiar warmth of true love wash over him. Making his way into the kitchen, he spotted two dinner plates left out from last night. One was picked clean and the other still had a pile of spaghetti on it, like it hadn't even been touched. He took hold of the one with the spaghetti and dumped the leftover food into the trash.

"Tara should do a better job of eating today," he whispered. "She needs her strength."

Placing both plates in the sink, he then tossed six empty beer cans into the trash and put his empty whisky glass in there too. He then took the frying pan down from its hook on the wall and set it on a stove burner.

Opening the door to the fridge, he bent over to grab the eggs, but got so dizzy, he nearly collapsed. Standing up straight, he inhaled a calming breath.

"You'd better take a nap after breakfast, Lynn," he spoke to himself. "Or there will be no writing for you today."

Carefully bending at the hips one more time, he took hold of the carton of eggs. This time, he didn't feel like passing out. He set the carton on the wood counter, opened it, and cracked six of them into a white bowl. He whisked them up with a fork. Adding some butter to the frying pan, he turned on the burner. When the butter was melted and sizzling, he added the eggs.

"Breakfast will be ready in a jiff," he shouted pleasantly.

"Almost there, honey," Tara responded. "Just getting out of the shower."

When the eggs were done, Lynn spooned an equal portion of the eggs onto two clean plates and set them on the counter. He went back into the fridge for some orange juice, but when he saw some fresh beer cans, he thought, "What the hell. It's five o'clock somewhere in the world."

That's when Tara came in. She had a towel wrapped around her head that looked like a white turban. She was also wearing one of Lynn's robes. She looked ravishing to the writer.

"Well doesn't this just smell delicious," she said taking her seat on one of the two wood stools. "I'm so famished, I could eat a horse."

Together, the two ate their eggs while Lynn drank his beer and they laughed about baby names and they made plans for adding a nursery to the cabin. When breakfast was finished, Lynn got up and went to grab Tara's empty plate, but she gently pushed him away.

"I'll do the dishes," she said. "Don't you have some writing to do, lover?"

"I guess I do," he said. Then kissing her on the top of the head, "Thanks, baby."

Turning, he entered into his writing room and closed the door behind him. Something happened to him then. Now that he was alone behind closed doors, the weight of the end of the end of the world returned. Once more, it settled onto his shoulders. He felt so heavy, it took a great effort just to walk the length of the room to his swivel chair. When he finally came to it, he didn't sit down in it, so much as dropped deadweight into it.

For a time, he stared at the blank screen on his laptop. But he didn't have the strength to raise his hands and position them over the keys. He gazed out the window onto the backyard and the pond and the tall, thick trees beyond it. The ash was falling and covering everything. The dead deer, a couple of dead coy dogs, an elk, maybe a fox or two, more birds, another human being, identity unknown. Even sex unknown. The pond was even covered along with the treetops. Everything was dead or dying.

Lynn shifted his eyes back to the screen. It seemed to take an enormous effort, but he managed to bring his hands to the keyboard.

This is how it ends, he typed.

He then dropped his hands back into his lap. He thought about last evening, about making love to Tara. It was one of the most wonderful nights he'd ever experienced in his life. One of the most magical. It occurred on the day the world came to an end.

"Oh, the bitter irony," Lynn thought.

He didn't see any point in writing anymore words since all the readers were dead. He yawned again, and slowly got up from his chair.

"At least I have my Tara to keep me company," he said as he made the journey from his desk to the writing room door. "At least we'll have our baby."

Entering the kitchen, he noticed that the two breakfast plates were still occupied the counter. One of them was empty, but the other still supported a portion of scrambled eggs. He also saw his empty beer can.

"That's strange," he said. "Must be Tara was too tired to clean up. She must have gone back to bed. Can't say I blame her."

He shuffled over the living area floor to the bedroom. Coming around the bed, he sat himself down on the edge, and took off his boots. He then slipped out of his jeans and let them lie in a clump on the cold wood floor. For a long beat, he stared at the semi-automatic set on the nightstand. His imagination ran wild with the thought of swallowing the barrel and pulling the trigger. But then, where would that leave Tara? All alone in a dying wilderness with a little baby to take care of.

He then heard something that caught his attention. He heard total silence. The generator…it had shut off. With the sun being completely blocked by a sky filled with ash, the solar panels were useless.

"Damn thing must be out of gas," Lynn muttered.

He tried turning on the light to see if there was any power. But the light wouldn't come on. They were in the dark. That is, they would be in the dark when nightfall came. He didn't have the strength to go down in the basement to refill the generator. Nor did he have the strength to put more logs on the dying fire. Soon they would be in the dark and they would be freezing in this now never ending winter.

"But at least we'll be together," Lynn said.

He lay on his side and faced his love. Reaching for the edge of the comforter, he pulled it down exposing her face. Even now, he took no notice of her stillness, her coldness, her lifelessness, her missing left eye, and the purple and blood red gash on her left cheek where a piece of flying shrapnel had pierced it. Her lack of life didn't seem to have slightest effect on the Lynn. It didn't affect him now, anymore than it had affected him yesterday afternoon when she ran away from him at the gate, only to have stepped on the landmine.

Her body was damaged beyond repair, but she remained alive long enough for Lynn to carry her into the house and to place her in his bed. She was alive long enough for him show his undying love and affection for her. Even now, when he looked at Tara, he saw someone so entirely beautiful and alive with his child. He ran his hand through her blood-caked hair, and he spooned into her.

"I love you, Tara," he whispered into her ear.

"I love you too, Lynn," she said.

He closed his eyes, and for the very last time, prayed for the swift and painless end of his world.

THE END

ASK ME TOMORROW

FRANK ZAFIRO

THE BAR HUMS with low light and easy talk, the kind of place where men come to feel less alone without admitting it. Sam sits near the end of the counter, bourbon half gone, smoke curling from the ashtray. The hour's soft and tired. He's watching the mirror behind the bottles, not for himself but for anyone who might be watching him.

Then she walks in.

Not like she owns the room—more like she's been here before and it owed her something. She moves with a quiet certainty, the kind that doesn't need an audience, yet still demands one. The coat she wears is thin for the weather, and the rain still clings to her hair. She takes a stool two down from him and orders a whiskey neat. No ice, no flourish. Just a clean pour and a nod.

Sam glances over once. Enough. The mirror does the rest.

When her drink comes, she lifts it, sips, sets it down with a precision that's almost studied. That's what catches him—the sense of someone performing. But for whom?

He takes out his lighter, silver and worn smooth. He flicks it once, lets the flame dance. She notices. Her mouth curves, faintly. Sam makes eye contact and lifts the cigarette pack.

"You want one?" he asks her.

"I don't smoke," she says.

Sam shrugs and puts the pack away. He takes in a drag and lets the smoke out in a slow billowing cloud, directing it away from her.

"Do you kiss?" he asks casually.

She smirks, but behind the smirk she studies him, and after a moment, he can tell she finally sees the same thing he does. Another grifter.

"No lips that touch a cigarette ever touch mine," she says, her tone somehow curt and playful at the same time.

Wordlessly, Sam drops the pack of cigarettes on the bar and pushes them away. He pockets the lighter, though. It had been his father's.

"Just like that?" Rachel asks.

"Just like that."

He picks up his drink and slides one stool to the left, closer to her and further from the abandoned cigarettes.

She watches him but doesn't object. "Most decisions men make in bars are ones they live to regret," she says dryly.

"Most men aren't me."

The smirk is back. "Are you sure of that?"

"Ask me tomorrow," he says. His bravado doesn't put her off. She keeps her eyes on him, waiting. He lets a slight grin touch his lips. "I'm Sam."

She pauses before answering. "Rachel."

"Stage name, Rachel?"

"They say all the world's a stage," she replies.

"So you're an English Lit professor, then."

She arched a brow. "Can you really see me in front of a classroom, reading some shitty poem to a bunch of entitled kids?"

He wants to say something clever—maybe how, right now, he can't see her anywhere but here with him—but stops himself. There's a rhythm here he doesn't want to break. Instead, he studies her in the mirror's reflection—the line of her jaw, the way her hand circles her glass, thumb tracing condensation. Again with the sense she knows she's being watched and doesn't mind.

The first silence between them feels deliberate, built like part of a script. He's certain she feels it too.

"Buy you another?" he says.

She tilts her head, considering. "You think I can't buy my own?"

"I think you like seeing who'll try."

That earns a small laugh. She lets him order the next round.

They continue the dance for another half hour, though to Sam, it could have been a minute or a millennium. Her eyes are deep and guarded, but some of her genuine self trickles from them as they speak. The words aren't memorable, but the conversation is. It is punctuated by the occasional light chuckle and periodic silences. Sam takes these moments to fully appreciate what is happening.

It is special.

It is real.

He should know. Everything else in his life is grift.

The smoldering looks between them as they talk should have put off anyone with half a clue, but Sam thanks God the world over that he created so many marks who don't meet that minimum criteria.

Two stools down, a man in a gray sport coat has been watching her since she walked in. Mid-forties, soft around the eyes, confidence practiced. The kind of man who likes being seen with a woman who makes other men jealous. Sam clocks him in the mirror as he approaches.

"This guy bothering you?" he asks Rachel, his voice full of the bravado that comes with money.

Sam thinks—almost hopes—she will tell him to fuck off, whether politely or subtly. Then the evening will almost certainly end—no, not an end, a beginning—with her coming back to his hotel room. But then a touch of a smile tugs at the corners of Rachel's mouth, and her eyes flick to his. That is all it takes for Sam to understand.

As Porter always said, a grifter's gonna grift. And you never pass up a chance at the game.

"Yes," Rachel tells the mark evenly, still looking at Sam. "Yes, he is."

Sam lifts his hands, palms up. "Nice, Helene. Really nice."

Rachel laughs, then flashes a half smile at the mark. "Tom's a little sensitive. I seem to attract the delicate ones."

The man seems confused. "So, is he bothering you, or not?"

"He is," Rachel says. "But that's the bother I chose."

Sam smirks and shakes his head. "Relationships," he mutters, and takes a slug of his drink.

The man's confusion sifts into a mix of irritated disappointment.. "Whatever. I'll leave you to it, then."

"No," Rachel says. "Stay. We could use some company."

He stares at her, unsure. Not answering.

"Seriously," Rachel says. "We need a distraction."

The man grins, his doubt falling away. "Well, I'm good at being that," he says. "Name's Campbell."

Rachel tilts her head. "That right?"

"Campbell Erickson," he says, extending a hand. "Friends call me Camp."

"Friends, huh?" She takes his hand, holds it a moment too long. "You might be getting ahead of yourself."

Sam says nothing. He lets the moment hang. There's something in the way she draws the man in—smooth, instinctive. A current he recognizes.

Erickson laughs, embarrassed but charmed. "Fair enough. Let me buy the next round then. Call it a peace offering, for the intrusion. I didn't know you all were a couple."

Rachel glances at Sam. The smallest flick of her eyes— permission, invitation, maybe both. Sam nods once, slow. He can't resist the lure of the game. Doubts she can, either.

She turns back to Erickson. "Why not?"

The bartender sets up the drinks. Erickson insists on paying, as promised. Despite his acknowledgment of Sam and Rachel's status, he still leans closer to Rachel, voice lowering into what he thinks is intimacy. Sam watches, listens, measuring the rhythm. He can almost hear the gears in her head turning, matching his own. Neither needs to speak to know where this might go. Her the femme fatale, him the cuckold?

No, he decides. She'll play it more subtly than that. But the hint of it is there, so Sam will lean into it.

Rachel asks Erickson questions that sound simple but aren't. What line of work? How long in town? Married? Each one a feeler, subtle as a pickpocket's touch. Sam lets her lead. He plays the quiet one, the background man. The one who makes her seem more available by not pressing his claiming to her.

Strangely, he feels a flash of jealousy. Then it is gone and, in its place, there is only the two of them and the game. Nothing else matters. He has no idea how this is true so immediately, but he doesn't question it. The grift is an art, and you don't question art. You absorb it.

Erickson puffs up. Talks about a deal that went through, a massive bonus check, a trip he's planning. The kind of story meant to impress, but that only shows the seams. Rachel laughs at the right moments, leans in just enough. Every gesture rehearsed, yet alive.

Sam wishes for another cigarette. Instead, he focuses on his drink, fingering the lighter. The top clicks as he fidgets with it, a metronome for their unspoken timing.

After the third drink, Erickson's voice gets louder. His hand rests on Rachel's arm too comfortably. Sam catches her glance, quick and sharp, then she looks back to the man and smiles again. The signal's there. She's got the bite; now comes the line.

Sam finishes his drink, motions to the bartender for his tab. Rachel lays a hand on his wrist. "Where are you off to?"

He meets her eyes. "Just need some air."

Erickson grins, misunderstanding. "You two fighting?"

Rachel shakes her head, all soft amusement. "Not yet."

That makes Erickson laugh. Sam hears the code in it. Erickson thinks he's signaling understanding, but the true message is one he doesn't realize he's sending. Sam sets his jaw and steps outside.

The rain's eased, leaving the air damp and metallic. He leans against the wall, waits, watching the streetlights blur in puddles.

He counts out a slow minute, then two. Waits a little longer, same as if he'd smoked a cigarette. Then he goes back in.

Rachel has moved closer to Erickson, their heads nearly touching. Perfect. She looks up as Sam passes behind them, catches his eye. Another signal—quick, precise. Time to set the hook.

He stops by the bar again, motions the bartender over. "You still open for change?"

"Depends what kind," the bartender says.

Sam lays a fifty on the counter. "Twenties, if you got 'em."

Erickson glances over. "Hell, you carrying cash? Thought I was the only one. Hardly anyone does that anymore."

"Some habits die hard," Sam says. "Plastic makes me nervous."

Rachel eyes him. "You seem nervous about more than that."

"I don't want it to end up like last time."

"Last time didn't include *camp*ing," she says, and chuckles.

Erickson laughs too, eager to join the current she's creating, keeping his chances alive. "You know what makes me nervous?" he offers. "The craps table over at the Lakeside. Can't stay away from it."

Rachel brightens. She turns to him. "You gamble?"

He grins. "Let's say I have my nights."

She tilts her head. "Maybe tonight's one of them."

That's all it takes. Sam knows the pattern. The mark wants to prove himself and show he can afford a thrill. Get the energy up to burst through to the kink he's more and more certain is waiting on the other side. Rachel gives him the stage; Sam keeps the lights steady.

Erickson waves to the bartender for another round. "You two up for a little action? Nothing crazy, just some fun."

Rachel's smile widens. "What kind of fun?"

He takes out his wallet, an oversized leather monstrosity, and fans a few hundreds like playing cards. "Let's say a quick game. Winner takes the tab. Keeps things interesting."

Sam shrugs. "It's your money."

The man laughs. "You sound like you expect me to lose."

"Only one way to find out," Sam says.

The bartender brings a deck of cards, happy for the extra tip. Simple game, three hands of blackjack. Erickson insists on dealing. Sam watches the way his fingers move—confident, not practiced, the kind of guy who thinks luck is a skill.

Rachel leans close enough to Erickson that Sam knows the man has to smell her intoxicating perfume. "Better be gentle, Campbell. I bruise easy."

He grins, already off balance.

Sam takes his cards, plays loose. Rachel folds when she should stay, stays when she should fold. They let him win two small pots, just enough to feel clever. Then Sam scratches his jaw, glances at her. "You really want to let him walk with our tab?"

She pouts. "You got a better idea?"

"Double or nothing," Erickson says before Sam can answer. "Let's make it worth staying up for."

Rachel sighs, feigned reluctance. "You boys and your luck."

Sam leans back, watching her. The line between them hums now—not just the con but something warmer, stranger. She knows it too. That's the trick of it: they're not pretending attraction; they're channeling it.

Erickson loses the next hand. Not by much, but enough for him to laugh it off. "Guess I'm paying for the night, then."

Rachel brushes his arm. "You sure you can afford it?"

He smirks. "My bonus hit this week. I'll survive."

She tilts her head, smiling like a secret. "Maybe we should make it a real game."

His eyes sharpen. "What do you have in mind?"

She looks at Sam, then back to Erickson. "Something that costs enough to mean something."

That's where Sam sees it—her rhythm syncing with his. They're past the test now. The rest will be easy.

Rachel watches Campbell Erickson take the bait and feels that small click inside her chest — the one that happens when the mark's heartbeat starts to sync with hers. Every con is a conversation; every sentence, a test. She's fluent in this language.

He leans closer now, shoulders loosening as the whiskey softens the sharp edges of his self-consciousness. His smile widens when she laughs. Men like him always need a mirror, someone who reflects the version they're proud of. Tonight, she'll be that mirror for a little while.

She traces the rim of her glass with one finger, lets her eyes drop just long enough to make him wonder what she's thinking. Then she looks back up, meets his gaze, and he's already leaning forward again. Predictable. Reliable.

"What did you have in mind?" he asks, pretending control.

She shrugs like it doesn't matter, though it matters more than he'll ever know. "Something easy. Something fun."

He chuckles. "You sound like trouble."

"Only if you ask nicely."

The line lands exactly where she wants it to — on the edge between flirtation and challenge. Coupled with the earlier conversation, there is more than a hint of promise, all of it contrived, though Erickson won't ever know. Not even after he's been taken off.

Sam, sitting quiet on her right, doesn't move or speak, but she can feel him watching. His stillness works like gravity. The kind that holds her in orbit even while she's pretending to circle Erickson.

She thinks of how Sam looked earlier, flame flickering between them, patience steady as a metronome. The way he didn't flinch when she tested him, just pushed the cigarettes away. That kind of control is rare. Dangerous, maybe. But it makes her pulse quicken.

Erickson takes out his massive wallet again. Flashy move. Bills folded fat, too many hundreds pressed together. Rachel's pulse slows instead of speeding up — calculation replacing heat. He wants her to see it. Wants her to imagine what else he can afford. That's the mistake.

"You ever flip a coin for keeps?" she asks, smiling.

He raises an eyebrow. "A coin?"

She pulls one from her pocket — a silver dollar she keeps for luck, or maybe for theater. She spins it once on the counter, watches it shimmer under the bar light. "Call it. Heads or tails."

He laughs. "What do I get if I win?"

"Depends how brave you are."

He leans back, grinning. "And if I lose?"

Her voice softens, barely above the music. "Then you'll owe me something that stings just enough to remember."

He's grinning wider now, drunk enough to think he's in on the joke. "Alright, sweetheart. You're on."

She flips the coin high. It arcs, catches the light, and lands on the back of her hand — heads. She lifts her palm to show him.

He sighs, mock wounded. "Guess I'm paying."

"Not yet," she says, pocketing the coin. "We'll get there."

Sam's drink sits untouched. When she glances his way, he nods — once, barely perceptible. A private acknowledgment that she's moving him, too, even as she moves the mark. Their connection hums under her skin.

Erickson orders another round, his wallet staying on the bar now, a bold and careless move. That's where it needs to be.

She leans close, voice dropping to a whisper meant for only him. "You said you liked games. Let's make one worth winning."

He licks his lips. "Go on."

She smiles, all promise, and tilts her head, letting her hair brush her shoulder. "You and Tom each put something down. Cash, watch, whatever says you've got faith in your luck. We let the bartender hold it. One hand of cards, closest to twenty-one takes it."

Erickson grins, glancing at Sam. "You in, quiet man?"

"In?" Sam feigns ignorance. He may not have heard her words but he knew her intent. She is certain of it. That's what makes him dangerous — not his looks, not his calm — but the way he reads her signals like they're his own thoughts.

Erickson repeats the terms. Rachel can hear the beginnings of a slur in his words, something most cops wouldn't even catch if they stopped the man on his way home. But it's there and works in their favor.

Sam answers, his tone steady. "Sure. I've lost worse bets."

Rachel marvels for a moment that he's following her lead with no need for details. So fast, she thinks. So… inexorably *real*. Then she pushes the contemplation aside. She needs to focus on right now, on the game.

She watches Erickson pull out a wad of cash, peel off six crisp hundreds, and slap them on the counter. "How's that for faith?"

Rachel whistles softly. "That's bold."

He laughs. "Your turn."

Sam lays down three hundreds. "Call it a gesture."

"Not quite even," Erickson says.

"I'll cover." Rachel reaches for her purse, draws out a stack of smaller bills, and sets them beside Sam's. "Now it is."

The bartender shakes his head, half amused. "You kids sure about this?"

Rachel smiles. "We're adults, aren't we?"

The bartender shrugs and stows the money.

Erickson deals. Three cards each. Erickson's first two are good — a nine and a seven. He smirks. Rachel's heart beats once, twice, and she sees the future line by line.

Sam's cards add to twelve. He asks for one more. A face card. Too much. He folds with a grimace that looks genuine. Rachel catches his eye and feels the pulse of the con quicken.

Erickson's turn. He hits once more, draws a four, and slaps the cards down like a man planting a flag. "Twenty! Guess that makes me lucky after all."

He's laughing, relaxed. Rachel smiles back, lets him have his victory for three slow breaths. Then she picks up her cards, fans them open, and tilts her head as if puzzled. "Wait," she says softly, "you dealt from the bottom."

Erickson freezes. "What?"

"Right here," she says, pointing to the deck. "That flash—everyone saw it."

The bartender frowns. "I didn't see nothing."

"Maybe you weren't looking," she says, voice hardening just enough. "But he saw it." She nods toward Sam.

Sam shrugs. "Looked odd to me."

Erickson's smile falters. "Hey, I wouldn't—"

Rachel cuts in, gentle again. "It's okay. Maybe it was an accident."

He blusters. "No accident! You're accusing me—"

She leans closer, voice low and intimate. "Relax, Camp. Nobody here's looking to start anything."

"Then don't say shit like I cheated."

"I don't think it was intentional," she assures him. "We just need to make it right."

He stares, confused. "Make it right how?"

"Simple," she says. "You put up another six. If you win clean, you walk with all of it. If not—well, you've proven you're honest."

It's the pivot, the invisible line between pride and fear. She watches him teeter. The whiskey, the flirtatious hints promising something more, but most of all, the challenge — all of it pushes him toward the only choice that feels safe to his ego: doubling down.

He sighs, mutters something about fairness, and counts out six more hundreds. The bartender hesitates but takes them, tucking the money under the bar.

Rachel deals this time, hands steady. Two quick rounds. Erickson stares at his cards intently but completely misses where they come from. He loses the first with a bust. The second, he holds on nineteen but Sam rolls over two queens.

He laughs too loudly, shakes his head, cheeks flushed. "Guess all the ladies are on your side, Tom."

Sam shrugs. "On any given day..."

Erickson casts a sideways glance at Rachel. There is hope in his eyes but also defeat. She mirrors back the defeat. Even drunk, he gets her meaning. The chance at whatever kink was in the air was gone along with his money. He simply didn't size up.

He polishes off his drink and shakes his head. "Hell of a price to prove I'm an honest man."

Rachel smiles, sympathetic. "Character is worth paying for, don't you think?"

He waves a hand. "You got me, sweetheart. Drinks are on me."

When he stands, his wallet sits on the counter, forgotten. Sam moves to help steady him, a friendly hand on the shoulder. In that moment, she palms the wallet, slides out the cash with the same smooth grace she used lighting her cigarette earlier. Practice, not hesitation. She presses the empty wallet into Sam's hand. He takes it without looking her way.

Erickson staggers toward the door, Sam at his elbow, humming a tune that doesn't exist. She finishes her drink slowly after they're gone. Meanwhile, the bartender lays their winnings on the counter. Rachel slides five hundred his direction.

Wordlessly, the bartender accepts the money and moves away. Not an unwitting confederate, she realizes. Just a roll with the punches sort of guy. She figures every good bartender probably is.

Sam returns and sits next to her, an unreadable expression somewhere between admiration and warning. "Five, six grand?"

"Somewhere in there," she says. "Minus five bills for the bartender."

"Never tip light," Sam says, approving.

"Or too much."

The corner of his mouth lifts. "You sure you weren't born for this?"

She meets his gaze. "Pretty sure I was made for it."

For the first time tonight, she feels the heat behind her own words.

Outside, the rain's started again, a soft hiss against the

windows. She reaches for her coat. Sam gets his too. Neither says it, but they both know the night doesn't end here.

She nods toward the door. "You coming?"

He nods once in return, that quiet patience still intact. "After you."

She walks ahead, smiling to herself as the door swings shut behind them.

Rain needles his collar as they step into the street. Sam follows a half-step behind, watching Rachel move through the puddles like the water parts for her. The bar's neon sign spills light across the sidewalk, a broken reflection of red and gold.

He still feels the pulse of the con in his fingers, the electricity that comes after the take, no matter the size—part relief, part wanting. She doesn't look back, just heads toward the corner where the cheap hotels cluster near the river. Her purse swings lightly at her side. He wonders if she can feel the weight of the cash inside.

"You always walk this fast after a score?" he asks.

Rachel glances over her shoulder. "You always follow this close after one?"

"Habit," he says. "You never know who's watching."

"Someone's always watching." She stops under the yellow glow of a streetlight, turns to face him. Her hair's damp again, darkening in the rain. "Question is, why do you care?"

Sam searches her face. The right answer would be the practical one—because he doesn't want loose ends, because getting sloppy means getting caught. But that isn't the truth, and both of them know it.

"Maybe I just don't like walking away too soon," he says. "Not from a good thing, anyway."

She studies him a second longer than comfort allows. Then she starts walking again.

At the next corner, a cab rolls past. She lifts a hand, and the car pulls over with a hiss of brakes. The driver leans out, asks where to. She says, "Riverside Inn," like she's said it a hundred times.

Sam opens the door for her. She slides in first, the scent of smoke and rain following. He gets in beside her, closes the door, and the city's noise cuts off.

They don't talk on the ride. The meter ticks softly, the wipers keeping time. Sam watches the lights smear across the glass, thinks about how easy it was—the rhythm between them, the wordless coordination. That kind of connection doesn't happen by accident.

Rachel looks straight ahead, face calm, hands folded in her lap. But her reflection in the window tells a different story: her pupils wide, a faint tremor in the pulse at her throat. She feels it too—the charge, the danger of recognition.

When the cab stops, Sam pays. She doesn't argue. They step under the hotel's flickering awning.

Inside, the lobby smells like bleach and old carpet. A bored clerk hands her a key with an oversized room tag stamped with 412 without asking for ID. Sam raises an eyebrow.

"Regular here?" he says.

"I travel light," she answers.

The elevator hums them up four floors. She leans against the wall, eyes half-closed. "You ever think about stopping?" she asks suddenly.

He shakes his head. "The game, you mean?"

"Yes." She opens her eyes. "The work, the pretending. Walking into rooms just to walk out richer and emptier."

He wants to tell her no, that the grift is the only thing that ever makes sense. But the words feel thin in his mouth. "Doesn't sound like you want to stop either," he says.

She smiles faintly. "Maybe I just want someone who understands why I don't."

The elevator dings. She leads him down a narrow hall that smells of dust and disinfectant. The carpet muffles their footsteps. Room 412 waits at the end.

She unlocks it, pushes the door open, and the light from the hallway spills inside—bed, table, a single chair, nothing else. The kind of room where things start or end but never last.

Rachel steps in first, drops her purse on the table, and takes out the cash. She flips through the hundreds, counting the money. "Six thousand two hundred," she says softly. "About what I figured."

Sam stands at the door, propping it open with his foot. He doesn't know why he does this, only knows it feels right. Everything that's happened tonight has been by feel, so he doesn't question it.. "Not bad for an hour's work."

"Even if burns the bar?"

He shrugs. "Seems like a fair trade."

She divides the bills, half to him, half to herself. Her fingers brush his when she hands his share over, light as a breath.

"Clean take," he says. "No witnesses."

"Except the bartender," she answers.

"You took care of that."

"And you took care of Camp?"

Sam nods. "Put him in a taxi. Gave the driver a fifty. Campbell probably won't realize his wallet's empty until the morning." He pauses. "We work well together."

"Together can be dangerous. More memorable."

"Worked for Bonnie and Clyde."

"Until it didn't." She tilts her head, though this time without the artifice he'd seen at the bar. The difference is barely perceptible, but goddamn if it isn't there. "I'm not interested in ending up dead in the front seat of a bullet-riddled car."

He waves a hand. "They were bank robbers. It's different. In comparison, we're… artists."

The room goes quiet again. Outside, the rain intensifies, pattering against the window like static. She sets the money aside and looks at him.

"That thing you said," she murmurs. "About not walking away too soon."

"Yeah?"

"You were right."

She reaches for his tie, slow enough that he could step back if he wanted. He doesn't. Her eyes hold his as she tugs gently, drawing him forward until they're inches apart. The smell of whiskey and the wispy remains of smoke lingers between them.

He hears his own heartbeat louder than the rain.

"You sure about this?" he asks.

Rachel smiles, small and certain. "Ask me tomorrow."

Then she pulls him fully into the room and steps backward toward the bed. Sam follows, fully entranced. The door latches shut behind them.

The rain outside keeps falling, steady as breathing.

ABOUT THE AUTHORS

REED FARREL COLEMAN

Called a hard-boiled poet by NPR's Maureen Corrigan and the noir poet laureate in the Huffington Post, Reed Farrel Coleman is the New York Times-bestselling author of thirty-one novels—including theNick Ryan series and six in Robert B. Parker's Jesse Stone series—short stories, poetry, and essays.

In addition to his acclaimed series characters, Moe Prager and Gus Murphy, he has written the stand-alone novel Gun Church and collaborated with decorated Irish crime writer Ken Bruen on the novel Tower.

Reed is a four time Edgar Award nominee in three different categories: Best Novel, Best Paperback Original, and Best Short Story. He is a four-time recipient of the Shamus Award for Best PI Novel of the Year. He has also won the Audie, Macavity, Barry, and Anthony Awards.

With their kids moved away to far off Brooklyn, Reed, his wife Rosanne, and their cats live in the wilds of Suffolk County on Long Island.

DANICA FAVORITE

Danica Favorite writes emotionally charged romance that celebrates women finding their way back to themselves. Known for emotionally rich stories grounded in hope, belonging, and second chances, she explores what happens when women stop living by other people's rules and start choosing their own truth. When she isn't writing, Danica supports authors in the publishing world and champions creativity as a path to freedom. Her work is a reminder that no one is alone—and it's never too late to rewrite the story.

REBELRY STONE

Rebelry Stone thrives in the shadows of dark contemporary romance, where love is ruthless and desire is a weapon. Her characters don't play nice, and neither do their hearts. If you crave stories that seduce, shatter, and consume, you're in the right place.

JE FISHMAN

Best known for his Bomb Squad NYC series of police thrillers, J.E. Fishman is author of a dozen books of fiction and nonfiction, including the novels Primacy, Cadaver Blues, The Dark Pool, We Once Were Giants, and, under the pen name Dana I. Wolff, The Prisoner of Hell Gate. A lifelong environmentalist, he also writes the Substack newsletter Backyard Stewardship. He divides his time between Pennsylvania and California.

CHARLES SALZBERG

Charles Salzberg is a former magazine journalist and nonfiction book writer. His articles have appeared in *New York, Esquire,* and *The New York Times.* .

His nonfiction books include, *Soupy Sez: My Zany Life and Times* (Soupy Sales) and *From Set Shot to Slam Dunk, An Oral History of the NBA.*

His first novel, *Swann's Last Song* was nominated for a Shamus Award, as was *Second Story Man* (winner of the Beverly Hills Book Award), and *Canary in the Coal Mine; Devil in the Hole,* was named one of the best crime novels of the year by *Suspense* magazine; *Man on the Run,* won the NYC Big Book Award for Crime Fiction. .

A founding member of New York Writers Workshop, he was also Visiting Professor at the S.I. Newhouse School of Public Communications.

LAWRENCE KELTER

Lawrence Kelter hails from New York but now calls North Carolina his home. He is the bestselling author of more than thirty novels including the Stephanie Chalice Mystery Series that has topped bestseller lists in the US, UK, and Australia. In 2017 he penned BACK TO BROOKLYN, the studio-authorized sequel to the cult comedy classic "My Cousin Vinny."

Early in his writing career he received direction from literary icon, Nelson DeMille, who edited portions of his early work. Well before he said, "Lawrence Kelter is an exciting new novelist, who reminds me of an early Robert Ludlum," he said, "Kid, your work needs editing, but that's a hell of a lot better than not having talent. Keep it up!"

His novels are quickly paced and crammed full of twists, turns, and laughs.

SAMANTHA RIPLEY

Samantha Ripley is primarily a horror comedy and urban fantasy author. Her stories live in the spaces between adrenaline and intimacy, where characters discover love not in spite of the chaos around them, but because of it.

With a style that blends cinematic action and emotional vulnerability, Ripley crafts narratives where every bullet casing glints with metaphor and every kiss carries weight. Her work thrives on contradiction—the tenderness in violence, the softness hidden beneath steel, the way desire burns brightest against the backdrop of danger.

Characters who should be enemies find themselves drawn together, not only by the pull of passion but by a shared recognition of scars and resilience. In Ripley's hands, romance is never safe, never simple. It's explosive, jagged, and beautifully human.

PAUL D. BRAZILL

Paul D. Brazill's books include Stray Bullets, Guns Of Brixton, and Last Year's Man. He lives in Hartlepool. England. His writing has been translated into Portuguese, Spanish, Italian, Finnish, Polish, German and Slovene. He has had writing published in various magazines and anthologies, including 3 volumes of The Mammoth Books of Best British Crime

TROY LAMBERT

Troy Lambert is an award-winning author and story coach best known for his Max Boucher and Solitaire series. Over a decade of full-time writing has produced more than thirty novels, numerous short stories and several non-fiction guides.

His thrillers blend psychological depth with procedural suspense and have drawn comparisons to the works of Dean Koontz and Michael Connelly.

Troy now runs The Plot Abides, where he teaches story structure and mentors writers. Raised in southern Idaho he lives near Boise with his wife and a talented German Shepherd named McClane. When he's not plotting his next twist, Troy speaks at conferences and explores Idaho's mountains by bike, ski or hiking trail.

SCOTT KIKKAWA

Scott Kikkawa is the author of Kona Winds, Red Dirt, Char Siu and the upcoming Sporting Girl (to be released in early 2026), all from Bamboo Ridge Press, noir detective novels set in postwar Honolulu. He has contributed to Akashic Books' Honolulu Noir anthology (Chris McKinney, editor). His short stories have appeared in Bamboo Ridge: The Journal of Hawai'i Literature and Arts, the Colin Conway-edited anthology A Bag of Dick's and the Frank Zafiro-edited anthology Tattered Blue Line. His essays have appeared in The Hawai'i Review of Books and Kyoto Journal. Kikkawa has been honored with an Elliot Cades Award for Literature, and his short story "Joe Sukiyaki" from A Bag of Dick's was selected as one of the "Other Distinguished Stories of 2021" in the 2022 Best American Mysteries and Suspense anthology.

His first two novels, Kona Winds and Red Dirt, are among Honolulu Magazine's "Essential Hawai'i Books You Should Read: The Next 134".

His work was recommended in the 2024 New York Times piece "Read Your Way Through Hawai'i." He is a columnist and an Associate Editor for The Hawai'i Review of Books. Currently a federal law enforcement officer, the New York University Alumnus lives with his family in Honolulu.

VINCENT ZANDRI

Vincent Zandri is the New York Times and the USA Today bestselling ITW Thriller and PWA Shamus Award-winning author of hundreds of novels, novellas, and stories, including the Dick Moonlight PI series.

Said to be "…one of the most acclaimed thriller writers working today," by Publisher's Weekly, Zandri, a Derringer Award finalist, is a freelance journalist and the host of the Writer's Life Podcast.

For a FREE thriller,

Visit his official website, www.vinzandri.com.

FRANK ZAFIRO

Frank Zafiro writes gritty crime fiction from both sides of the badge. He was a police officer from 1993 to 2013, holding many different positions and ranks. He retired as a captain.

Frank is the author of more than fifty novels, most of them crime fiction. His mainstream work (mostly hockey or humorous/heartwarming dramas) appears under the name Frank Scalise, while his science fiction and fantasy is written as Frank Saverio.

In addition to writing, Frank has hosted the crime fiction podcast Wrong Place, Write Crime since 2017. He is an avid hockey fan, martial artist, and a tortured guitarist. He currently lives in Redmond, Oregon, with his wife and a pair of cats. Two of the three are mildly impressed with his literary achievements.

ACKNOWLEDGMENTS

True Romance wouldn't exist without a community of storytellers and supporters. As co-founders of Alibi Syndicate Press, Troy Lambert and I, Stacey Smekofske, tip our fedoras to everyone who brought this anthology to life.

First, a nod to our Editor at Large, Vincent Zandri—your sharp eye and noir sensibilities kept us on track. To our remarkable authors—Reed Farrel Coleman, Danica Favorite, Rebelry Stone, J.E. Fishman, Charles Salzberg, Lawrence Kelter, Samantha Ripley, Paul D. Brazill, Scott Kikkawa, Frank Zafiro, and yes, Vincent Zandri & Troy Lambert—your words define the dark side of True Romance.

We extend special thanks to Ashley Brown for steering our marketing ship and to Sydney at Meirawood Productions for fixing our Kickstarter trailer with flair.

To our Kickstarter backers who believed in this project early; you're part of the Syndicate now.

And finally, to you, the readers. Thank you for making space in your hearts for these tales.

COMING SOON FROM
ALIBI SYNDICATE PRESS

When bestselling author Norman Kelleher wakes up on a speeding train with blood on his hands and no memory, a surreal nightmare of sleepwalking, secrets, and a desperate escape unfolds—where the line between dream and danger blurs with every step.

Watch for
<u>Quietly Into the Night</u>
a New Thrilling Novel by Vincent Zandri

Follow us at AlibiSyndicatePress.com